ABOUT THE AUTHOR

Xiao Hong (Hsiao Hung) was the penname of Zhang Naiying, a novelist from the town of Hulan (called Hulan River by its inhabitants), near the Manchurian city of Harbin. Born in 1911, the year Sun Yat-sen launched his Republican Revolution, she left her homeland shortly after its occupation by the Japanese in 1931. She was a well traveled writer during the ten years left to her, although, ironically, she died in Hong Kong only a month after it too was occupied militarily by the Japanese, as the war in the Pacific began. Xiao Hong authored four novels, four collections of stories and essays, some miscellaneous writings, and an autobiography. All her major works are currently or soon will be available in English in Howard Goldblatt's translations.

Tales of Hulan River

Xiao Hong
Tales of Hulan River

Translated by Howard Goldblatt

Joint Publishing (H.K.) Co., Ltd.

This edition is published with the permission of Indiana University Press

Copyright © 1988 Joint Publishing (H.K.) Co., Ltd.

Published by
Joint Publishing (H.K.) Co., Ltd.
9 Queen Victoria Street, Hongkong

First published April 1988

Printed in Hongkong by
C & C Joint Printing Co., (H.K.) Ltd.
75 Pau Chung Street, Kowloon, Hong Kong

Paperback ISBN 962·04·0622·2

Nancy ☺ 9-14

–Acct. mgr. Johnson

8 p.m. @ USC

150-157

–Reservation @ $150

– there are (Abc

Contents

Translator's Note

This is the first complete English translation of Xiao Hong's autobiographical novel *Tales of Hulan River* (Hulanhe zhuan). In the original hardcover edition (Indiana University Press, 1979), which was published together with Xiao Hong's first novel, *The Field of Life and Death* (Shengsi chang) in a single volume, the final two chapters were deleted. They have been restored for this edition, for which some minor changes were also made, including a conversion to the *pinyin* system of romanization. The translator is grateful to Joint Publishing Company for reissuing the novel in an affordable, complete edition, and to Indiana University Press for making it possible.

Preface to the Second Edition

Xiao Hong completed *Tales of Hulan River* slightly more than a year before she died at the age of thirty. The novel presents a number of paradoxes: written in the midst of China's struggle for survival as an independent nation, it has nothing to do with war or with contemporary events; begun in the wartime capital of Chongqing and completed in Hong Kong prior to its occupation by the Japanese, it is set exclusively in Northeast China during the waning years of the Manchu Dynasty; and conceived in an era characterized by brutality and the ugliness of death and destruction, it is filled with considerable beauty and innocence. Viewed in light of the times, it is certainly an enigma, although it is the novel for which Xiao Hong is best remembered, her autobiographical masterpiece; as Mao Dun wrote in his preface to the 1947 Chinese edition, it is "a narrative poem, a colorful genre painting, a haunting poem."

Xiao Hong devoted much of her adult life to a frequently desperate quest for the elusive "warmth and love" whose existence was affirmed to her by her adored "Granddad" as a child and later reaffirmed by her friend and benefactor. Lu Xun. The fact that she ultimately found little of either probably accounts for why she returned to her childhood as the setting for her most moving novel, and why *Tales of Hulan River* is unquestionably one of her most intensely personal works.

The region beyond the Great Wall (known in the West as Manchuria and to the Chinese as Northeast China) is unique in China for many reasons, including its isolation from the rest of the country, its history, and, of course, its climate. Not all of this is apparent in *Tales of Hulan River,* and much of what appears in the novel is more universal than regional. Except for climate, that is. Somehow, a description of the weather in a place where the thermometer can fall to -50° in the dead of winter seems a fitting way to begin a narrative such as this:

> After the harsh winter has sealed up the land, the earth's crust begins to crack and split. From south to north, from east to west; from a few feet to several yards in length; anywhere, anytime, the cracks run in every direction. As soon as harsh winter is upon the land, the earth's crust opens up.
> The severe winter weather splits the frozen earth.

From this point of the narration on, the frozen earth gives up its cultural secrets, revealing to the reader glimpses of life in the author's childhood home. Xiao Hong, who spent all of her childhood winters in the frozen Northeast, takes her readers on a cultural tour of small-town life in a region that, in many respects, still remains a mystery to the rest of China, let alone the outside world. It is a fascinating tour in which ordinary events assume extraordinary dimensions through a simplicity of style that reveals the complexity of the society, and an evocation of childish innocence that is frequently the vehicle for the transmission of deeply felt adult convictions.

Shortly before her death in Hong Kong of a throat infection and ensuing complications on January 22, 1942, Xiao Hong told a friend that she intended to write a sequel to *Tales of Hulan River.* That she was not able to do so only compounds the tragedy of her death, for with the exception of Chapter Five, which remains an extremely powerful indictment of traditional Chinese misogyny and superstition, the writing of this novel must have brought Xiao Hong a large measure of the meager pleasure she enjoyed in her adult years, particularly after 1936. The death in that year of Lu Xun, Xiao Hong's patron, friend, and, some would say, surrogate father, removed from the scene the second most powerful influence in her life (after her grandfather); according to all accounts, she knew little peace from that time forward. Yet she was able to create a literary work that has beautifully memorialized the place where she was born and the time of her childhood, giving readers then and now glimpses of many universal aspects of humanity — good and bad — while she describes other aspects peculiar to that place and time. Xiao Hong is a master of description, and rare is the reader who does not come away from this novel with a host of images of the land and the people, a sadness over the fate of victims like the child bride and Second Uncle You, and a sense of gratitude to Xiao Hong for making them all available through her evocation of the past.

1

Hulan River

I

After the harsh winter has scaled up the land, the earth's crust begins to crack and split. From south to north, from east to west; from a few feet to several yards in length; anywhere, anytime, the cracks run in every direction. As soon as harsh winter is upon the land, the earth's crust opens up.

The severe winter weather splits the frozen earth.

Old men use whisk brooms to brush the ice off their beards the moment they enter their homes. "Oh, it's cold out today!" they say. "The frozen ground has split open."

A carter twirls his long whip as he drives his cart sixty or seventy *li* under the stars, then at the crack of dawn he strides into an inn, and the first thing he says to the inn-keeper is: "What terrible weather. The cold is like a dagger."

After he has gone into his room at the inn, removed his dogskin cap with earflaps, and smoked a pipeful of tobacco, he reaches out for a steamed bun; the back of his hand is a mass of cracked, chapped skin.

The skin on people's hands is split open by the freezing cold. The man who sells cakes of bean curd is up at dawn to go out among the people's homes and sell his product. If he carelessly sets down his square wooden tray full of bean curd it sticks to the ground, and he is unable to free it. It will have quickly frozen to the spot.

The old steamed-bun peddler lifts his wooden box filled with the steaming buns up onto his back, and at the first light of day he is out hawking on the street. After emerging from his house he walks along at a brisk pace shouting at the top of his voice. But before too long, layers of ice have formed on the bottoms of his shoes, and he walks as though he were treading on rolling and shifting eggs. The snow and ice have encrusted the soles of his shoes. He walks with an unsure step, and if he is not altogether careful he will slip and fall. In fact, he slips and falls despite all his caution. Falling down is the worst thing that can happen to him, for his wooden box crashes to the ground, and the buns come rolling out of the box, one on top of the other. A witness to the incident takes advantage of the old man's inability to pick himself up and scoops up several of the buns, which he eats as he leaves the scene. By the time the old man has struggled to his feet, gathered up his steamed buns — ice, snow, and all — and put them back in the box, he counts them and discovers that some are missing. He understands at once and shouts to the man who is eating the buns, but has still not left the scene: "Hey, the weather's icy cold, the frozen ground's all cracked, and my buns are all gone!"

Passersby laugh when they hear him say this. He then lifts the box up onto his back and walks off again, but the layers of ice on the soles of his shoes seem to have grown even thicker, and he finds the going more difficult than before. Drops of sweat begin to form on his back, his eyes become clouded with the frost, ice gathers in even greater quantity on his beard, and the earflaps and front of his tattered cap are frosting up with the vapor from his breath. The old man walks more and more slowly, his worries and fears causing him to tremble in alarm; he resembles someone on iceskates for the first time who has just been pushed out onto the rink by a friend.

A puppy is so freezing cold it yelps and cries night after night, whimpering as though its claws were being singed by flames.

The days grow even colder:

Water vats freeze and crack;

Wells are frozen solid;

Night snowstorms seal the people's homes; they lie down at night to sleep, and when they get up in the morning they find they cannot open their doors.

Once the harsh winter season comes to the land everything undergoes a change: the skies turn ashen gray, as though a strong wind has blown through, leaving in its aftermath a turbid climate accompanied by a constant flurry of snowflakes whirling in the air. People on the road walk at a brisk pace as their breath turns to vapor in the wintry cold. Big carts pulled by teams of seven horses form a caravan in the open country, one following closely upon the other, lanterns flying, whips circling in the air under the starry night. After running two *li* the horses begin to sweat. They run a bit farther, and in the midst of all that snow and ice the men and horses are hot and lathered. The horses stop sweating only after the sun emerges and they are finally turned into their stalls. But the moment they stop sweating a layer of frost forms on their coats.

After the men and horses have eaten their fill they are off and running again. Here in the frigid zones there are few people; unlike the southern regions, where you need not travel far from one village to another, and where each township is near the next, here there is nothing but a blanket of snow as far as the eye can see. There is no neighboring village within the range of sight, and only by relying on the memories of those familiar with the roads can one know the direction to travel. The big carts with their seven-horse teams transport their loads of foodstuffs to one of the neighboring towns. Some have brought in soybeans to sell, others have brought sorghum. Then when they set out on their return trip they carry back with them oil, salt, and dry goods.

Hulan River is one of these small towns, not a very prosperous place at all. It has only two major streets, one running north and south and one running east and west, but the best-known place in town is The Crossroads, for it is the heart of the whole town. At The Crossroads there is a jewelry store, a yardage shop, an oil store, a salt store, a teashop, a pharmacy, and the office of a foreign dentist. Above this dentist's door hangs a large shingle about the size of a rice-measuring basket, on which is painted a row of oversized teeth. The advertisement is hopelessly out of place in this small town, and the people who look at it cannot figure out just what it's supposed to represent. That is because neither the oil store, the yardage shop, nor the salt store displays any kind of advertisement; above the door of the salt store, for example, only the word "salt" is written, and hanging above the door of the yardage shop are two curtains that are as old as the hills. The remainder of the signs are like the one at the pharmacy, which gives nothing more than the name of the bespectacled physician whose job it is to feel women's pulses as they drape their arms across a small pillow. To illustrate: the physician's name is Li Yongchun, and the name of his pharmacy is simply "Li Yongchun." People rely on their memories, and even if Li Yongchun were to take down his sign, the people would still know that he was there. Not only the townsfolk, but even the people from the countryside are more or less familiar with the streets of the town and what can be found there. No advertisement, no publicity is necessary. If people are in need of something, like cooking oil, some salt, or a piece of fabric, then they go inside and buy it. If they don't need anything, then no matter how large a sign is hung outside, they won't buy anything.

That dentist is a good case in point. When the people

from the countryside spot those oversized teeth they stare at them in bewilderment, and there are often many people standing in front of the large sign looking up at it, unable to fathom its reason for being there. Even if one of them were standing there with a toothache, under no circumstances would he let that dentist, with her foreign methods, pull his tooth for him. Instead he would go over to the Li Yongchun Pharmacy, buy two ounces of bitter herbs, take them home and hold them in his mouth, and let that be the end of that! The teeth on that advertisement are simply too big; they are hard to figure out, and just a little bit frightening.

As a consequence, although that dentist hung her shingle out for two or three years, precious few people ever went to her to have their teeth pulled. Eventually, most likely owing to her inability to make a living, the woman dentist had no recourse but to engage in midwifery on the side.

In addition to The Crossroads, there are two other streets, one called Road Two East and the other called Road Two West. Both streets run from north to south, probably for five or six *li*. There is nothing much on these two streets worth nothing — a few temples, several stands where flat-cakes are sold, and a number of grain storehouses.

On Road Two East there is a fire mill standing in a spacious courtyard, a large chimney made of fine red brick rising high above it. I have heard that no one is allowed to enter the fire mill, for there are a great many knobs and gadgets inside which must not be touched. If someone did touch them, he might burn himself to death. Otherwise, why would it be called a fire mill? Because of the flames inside, the mill is reportedly run neither by horses nor donkeys — it is run by fire. Most folk wonder why the mill itself doesn't go up in flames since only fire is used. They ponder this over and over, but are unable to come up with an answer, and the more they ponder it, the more confused they become, especially since they are not allowed to go inside and check things out for themselves. I've heard they even have a watchman at the door.

There are also two schools on Road Two East, one each at the southern and northern ends. They are both located in temples — one in the Dragon King Temple and one in the Temple of the Patriarch — and both are elementary schools.

The school located in the Dragon King Temple is for the study of raising silkworms, and is called the Agricultural School, while the one in the Temple of the Patriarch is just a regular elementary school with one advanced section added, and is called the Higher Elementary School.

Although the names of these two schools vary, the only real difference between them is that in the one they call the Agricultural School the silkworm pupae are fried in oil in the autumn, and the teachers there enjoy several sumptuous meals.

There are no silkworms to be eaten in the Higher Elementary School, where the students are definitely taller than those in the Agricultural School. The students in the Agricultural School begin their schoolwork by learning the characters for "man", "hand", "foot", "knife", and "yardstick", and the oldest among them cannot be more than sixteen or seventeen years of age. But not so in the Higher Elementary School; there is a student there already twenty-four years old who is learning to play the foreign bugle and who has already taught in private schools out in the countryside for four or five years, but is only now himself attending the Higher Elementary School. Even the man who has been manager of a grain store for two years is a student at the school.

When this elementary school student writes a letter to his family he asks questions like: "Has Little Baldy's eye infection gotten better?" Little Baldy is the nickname of his eldest son, who is eight. He doesn't mention his second son or his daughters, because if he were to include all of them the letter would be much too long. Since he is already the father of a whole brood of children — the head of a family — whenever he sends a letter home he is mainly concerned with household matters: "Has the tenant Wang sent over his rent yet?" "Have the soybeans been sold?" "What is the present market situation?" and the like.

Students like him occupy a favored position in the class; the teacher must treat them with due respect, for if he drops his guard, this kind of student will often stand up, classical dictionary in hand, and stump the teacher with one of his questions. He will smugly point out that the teacher has used the wrong character in a phrase he has written on the board.

As for Road Two West, not only is it without a fire mill, it has but one school, a Moslem school situated in the Temple of the City God. With this exception, it is precisely like Road Two East, dusty and barren. When carts and horses pass over these roads they raise up clouds of dust, and whenever it rains the roads are covered with a layer of mud. There is an added feature on Road Two East: a five- or six-foot-deep quagmire. During dry periods the consistency of the mud inside is about that of gruel, but once it starts to rain the quagmire turns into a river. The people who live nearby suffer because of it: When they are splashed with its water, they come away covered with mud; and when the waters subside as the sun reappears in the clearing sky, hordes of mosquitos emerge and fly around their homes. The longer the sun shines, the more homogenized the quagmire becomes, as though something were being refined in it; it's just as though someone were trying to refine something inside it. If more than a month goes by without any rain, that big quagmire becomes even more homogenized in makeup. All the water having evaporated, the mud has turned black and has become stickier than the gummy residue on a gruel pot, stickier even than paste. It takes on the appearance of a big melting vat, gummy black with an oily glisten to it, and even flies and mosquitos that swarm around stick to it as they land.

Swallows love water, and sometimes they imprudently fly down to the quagmire to skim their wings over the water. It is a dangerous maneuver, as they nearly fall victim to the quagmire, coming perilously close to being mired down in it. Quickly they fly away without a backward glance.

In the case of horses, however, the outcome is different: they invariably bog down in it, and even worse, they tumble down into the middle of the quagmire, where they roll about, struggling to free themselves. After a period of floundering they lie down, their energy exhausted, and the moment they do so they are in real danger of losing their lives. But this does not happen often, for few people are willing to run the risk of leading their horses or pulling their carts near this dangerous spot.

Most of the accidents occur during drought years or after two or three months without any rainfall, when the big quagmire is at its most dangerous. On the surface it would seem that the more rain there is, the worse the situation, for with the rain a veritable river of water is formed, nearly ten feet in depth. One would think this would make it especially perilous, since anyone who fell in would surely drown. But such is not the case. The people of this small town of Hulan River aren't so stupid that they don't know how brutal this pit can be, and no one would be so foolhardy as to try leading a horse past the quagmire at such times.

But if it hasn't rained for three months the quagmire begins to dry up, until it is no more than two or three feet deep, and there will always be those hardy souls who will attempt to brave the dangers of driving a cart around it, or those with somewhat less courage who will watch others make their way past, then follow across themselves. One here, two there, and soon there are deep ruts along both sides of the quagmire formed by the passage of several carts. A late arrival spots the signs of previous passings, and this erstwhile coward, feeling more courageous than his intrepid predecessors, drives his cart straight ahead. How could he have known that the ground below him is uneven? Others had safely passed by, but his cart flips over.

The carter climbs out of the quagmire, looking like a mud-spattered apparition, then begins digging to free his horse from the mud, quickly making the sad discovery that it is mired down in the middle of the quagmire. There are people out on the road during all of this, and they come over to lend a helping hand.

These passersby can be divided into two types. Some are attired in traditional long gowns and short overjackets and are spotlessly clean. Apparently none of them will move a finger to assist in this drama because their hands are much too clean. Needless to say, they are members of the gentry class. They stand off to the side and observe the goings-on. When they see the horse trying to stand up they applaud and shout, "Oh! Oh!" several times. But then they see that the horse is unable to stand and falls back down; again they clap their hands and again they shout several times, "Oh! Oh!" But this time they are registering their displeasure. The excitement surrounding the horse's attempts to stand and its inability to do so continues for some time, but in the end it cannot get to its feet and just lies there pitifully. By this time those who have only been watching the feverish activity conclude that this is about all that will happen, that nothing new will materialize, and they begin to disperse, each heading off to his home.

But let us return to the plight of the horse lying there. The passersby who are trying to free it are all common folk, some of the town's onion peddlers, food sellers, tile masons, carters, and other workers. They roll up their trouser cuffs, remove their shoes, and seeing no alternative, walk down into the quagmire with the hope that by pooling their strength they will be able to hoist the horse out. But they fail in their attempts, and by this time the horse's breathing has become very faint. Growing frantic, they hasten to free the horse from its harness, releasing it from the cart on the assumption that the horse will be able to get up more easily once it is freed from that burden. But contrary to their expectations, the horse still cannot stand up. Its head is sticking up out of the mire, ears twitching, eyes shut, snorts of air coming from its nostrils.

Seeing this sad state of affairs, people from the neighborhood run over with ropes and levers. They use the ropes to secure the horse and the levers to pry it free. They bark out orders as though they were building a house or constructing a bridge, and finally they manage to lift the animal out. The horse is still alive, lying at the side of the road. While some individuals are pouring water over it and washing the mud off its face, there is a constant flow of people coming and going at the scene of the spectacle.

On the following day everyone is saying: "Another horse has drowned in the big quagmire!" As the story makes its rounds, although the horse is actually still alive, it is said to have died, for if the people didn't say so, the awe in which they held that big quagmire would suffer.

It's hard to say just how many carts flip over because of that big quagmire. Throughout the year, with the exception of the winter season when it is sealed up by the freezing weather, this big quagmire looks as though it has acquired a life of its own — it is alive. Its waters rise, then subside; now it has grown larger, in a few days it recedes again. An intimate bond between it and the people begins to form.

When the water is high, not only are horses and carts impeded, it is an obstacle even to pedestrians. Old men pass along its edge on trembling legs, children are scared out of their wits as they skirt around it.

Once the rain begins to fall, the water quickly fills the now glistening quagmire, then overflows and covers the bases of neighboring walls. For people out on the street who approach this place, it is like being dealt a setback on the road of life. They are in for a struggle: sleeves are rolled up, teeth are ground tightly, all their energy is called forth; hands clutch at a wooden wall, hearts pound rapidly; keep your head clear, your eyes in focus . . . the battle is joined.

Why is it that this, of all walls, has to be so smooth and neatly built, as though its owners have every intention of not coming to anyone's aid in this moment of distress? Regardless of how skillfully these pedestrains reach out, the wall offers them no succor; clawing here and groping there, they grab nothing but handfuls of air. Where in the world is there a mountain on which wood like this grows, so perfectly smooth and devoid of blemishes or knots?

After five or six minutes of struggling, the quagmire has been crossed. Needless to say, the person is by then covered with sweat and hot all over. Then comes the next individual, who must prepare himself for a dose of the same medicine. There are few choices available to him — about all he can do is grab hold here and clutch there, till after five or six minutes he too has crossed over. Then, once he is on the other side he feels revitalized, bursts out laughing, and looks back to the next person to cross, saying to him in the midst of his difficult struggle: "What's the big deal? You can't call yourself a hero unless you've faced a few dangers in your life!"

But that isn't how it always goes — not all are revitalized; in fact, most people are so frightened that their faces are drained of color. There are some whose trembling legs are so rubbery after they have crossed the quagmire that they cannot walk for some time. For timid souls like this, even the successful negotiating of this dangerous stretch of road cannot dispel the mood of distress that has involuntarily settled upon them; their fluttering hearts seemingly put into motion by this big quagmire, they invariably cast a look behind them and size it up for a moment, looking as though they have something they want to say. But in the end they say nothing, and simply walk off.

One very rainy day a young child fell into the quagmire and was rescued by a bean-curd peddler. Once they got him out they discovered he was the son of the principal of the Agricultural School. A lively discussion ensued. Someone said that it happened because the Agricultural School was located in the Dragon King Temple, which angered the venerable Dragon King. He claimed it was the Dragon King who caused the heavy downpour in order to drown the child.

Someone disagreed with him completely, saying that the cause of the incident rested with the father, for during his highly animated lectures in the classroom he had once said that the venerable Dragon King was not responsible for any rainfall, and, for that matter, did not even exist. "Knowing how furious this would make the venerable Dragon King, you can imagine how he would find some way to vent his anger! So he grabbed hold of the son as a means of gaining retribution."

Someone else said that the students at the school were so incorrigible that one had even climbed up onto the old Dragon King's head and capped him with a straw hat. "What are the times coming to when a child who isn't even dry behind the ears would dare to invite such tremendous calamities down upon himself? How could the old Dragon King not seek retribution? Mark my word, it's not finished yet; don't you get the idea that the venerable Dragon King is some kind of moron! Do you think he'd just let you off once you've provoked his anger? It's not like dealing with a ricksha boy or a vegetable peddler whom you can kick at will, then let him be on his way. This is the venerable Dragon

King we're talking about! Do you think that the venerable Dragon King is someone who can easily be pushed around?''

Then there was someone who said that the students at that school were truly undisciplined, and that with his own eyes he had once seen some of them in the main hall putting silkworms into the old Dragon King's hands. "Now just how do you think the old Dragon King could stand for something like that?''

Another person said that the schools were no good at all, and that anyone with children should on no account allow them to go to school, since they immediately lose respect for everyone and everything.

Someone remarked that he was going to the school to get his son and take him home — there would be no more school for him.

Someone else commented that the more the children study, the worse they become. "Take, for example, when their souls are frightened out of their bodies; the minute their mothers call for the souls to return, what do you think they say? They announce that this is nothing but superstition! Now what in the world do you think they'll be saying if they continue going to school?''

And so they talked, drifting further and further away from the original topic.

Before many days had passed, the big quagmire receded once again and pedestrians were soon passing along either side unimpeded. More days passed without any new rainfall, and the quagmire began to dry up, at which time carts and horses recommenced their crossings; then more overturned carts, more horses falling into it and thrashing around; again the ropes and levers appeared, again they were used to lift and drag the horses out. As the righted carts drove off, more followed: into the quagmire, and the lifting began anew.

How many carts and horses are extricated from this quagmire every year may never be known. But, you ask, does no one ever think of solving the problem by filling it in with dirt? No, not a single one.

An elderly member of the gentry once fell into the quag-mire at high water. As soon as he crawled out he said: "This street is too narrow. When you have to pass by this water hazard there isn't even room to walk. Why don't the two families whose gardens are on either side take down their walls and open up some paths?"

As he was saying this, an old woman sitting in her garden on the other side of the wall chimed in with the comment that the walls could not be taken down, and that the best course of action would be to plant some trees; if a row of trees were planted alongside the wall, then when it rained the people could cross over by holding on to the trees.

Some advise taking down walls and some advise planting trees, but as for filling up the quagmire with dirt, there isn't a single person who advocates that.

Many pigs meet their end by drowning in this quagmire; dogs are suffocated in the mud, cats too; chickens and ducks often lose their lives there as well. This is because a crust has formed on top of the quagmire; the animals are unaware that there is a trap lying below, and once they realize that fact it is already too late. Whether they come on foot or by air, the instant they alight on the husk-covered mire they cannot free themselves. If it happens in the daytime there is still a chance that someone passing by might save them, but once night falls they are doomed. They struggle all alone until they exhaust their strength, then begin to sink gradually into the mire. If, on the contrary, they continue to struggle, they might sink even faster. Some even die there without sinking below the surface, but that's the sort of thing that happens when the mud is gummier than usual.

What might happen then is that some cheap pork will suddenly appear in the marketplace, and everyone's thoughts turn to the quagmire. "Has another pig drowned in that quagmire?" they ask.

Once the word is out, those who are fast on their feet lose no time in running to their neighbors with the news: "Hurry over and get some cheap pork. Hurry, hurry, before it's all gone."

After it is bought and brought home, a closer look reveals that there seems to be something wrong with it. Why is the meat all dark and discolored? Maybe this pork is infected. But on second thought, how could it really be infected? No, it must have been a pig that drowned in the quagmire. So then family after family sautes, fries, steams, boils, and then eats this cheap pork. But though they eat it, they feel always that it doesn't have a fragrant enough aroma, and they fear that it might have been infected after all. But then they think: "Infected pork would be unpalatable, so this must be from a pig that drowned in the quagmire!"

Actually, only one or two pigs drown each year in the quagmire, perhaps three, and some years not a single one. How the residents manage to eat the meat of a drowned pig so often is hard to imagine, and I'm afraid only the Dragon King knows the answer.

Though the people who eat the meat say it is from a pig drowned in the quagmire, there are still those who get sick from it, and those unfortunates are ready with their opinions: "Even if the pork was from a drowned pig, it still shouldn't have been sold in the marketplace; meat from animals that have died isn't fresh, and the revenue office isn't doing its job if it allows meat like this to be sold on the street in broad daylight!"

Those who do not become ill are of a different opinion: "That's what you say, but you're letting your suspicions get the best of you. If you'd just eat it and not give it another thought, everything would be all right. Look at the rest of us; we ate it too, so how come we're not sick?"

Now and then a child lacking in common sense will tell people that his mother wouldn't allow him to eat the pork since it was infected. No one likes this kind of child. Everyone gives him hard looks and accuses him of speaking nonsense.

For example, a child says that the pork is definitely infected — this he tells a neighbor right in front of his mother. There is little reaction from the neighbor who hears him say this, but the mother's face immediately turns beet-red. She reaches out and smacks him.

But he is a stubborn child, and he keeps saying: "The pork is infected! The pork is infected!"

His mother, feeling terribly embarrassed, picks up a poker that is lying by the door and strikes him on the shoulder, sending him crying into the house. As he enters the room he sees his maternal grandmother sitting on the edge of the *kang,* so he runs into her arms. "Grannie," he sobs, "wasn't that pork you ate infected? Mama just hit me."

Now this maternal grandmother wants to comfort the poor abused child, but just then she looks up to see the wet nurse of the Li family who shares the compound standing in the doorway looking at her. So she lifts up the back of the child's shirttail and begins spanking him loudly on the behind. "Whoever saw a child as small as you speaking such utter nonsense!" she exclaims. She continues spanking him until the wet nurse walks away with the Li's child in her arms. The spanked child is by then screaming and crying uncontrollably, so hard that no one can make heads or tails of his shouts of "infected pork this" and "infected pork that."

In all, this quagmire brings two benefits to the residents of the area: The first is that the overturned carts and horses and the drowned chickens and ducks always produce a lot of excitement, which keeps the inhabitants buzzing for some time and gives them something to while away the hours.

The second is in relation to the matter of pork. Were there no quagmire, how could they have their infected pork? Naturally, they might still eat it, but how are they to explain it away? If they simply admit they are eating infected pork, it will be too unsanitary for words, but with the presence of the quagmire their problem is solved: infected pork becomes the meat of drowned pigs, which means that when they buy the meat, not only is it economical, but there are no sanitation problems either.

II

Besides the special attraction of the big quagmire, there is little else to be seen on Road Two East: one or two grain-mills, a few bean-curd shops, a weaving mill or two, and perhaps one or two dyeing establishments. These are all operated by people who quietly do their own work there, bringing no enjoyment to the local inhabitants, and are thus unworthy of any discussion. When the sun sets these people go to bed, and when the sun rises they get up and begin their work. Throughout the year — warm spring with its blooming flowers, autumn with its rains, and winter with its snows — they simply follow the seasonal changes as they go from padded coats to unlined jackets. The cycle of birth, old age, sickness, and death governs their lives as they silently manage their affairs.

Take, for example, Widow Wang, who sells bean sprouts at the southern end of Road Two East. She erected a long pole above her house on top of which she hangs a battered old basket. The pole is so tall it is nearly on a level with the iron bell at the top of the Dragon King Temple. On windy days the *clang-clang* of the bell above the temple can be heard, and although Widow Wang's battered basket does not ring, it nonetheless makes its presence known by waving back and forth in the wind.

Year in and year out that is how it goes, and year in and year out Widow Wang sells her bean sprouts, passing her days tranquilly and uneventfully at an unhurried pace.

But one summer day her only son went down to the river to bathe, where he fell in and drowned. This incident caused a sensation and was the talk of the town for a while, but before many days had passed the talk died away. Not only Widow Wang's neighbors and others who lived nearby, but even her friends and relatives soon forgot all about it.

As for Widow Wang herself, even though this caused her to lose her mind, she still retained her ability to sell bean sprouts, and she continued as before to live an uneventful and quiet life. Occasionally someone would steal her bean sprouts, at which time she was overcome by a fit of wailing on the street or on the steps of the temple, though it soon passed, and she would return to her uneventful existence.

Whenever neighbors or other passersby witnessed the scene of her crying on the temple steps, their hearts were momentarily touched by a slight feeling of compassion, but only momentarily.

There are some people who are given to lumping together misfits of all kinds, such as the insane and the slow-witted, and treating them identically.

There are unfortunates in every district, in every county, and in every village: the tumorous, the blind, the insane, the slow-witted. There are many such people in our little town of Hulan River, but the local inhabitants have apparently heard and seen so much of them that their presence does not seem the least bit unusual. If, unhappily, they encounter one of them on the temple steps or inside a gateway alcove, they feel a momentary pang of compassion for that particular individual, but it is quickly supplanted by the rationalization that mankind has untold numbers of such people. They then turn their glances away and walk rapidly past the person. Once in a while someone stops there, but he is just one of those who, like children with short memories, would throw stones at the insane or willfully lead the blind into the water-filled ditch nearby.

The unfortunates are beggars, one and all. At least that's the way it is in the town of Hulan River. The people there treat the beggars in a most ordinary fashion. A pack of dogs is barking at something outside the door; the master of the house shouts out: "What are those animals barking at?"

"They're barking at a beggar," the servant answers.

Once said, the affair is ended. It is obvious that the life of a beggar is not worth a second thought.

The madwoman who sells bean sprouts cannot forget her grief even in her madness, and every few days she goes to wail at the steps of the temple; but once her crying has ended, she invariably returns home to eat, to sleep, and to sell her bean sprouts. As ever, she returns to her quiet existence.

III

A calamity once struck the dyer's shop: Two young apprentices were fighting over a woman on the street, when one of them pushed the other into the dyeing vat and drowned him. We need not concern ourselves here with the one who died, but the survivor was sent to jail with a life sentence.

Yet this affair, too, was disposed of silently and without a ripple. Two or three years later, whenever people mentioned the incident they discussed it as they would the famous confrontation between the heroic general Yue Fei and the evil prime minister Qin Hui, as something that had occurred in the long distant past.

Meanwhile the dyer's shop remains at its original location, and even the big vat in which the young man drowned is quite possibly still in use to this day. The bolts of cloth that come from that dye shop still turn up in villages and towns far and near. The blue cloth is used to make padded cotton pants and jackets, which the men wear in the winter to ward off the severe cold, while the red cloth is used to make bright red gowns for the eighteen- and nineteen-year-old girls on their wedding days.

In short, though someone had drowned in the dyer's shop on such and such a day during such and such a month and year, the rest of the world goes on just as before without the slightest change.

Then there was the calamity that struck the bean-curd shop: During a fight between two of the employees the donkey that turned the mill suffered a broken leg. Since it was only a donkey, there wasn't much to be said on that score, but a woman lost her sight as a result of crying over the donkey (she turned out to be the mother of the one who had struck the animal), so the episode could not simply be overlooked.

Then there was the paper mill in which a bastard child was starved to death. But since it was a newborn baby, the incident didn't amount to much, and nothing more need be said about it.

IV

Then, too, on Road Two East there are a few ornament shops, which are there to serve the dead.

After a person dies his soul goes down to the nether world, and the living, fearing that in that other world the dear departed will have no domicile to live in, no clothes to wear, and no horse to ride, have these things made of paper, then burn them for his benefit; the townspeople believe that all manner of things exist in the nether world.

On display are grand objects like money-spewing animals, treasure-gathering basins, and great gold and silver mountains; smaller things like slave girls, maidservants, cooks in the kitchen, and attendants who care for the pigs; and even smaller things like flower vases, tea services, chickens, ducks, geese, and dogs. There are even parrots on the window ledges.

These things are enormously pleasing to the eye. There is a courtyard surrounded by a garden wall, the top of which is covered with gold-colored glazed tiles. Just inside the courtyard is the principal house with five main rooms and three side rooms, all topped with green- and red-brick tiles; the windows are bright, the furniture spotless, and the air fresh and clean as can be. Flower pots are arranged one after another on the flower racks; there are cassias, pure-white lilies, purslanes, September chrysanthemums, and all are in bloom. No one can tell what season it is — is it summer or is it autumn? — since inexplicably the flowers of the purslanes and the chrysanthemums are standing side by side; perhaps the year is not divided into spring, summer, autumn, and winter in the nether world. But this need not concern us.

Then there is the cook in his kitchen, vivid and lifelike; he is a thousand times cleaner than a true-to-life cook. He has a white cap on his head and a white apron girding his body as he stands there preparing noodles. No sooner has lunchtime arrived than the noodles have been cooked, and lunch is about to be served.

In the courtyard a groom stands beside a big white horse, which is so large and so tall that it looks to be an Arabian; it stands erect and majestic, and if there were to be a rider seated upon it, there is every reason to believe it could outrun a train. I'm sure that not even the general here in the town of Hulan River has ever ridden such a steed.

Off to one side there is a carriage and a big mule. The mule is black and shiny, and its eyes, which have been made out of eggshells, remain stationary. There is a particularly fetching little mule with eyeballs as large as the big mule's standing alongside it.

The carriage, with its silver-colored wheels, is decorated in especially beautiful colors. The curtain across the front is rolled halfway up so that people can see the interior of the carriage, which is all red and sports a bright red cushion. The driver perched on the running board, his face beaming with a proud smile, is dressed in magnificent attire, with a purple sash girding his waist over a blue embroidered fancy gown, and black satin shoes with snow-white soles on his feet. (After putting on these shoes he probably drove the carriage over without taking a single step on the ground.) The cap he is wearing is red with a black brim. His head is raised as though he were disdainful of everything, and the more the people look at him, the less he resembles a carriage driver — he looks more like a bridegroom.

Two or three roosters and seven or eight hens are in the courtyard peacefully eating grain without making a sound, and even the ducks are not making those quacking noises that so annoy people. A dog is crouching next to the door of the master's quarters maintaining a motionless vigil.

All of the bystanders looking on comment favorably, every one of them voicing his praise. The poor look at it and experience a feeling that it must be better to be dead than alive.

The main room is furnished with window curtains, four-poster bed frames, tables, chairs, and benches. Everything is complete to the last detail.

There is also a steward of the house who is figuring accounts on his abacus; beside him is an open ledger in which is written:

"Twenty-two catties of wine owed by the northern distillery.

"Wang Family of East Village yesterday borrowed 2,000 catties of rice.

"Ni Renzi of White Flag Hamlet yesterday sent land rent of 4,300 coppers."

Below these lines is written the date: "April twenty-eighth."

This page constitutes the running accounts for the twenty-seventh of April; the accounts for the twenty-eighth have evidently not yet been entered. A look at this ledger shows that there is no haphazard accounting of debts in the nether world, and that there is a special type of individual whose job it is to manage these accounts. It also goes without saying that the master of this grand house is a landlord.

Everything in the compound is complete to the last detail and is very fine. The only thing missing is the master of the compound, a discovery that seems puzzling: could there be no master of such a fine compound? This is certainly bewildering.

When they have looked more closely the people sense that there is something unusual about the compound: how is it that the slave girls and maidservants, the carriage drivers and the groom all have a piece of white paper across their chests on which their names are written? The name of the carriage driver whose good looks give him the appearance of a bridegroom is:

"Long Whip."

The groom's name is:

"Fleet of Foot."

The name of the slave girl who is holding a water pipe in her left hand and an embroidered napkin in her right is:

"Virtuous Obedience."

The other's name is:

"Fortuitous Peace."

The man who is figuring accounts is named:

"Wizard of Reckoning."

The name of the maid who is spraying the flowers with water is:

"Flower Sister."

A closer look reveals that even the big white horse has a name; the name tag on his rump shows that he is called:

"Thousand-*Li* Steed."

As for the others — the mules, the dogs, the chickens, and the ducks — they are nameless.

The cook who is making noodles in the kitchen is called "Old Wang," and the strip of paper on which his name is written flaps to and fro with each gust of wind.

This is all rather strange: the master of the compound doesn't even recognize his own servants and has to hang name tags around their necks! This point cannot but confuse and bewilder people; maybe this world of ours is better than the nether world after all!

But though that is the opinion of some, there are still many others who are envious of this grand house, which is so indisputably fine, elegant, peaceful and quiet (complete silence reigns), neat and tidy, without a trace of disorder. The slave girls and maidservants are fashioned exactly like those in this world; the chickens, dogs, pigs, and horses, too, are just like those in this world. Everything in this world can also be found in the nether world: people eat noodles in this world, and in the nether world they eat them, too; people have carriages to ride in this world, and in the nether world they also ride them; the nether world is just like this world — the two are exactly alike.

That is, of course, except for the big quagmire on Road Two East. Everything desirable is there; undesirable things are simply not necessary.

V

These are the objects that the ornament shops on Road Two East produce. The displayed handiwork is both dignified-looking and eye-catching, but the inside of the shop is a mass of confusion. Shredded paper is everywhere; there are rods and sticks all in a heap; crushed boxes and a welter of cans, paint jars, paste dishes, thin string, and heavy cord abound. A person could easily trip just walking through the shop, with its constant activity of chopping and tying as flies dart back and forth in the air.

When making paper human figures, the first to be fashioned is the head; once it has been pasted together it is hung on a wall along with other heads — men's and women's — until it is taken down to be used. All that is needed then is to put it atop a torso made of rods and sticks on which some clothes have been added, and you have the figure of a human being. By cutting out white paper hair and pasting it all over a sticklike paper-mâché horse, you have a handsome steed.

The people who make their living this way are all extremely coarse and ugly men. They may know how to fashion a groom or a carriage driver, and how to make up women and young girls, but they pay not the slightest attention to their own appearance. Long scraggly hair, short bristly hair, twisted mouths, crooked eyes, bare feet and legs; it is hard to believe that such splendid and dazzlingly beautiful lifelike human figures could have been created by those hands.

Their daily fare is coarse vegetables and coarse rice, they are dressed in tattered clothes, and they make their beds among piles of carriages, horses, human figures, and heads. Their lives seemingly are bitter ones, though they actually just muddle their way through, day by day, the year round, exchanging their unlined jackets for padded coats with each seasonal change.

Birth, old age, sickness, death — each is met with a stoic

absence of expression. They are born and grow in accord-
ance with nature's dictates. If they are meant not to grow
old, then so be it.

Old age — getting old has no effect on them at all: when
their eyesight fails they stop looking at things, when their
hearing fades they stop listening, when their teeth fall out
they swallow things whole, and when they can no longer
move about they lie flat on their backs. What else can they
do? Anyone who grows old deserves exactly what he gets!

Sickness — among people whose diet consists of a random
assortment of grains, who is there who does not fall prey
to illness?

Death — this, on the other hand, is a sad and mournful
affair. When a father dies, his sons weep; when a son dies,
his mother weeps; when a brother dies, the whole family
weeps; and when a son's wife dies, her family comes to weep.

After crying for one, or perhaps even three, days, they
must then go to the outskirts of town, dig a hole, and bury
the person. After the burial the surviving family members
still have to make their way back home and carry on their
daily routine. When it's time to eat, they eat; when it's
time to sleep, they sleep. Outsiders are unable to tell that
this family is now bereft of a father or has just lost an elder
brother. The members of that particular family even fail
to lock themselves in their home each day and wail. The
only expression of the grief they feel in their hearts is joining
the stream of people who go to visit the graves on the various
festivals each year as prescribed by local custom. During the
Qingming Festival — the time for visiting ancestral graves —
each family prepares incense and candles and sets out for the
family grave site. At the heads of some of the graves the
earth has settled and formed a small pit, while others have
several small holes in them. The people cast glances at one
another, are moved to sighing, then light the incense and

pour the wine. If the survivor is a close relative, such as a son, a daughter, or a parent, then they will let forth a fit of wailing, the broken rhythm of which makes it sound as though they were reading a written composition or chanting a long poem. When their incantation is finished they rise to their feet, brush the dirt from their behinds, and join the procession of returning people as they leave the grave sites and re-enter the town.

When they return to their homes in the town they must carry on life as before; all year round there is firewood, rice, oil, and salt to worry about, and there is clothing to starch and mend. From morning till evening they are busy without respite. Nighttime finds them exhausted, and they are asleep as soon as they lie down on the *kang*. They dream neither of mournful nor of happy events as they sleep, but merely grind their teeth and snore, passing the night like every other night.

If someone were to ask them what man lives for, they would not be confounded by the question, but would state unhesitatingly, directly, and unequivocally: "Man lives to eat food and wear clothes." If they were then asked about death, they would say: "When a man dies that's the end of it."

Consequently, no one has ever seen one of those ornament craftsmen fashion an underworld home for himself during his lifetime; more than likely he doesn't much believe in the nether world. And even if there were such a place, he would probably open an ornament shop when he got there; worse luck, he'd doubtless have to rent a place to open the shop.

VI

In the town of Hulan River, besides Road Two East, Road Two West, and The Crossroads, there remain only a number of small lanes. There is even less worth noting on these small byways; one finds precious few of the little stalls where flatcakes and dough twists are made and sold, and even the tiny stands that sell red and green candy balls are mainly located where the lanes give out onto the road — few find their way into the lanes themselves. The people who live on these small lanes seldom see a casual stroller. They hear and see less than other people, and as a result they pass their lonely days behind closed doors. They live in broken-down huts, buy two pecks of beans, which they salt and cook to go with their rice, and there goes another year. The people who live on these small lanes are isolated and lonely.

A peddler carrying a basket of flatcakes hawking his product at the eastern end of the lane can be heard at the western end. Although the people inside the houses don't care to buy, whenever he stops at their gates they poke their heads out to take a look, and may on occasion even ask a price or ask whether or not the glazed or fried dough twists still sell for the same price as before.

Every once in a while someone will walk over and lift up the piece of cloth that covers the basket, as though she were a potential customer, then pick one out and feel to see if it's still hot. After she has felt it she puts it right back, and the peddler is not the least bit angry. He simply picks up his basket and carries it to the next house.

The lady of this second house has nothing in particular to do, so she, too, opens up the basket and feels around for a while. But she also touches them without buying any.

When the peddler reaches the third house, a potential customer is there waiting for him. Out from the house comes a woman in her thirties who has just gotten up from a nap. Her hair is done up in a bun on top of her head, and probably because it isn't particularly neat, she has covered it with a black hairnet and fastened it on with several hairpins. But having just slept on it, not only is her hair all disheveled, but even the hairpins have worked their way out, so that the bun atop her head looks as though it has been shot full of darts.

She walks out of her house in high spirits, throwing the door open and virtually bursting through the doorway. Five children follow in her wake, each of them in high spirits; as they emerge they look every bit like a platoon marching in a column.

The first one, a girl of twelve or thirteen, reaches in and picks out one of the dough twists. It is about the length of a bamboo chopstick, and sells for fifty coppers. Having the quickest eye among them, she has selected not only the biggest one in the basket, but the only one in that size category.

The second child, a boy, chooses one that sells for twenty coppers.

The third child also chooses one that sells for twenty coppers; he, too, is a boy.

After looking them all over, the fourth child has no alternative but to choose one that sells for twenty coppers; and he, too, is a boy.

Then it is the fifth child's turn. There is no way of telling if this one is a boy or a girl — no hair on the head, an earring hanging from one ear, skinny as a dry willow branch, but with a large, protruding belly, it looks to be about five years old. The child sticks out its hands, which are far blacker than any of the other four children's — the hands of the other four are filthy black, all right, but at least they still look like human hands and not some other strange objects. Only this child's hands are indistinguishable. Shall we call them hands? Or what shall we call them? I guess we can call them anything we like. They are a mottled mixture of blacks and grays, darks and lights, so that looking at them, like viewing layers of floating clouds, can be a most interesting pastime.

The child sticks its hands into the basket to choose one of the fried dough twists, nearly each of which is touched and felt in the process, until the entire basket is soon a jumble. Although the basket is fairly large, not many dough twists had been put inside it to begin with: besides the single big one, there were only ten or so of the smaller ones. After this child has turned them all over, the ones that remain are strewn throughout the basket, while the child's black hands are now covered with oil as well as being filthy, and virtually glisten like shiny ebony.

Finally the child cries out: "I want a big one!"

A fight then erupts by the front door.

The child is a fast runner, and takes out after its elder sister. Its two elder brothers also take off running, both of them easily outdistancing this smallest child. The elder sister, holding the largest dough twist in her hand, is un-imaginably faster on her feet than the small child, and in an instant she has already found a spot where there is a break in the wall and has jumped through; the others follow her and disappear on the other side. By the time all the others have followed her past the wall, she has already jumped back across and is running around the courtyard like a whirlwind.

The smallest child — the one of indeterminate sex — cannot catch up with the others and has long since fallen behind, screaming and crying. Now and then, while the elder sister is being held fast by her two brothers, the child runs over and tries to snatch the dough twist out of her hand, but after several misses falls behind again, screaming and crying.

As for their mother, though she looks imposing, actually she cannot control the children without using her hands, and so, seeing how things are going, with no end in sight, she enters the house, picks up a steel poker, and chases after her children. But unhappily for her, there is a small mud puddle in her yard where the pigs wallow, and she falls smack into the middle of it, the poker flying from her hand and sailing some five feet or so away.

With that this little drama has reached its climax and every person watching the commotion is in stitches, delighted with the whole affair. Even the peddler is completely engrossed in what is going on, and when the woman plops down into the mud puddle and splashes muck all over, he nearly lets his basket fall to the ground. He is so tickled he has forgotten all about the basket in his hands.

The children, naturally, have long since disappeared from sight. By the time the mother gets them all rounded up she has regained her imposing parental airs. She has each of them kneel on the ground facing the sun so that they form a line, then has them surrender up their dough twists.

Little remains of the eldest child's dough twist — it was broken up in all the commotion.

The third child has eaten all of his.

The second one has a tiny bit left.

Only the fourth one still has his clenched in his hand.

As for the fifth child, well, it never had one to begin with.

The whole chaotic episode ends with a shouting match between the peddler and the woman before he picks up his basket and walks over to the next house to try to make another sale. Their argument is over the woman's wanting to return the dough twist that the fourth child had been holding onto all that time. The peddler flatly refuses to take it back, and the woman is just as determined to return it to him. The end result is that she pays for three dough twists and drives the peddler with his basket out of her yard.

Nothing more need be said about the five children who were forced to kneel on the ground because of those dough twists, and the remainder of the dough twists that had been taken into the lane to be handled and felt by nearly everyone are then carried over into the next lane and eventually sold.

A toothless old woman buys one of them and carries it back wrapped in a piece of paper, saying: "This dough twist is certainly clean, all nice and oily." Then she calls out to her grandchild to hurry on over.

The peddler, seeing how pleased the old lady is, says to her: "It's just come from the pan, still nice and warm!"

VII

In the afternoon, after the dough-twist peddler has passed by, a seller of rice pudding may come by, and like the other peddlers, his shouts from one end of the lane can be heard at the other end. People who want to buy his product bring along a small ceramic bowl, while others who are not interested in buying just sit inside their homes; as soon as they hear his shouts they know it is time to begin cooking dinner, since throughout the summer this peddler comes when the sun is setting in the west. He comes at the same time every day, like clockwork, between the hours of four and five. One would think that his sole occupation is bringing rice pudding to sell in this particular lane, and that he is not about to jeopardize his punctual appearance there in order to sell to one or two additional homes in another lane. By the time the rice-pudding peddler has gone, the sky is nearly dark.

Once the sun begins to set in the west the peddler of odds and ends, who announces his presence with a wooden rattle, no longer enters the lanes to peddle his wares. In fact, he does no more business on the quieter roadways either, but merely shoulders his load and makes his way home along the main streets.

The pottery seller has by then closed up shop for the day.

The scavengers and rag collectors also head for home.

The only one to come out at this time is the bean-curd peddler.

At dinnertime some scallions and bean paste make for a tasty meal, but a piece of bean curd to go along with it adds a pleasant finishing touch, requiring at least two additional bowlfuls of corn-and-bean gruel. The people eat a lot at each sitting, and that is only natural; add a little hot-pepper oil and a touch of bean sauce to the bean curd and the meal is greatly enhanced. Just a little piece of bean curd on the end of the chopsticks can last a half bowlful of gruel, and soon after the chopsticks have broken off another chunk of bean curd, another bowlful of gruel has disappeared. Two extra bowlfuls are consumed because of the addition of the bean curd, but that doesn't mean the person has overeaten; someone who has never tasted bean curd cannot know what a delightful flavor it has.

It is for this reason that the arrival of the bean-curd peddler is so warmly welcomed by everyone — men, women, young and old alike. When they open their doors, there are smiles everywhere, and though nothing is said, a sort of mutual affinity quietly develops between buyer and seller. It is as though the bean-curd peddler were saying: "I have some fine bean curd here."

And it is as though the customer were answering: "Your bean curd doesn't seem half bad."

Those who cannot afford to buy the bean curd are particularly envious of the bean-curd peddler. The moment they hear the sound of his shouts down the lane drawing near they are sorely tempted; wouldn't it be nice to have a piece of bean curd with a little green pepper and some scallions!

But though they think the same thought day in and day out, they never quite manage to buy a piece, and each time the bean-curd peddler comes, all his presence does for these people is confront them with an unrealizable temptation. These people, for whom temptation calls, just cannot make the decision to buy, so they merely eat a few extra mouthfuls of hot peppers, after which their foreheads are bathed in perspiration. Wouldn't it be wonderful, they dream, if a person could just open his own bean-curd shop? Then he could eat bean curd anytime he felt like it!

And sure enough, when one of their sons gets to be about

five years of age, if he is asked: "What do you want to do when you grow up?"

He will answer: "I want to open a bean-curd shop." It is obvious that he has hopes of realizing his father's unfulfilled ambition.

The fondness these people have for this marvelous dish called bean curd sometimes goes even beyond this; there are those who would even lead their families into bankruptcy over it. There is a story about the head of a household who came to just such a decision, saying: "I'm going for broke; I'll buy myself a piece of bean curd!" In the classical language, the words "going for broke" would be the equivalent of giving up one's all for charity, but in modern speech most people would just say: "I'm wiped out!"

VIII

Once the bean-curd peddler packs up and heads for home, the affairs of another day have come to an end.

Every family sits down to its evening meal, then after they have finished, some stay up to watch the sunset, while the others simply lie down on their *kangs* and go to sleep.

The sunsets in this place are beautiful to behold. There is a local expression here, "fire clouds"; if you say "sunset," no one will understand you, but if you say "fire clouds," even a three-year-old child will point up to the western sky with a shout of delight.

Right after the evening meal the "fire clouds" come. The children's faces all reflect a red glow, while the big white dog turns red, red roosters become golden ones, and black hens become a dark purple. An old man feeding his pigs leans against the base of a wall and chuckles as he sees his two white pigs turn into little golden ones. He is about to say: "I'll be damned, even you have changed," when a man out for a refreshing evening stroll walks by him and comments: "Old man, you are sure to live to a ripe old age, what with your golden beard!"

The clouds burn their way in the sky from the west to the east, a glowing red, as though the sky had caught fire.

The variations of the "fire clouds" here are many: one moment they are a glowing red, a moment later they become a clear gold, then half purple-half yellow, and then a blend of gray and white. Grape gray, pear yellow, eggplant purple – all of these colors appear in the sky. Every imaginable color is there, some that words cannot describe and others that you would swear you have never seen before.

Within the space of five seconds a horse is formed in the sky with its head facing south and its tail pointing west; the horse is kneeling, looking as though it is waiting for someone to climb up onto its back before it will stand up. Nothing much changes within the next second, but two or three seconds later the horse has gotten bigger, its legs have spread out, and its neck has elongated . . . but there is no longer any tail to be seen. And then, just when the people watching from below are trying to locate the tail, the horse disappears from sight.

Suddenly a big dog appears, a ferocious animal that is running ahead of what looks like several little puppies. They run and they run, and before long the puppies run from sight; then the big dog disappears.

A great lion is then formed, looking exactly like one of the stone lions in front of the Temple of the Immortal Matron. It is about the same size, and it, too, is crouching, looking very powerful and dominating as it calmly crouches there. It appears contemptuous of all around it, not deigning to look at anything. The people search the sky, and before they know it something else has caught their eye. Now they are in a predicament – they cannot be looking at something to the east and something to the west at the same time –

and so they watch the lion come to ruin. A shift of the eyes, a lowering of the head, and the objects in the sky undergo a transformation. But now as you search for yet something else, you could look until you go blind before finding a single thing. The great lion can no longer be seen, nor is there anything else to be found — not even, for example, a monkey, which is certainly no match for a great lion.

For a brief moment the sky gives the illusion of forming this object or that, but in fact there are no distinguishable shapes; there is nothing anymore. It is then that the people lower their heads and rub their eyes, or perhaps just rest them for a moment before taking another look. But the "fire clouds" in the sky do not often wait around to satisfy the children below who are so fond of them, and in this short space of time they are gone.

The drowsy children return home to their rooms and go to sleep. Some are so tired they cannot make it to their beds, but fall asleep lying across their elder sister's legs or in the arms of their grandmother. The grandmother has a horsehair fly swatter, which she flicks in the air to keep the bugs and mosquitos away. She does not know that her grandchild has fallen asleep, but thinks he is still awake.

"You get down and play; Grandma's legs are falling asleep." She gives the child a push, but he is fast asleep.

By this time the "fire clouds" have disappeared without a trace. All the people in every family get up and go to their rooms to sleep for the night after closing the windows and doors.

Even in July it is not particularly hot in Hulan River, and at night the people cover themselves with thin quilts as they sleep.

As night falls and crows fly by, the voices of the few children who are not yet asleep can be heard through the windows as they call out:

Raven, raven, work the grain-threshing floor;
Two pecks for you, not a tiny bit more.

The flocks of crows that cover the sky with their shouts of *caw-caw* fly over the town from one end to the other. It is said that after they have flown over the southern bank of the Hulan River they roost in a big wooded area. The following morning they are up in the air flying again.

As summer leads into autumn the crows fly by every evening, but just where these large flocks of birds fly to, the children don't really know, and the adults have little to say to them on the subject. All the children know about them is embodied in their little ditty:

Raven, raven, work the grain-threshing floor;
Two pecks for you, not a tiny bit more.

Just why they want to give the crows two pecks of grain doesn't seem to make much sense.

IX

After the crows have flown over, the day has truly come to an end.

The evening star climbs in the sky, shining brightly there like a little brass nugget.

The Milky Way and the moon also make their appearance.

Bats fly into the night.

All things that come out with the sun have now turned in for the night. The people are all asleep, as are the pigs, horses, cows, and sheep; the swallows and butterflies have gone to roost. Not a single blossom on the morning glories at the bases of the houses remains open — there are the closed buds of new blossoms and the curled up petals of the old. The closed buds are preparing to greet the morning sun of the following day, while the curled petals that have already greeted yesterday's sun are about to fall.

Most stars follow the moon's ascent in the sky, while the evening star is like her advance foot soldier, preceding her by a few steps.

As night falls the croaking of frogs begins to emerge from rivers, streams, and marshes. The sounds of chirping insects come from foliage in the courtyards, from the large fields outside the city, from potted flowers, and from the graveyard.

This is what the summer nights are like when there is no rain or wind, night after night.

Summer passes very quickly, and autumn has arrived. There are few changes as summer leads into autumn, except that the nights turn cooler and everyone must sleep under a quilt at night. Farmers are busy during the day with the harvest, and at night their more frequent dreams are of gathering in the sorghum.

During the month of September the women are kept busy starching clothes and removing the covers and fluffing the matted cotton of their quilts. From morning till night every street and lane resounds with the hollow twang of their mallets on the fluffing bows. When their fluffing work is finished, the quilts are re-covered, just in time for the arrival of winter.

Winter brings the snows.

Throughout the seasons the people must put up with wind, frost, rain, and snow; they are beset by the frost and soaked by the rain. When the big winds come they fill the air with swirling sand and pebbles, almost arrogantly. In winter the ground freezes and cracks, rivers are frozen over, and as the weather turns even colder the ice on the river splits with resounding cracks. The winter cold freezes people's ears, splits open their noses, chaps their hands and feet. But this is just nature's way of putting on airs of importance, and the common folk can't do a thing about it.

This is how the people of Hulan River are: when winter

comes they put on their padded clothes, and when summer arrives they change into their unlined jackets, as mechanically as getting up when the sun rises and going to bed when it sets.

Their fingers, which are chapped and cracked in the winter, heal naturally by the time summer arrives. For those that don't heal by themselves, there is always the Li Yongchun Pharmacy, where the people can buy two ounces of saffron, steep it, and rub the solution on their hands. Sometimes they rub it on until their fingers turn blood red without any sign of healing, or the swelling may even get progressively worse. In such cases they go back to the Li Yongchun Pharmacy, though this time, rather than purchasing saffron, they buy a plaster instead. They take it home, heat it over a fire until it becomes gummy, then stick it on the frostbite sore. This plaster is really wonderful, since it doesn't cause the least bit of inconvenience when it is stuck on. Carters can still drive their carts, housewives can still prepare food.

It's truly wonderful that this plaster is so sticky and gummy; it will not wash off in water, thereby allowing women to wash clothes with it on if they have to. And even if it does rub off, they can always heat it over a fire and stick it back on. Once applied it stays on for half a month.

The people of Hulan River value things in terms of strength and durability, so that something as durable as this plaster is perfectly suited to their nature. Even if it is applied for two weeks and the hand remains unhealed, the plaster is, after all, durable, and the money paid for it has not been spent in vain.

They go back and buy another, and another, and yet another, but the swelling on the hand grows worse and worse. People who cannot afford the plasters pick up the ones others have used and discarded and stick them on their own sores. Since the final outcome is always unpredictable, why not just muddle through the best one can!

Spring, summer, autumn, winter — the seasonal cycle

continues inexorably, and has since the beginning of time. Wind, frost, rain, snow; those who can bear up under these forces manage to get by; those who cannot must seek a natural solution. This natural solution is not so very good, for these people are quietly and wordlessly taken from this life and this world.

Those who have not yet been taken away are left at the mercy of the wind, the frost, the rain, and the snow . . . as always.

2

Festivals and Such

I

In Hulan River, besides these inconsequential and common realities of daily life, there are several special events that are not immediatcly related to the villagers' hand-to-mouth existence, such as:

The dance of the sorceress;

The harvest dances;

Releasing river lanterns;

Outdoor opera performances; and

The festival at the Temple of the Immortal Matron on the eighteenth day of the fourth lunar month.

We'll begin with the sorceress. The sorceress can cure diseases, and she dresses herself in peculiar clothing of a type that ordinary people do not wear. She is all in red — a red skirt — and the moment she puts this skirt around her waist she undergoes a transformation. Rather than starting by beating her drum, she wraps her embroidered red skirt around her and begins to tremble. Every part of her body, from her head down to her toes, trembles at once, then begins to quake violently. With her eyes closed, she mumbles constantly. Whenever her body begins to quake, she looks as though she is about to collapse to the ground, which throws a scare into the people watching her; but somehow she always manages to sit down properly.

The sorceress seats herself on a stool directly opposite a spirit tablet on which black letters are written on a piece of red paper. The older the spirit tablet, the better, for it gives evidence of the many occasions she has had during the course of a year to perform her dance, and the more dances she performs, the farther her reputation will spread, causing her business to prosper. Lighted incense is placed in front of the spirit tablet, from which smoke curls slowly upward.

Usually the spirit enters the sorceress' body when the incense has burned halfway down. As soon as she is possessed by the spirit her imposing airs undergo a change. It is as though she were in command of a huge army of soldiers and horses; invigorated, she rises to her feet and begins to cavort and jump around.

An assistant — a man — stands off to the sorceress' side. Unlike the woman, he presents a picture of orderliness, and is as organized and composed as the next man. He hurriedly places a round drum in the sorceress' hand, which she holds as she cavorts and begins to narrate the story of the descent from the mountain of the spirit that has possessed her: how it has ridden on the clouds, flown with the winds, and been carried by the mist on its journey. It is an impressive story. Whatever the sorceress asks the assistant standing alongside her, he answers. Appropriate answers will flow from the mouth of a good assistant, while the occasional careless response from a less competent one will throw the sorceress into a fit. She is then driven to beating on her drum and letting loose a volley of epithets. She will curse the afflicted person, saying that he will die before the night is out; that his ghost will not depart, but will wander endlessly; and that his immediate family, relatives, and neighbors will all be visited by fiery calamities. Members of the terror-stricken family that has requested the services of the sorceress frantically light incense and offer libations. But if these offerings fail to placate her, they must hurriedly make a presentation of red cloth, which they drape over the spirit tablet. If this too fails, they must then sacrifice a chicken. Once the tumult has reached the stage of sacrificing a chicken, it seldom goes any further, for there would be nothing more to be gained from continuing along this course.

The chicken and the cloth become the sorceress' property; after she has finished her dance she takes the chicken home to cook and eat; the red cloth she dyes a dark blue and makes into a pair of pants for her own use.

But no matter what some sorceresses do, the spirits fail to make an appearance. The family that has requested her services must then quickly sacrifice a chicken, for if they are even a little slow in doing so, the sorceress will come to a halt in mid-dance and begin haranguing them. Now since the sorceress has been invited to cure an illness, it is an unlucky omen if she begins to shout curses. As a result, she is both greatly respected and greatly feared.

The dance of the sorceress normally commences at dusk. At the sound of her drum, men, women, and children dash over to the house where she is engaged; on summer evenings crowds of people fill the rooms and the yard outside. Excited, shouting women drag or carry their children along as they clamber over walls to watch the dance of the sorceress, which continues late into the night until at last the spirit is sent back up the mountain. That moment is signaled by fiercely resounding drumbeats and the sorceress' enthralling chants, sounds that reach all the neighboring homes and produce in everyone within earshot a sense of desolation. The assistant begins to chant: "Return to your mountain, Great Fairy, proceed with care and deliberation."

The sorceress responds: "Assistant Fairy of mine . . . Green Dragon Mountain, White Tiger Peak . . . three thousand *li* in a single night is an easy task when riding on the winds."

The lyrics and melody of her incantation merge with the beat of the drum and carry a great distance; it is an eerie and depressing sound, which adds to the desolation of those who hear it. Often there are people who cannot sleep at night after hearing these pulsating sounds.

The sorceress has been requested by a family to drive away an illness, but has the patient been cured or not? This only produces anguished sighs throughout the neighborhood, and there are often those who lie awake all night troubled by this thought.

A star-filled sky, moonlight flooding the rooms; what is human existence and why must it be so desolate?

Ten days or two weeks later the thudding drumbeat of the sorceress' dance is heard again, and once more the people are aroused. They come over the walls and through the gate to take a look at the sorceress who has been summoned: What are her special talents? What is she wearing? Listen to hear what chants she is singing; look to see how beautiful her clothing is.

She dances into the still of the night, then the spirit is sent back up the mountain, escorted by a tantalizing cadence on the drum.

The feelings of desolation are particularly strong on rainy nights: widows are moved to tears, widowers wander aimlessly about. The beat of the drum seems designed to torment the unfortunates. Alternating between a rapid and a languid cadence, it calls forth the image of a lost traveler who is giving voice to his confusion, or of an unfortunate old man recalling the happier days of his all-too-brief childhood. It is also reminiscent of a loving mother sending her son off on a long journey, or of someone at the point of death who is unwilling to part with this world.

What is human existence all about? Why must there be nights of such desolation?

Seemingly, the next time the sound of drums is heard no

one would be willing to even listen, but such is not the case: at the first beat of the drum, people again clamber over the walls, straining their ears to the sound with more enthusiasm than people in Western countries on their way to a concert.

II

On the fifteenth day of the seventh month – during the Festival of the Hungry Ghosts – river lanterns are set adrift on the Hulan River. There are river lanterns shaped like cabbages, watermelons, and also lotuses.

Buddhist monks and Taoist priests, dressed in bright red satin robes with gold designs, play their reed organs, flutes, and panpipes along the riverbank, calling the people together to an open-air ritual. The music from their instruments can be heard at a distance of two *li* from the river. At dusk, before the sky has completely darkened, a continuous stream of people rushes to watch the river lanterns. Even people who never leave their homes at any other time fill the streets and lanes as they join the procession to the riverbank. The first arrivals squat at the edge of the river, until both banks are crowded with people resting on their haunches, while an unbroken line of people continues to emerge. Even the blind and the crippled come to see the river lanterns (no, I am wrong; the blind, of course, do not come to *see* the river lanterns), and a cloud of dust is raised over the roadway by the running people. There is no need to ask the maidens and the young married women who emerge from their gates in groups of twos and threes where they are headed. For they are all going to see the river lanterns.

By dusk during the seventh lunar month the "fire clouds" have just disappeared and a pale glow illuminates the streets; the bustle of activity disturbs the silence of the preceding days, as each roadway comes alive. It is as though a huge fire had broken out in the town and everyone was rushing to put it out. There is a sense of great urgency among the people surging forward on flying feet. The first to arrive at the river's edge squat down, and those who follow wedge themselves in and squat down on their haunches beside the others. Everyone waits; they are waiting for the moon to climb into the sky, at which time the river lanterns will be set adrift on the water.

The fifteenth day of the seventh lunar month, which is a festival devoted to spirits, is for the ghosts of the wronged who have been denied transmigration and cannot extricate themselves from their bitter existence in the nether world; they are unable to find the road that will release them. On this night each of them able to rest a river lantern on the palm of the hand can gain release — apparently the road leading from the nether world to this world is so dark that it cannot be seen without the aid of a lantern. Therefore the releasing of river lanterns is a charitable act. It is to show that the living — shall we call them the gentlefolk? — have not forgotten the ghosts of those who have been wronged.

But the day is not without its contradictions, for a child born on the fifteenth day of the seventh lunar month is held in low esteem, since it is thought that his soul is a wild ghost that has come to him on a lotus lantern. These children will grow up without the love of their parents. Now when boys and girls reach marrying age, their families must exchange and compare the children's horoscopes to determine their suitability before the nuptials can take place. If it is a girl who was born on the fifteenth day of the seventh lunar month, it will be difficult to arrange a marriage for her, and she must deceive the boy's family by altering her birth date. If it is a boy who was born on this day, the outlook is not much better, but if his family is a wealthy one, this short-coming can be overlooked and he is still considered marriageable. Possessed though he may be by an evil spirit, the fact that he is wealthy proves that it cannot be all that evil. But if it is the girl in this position, the situation is hopeless. That is, unless she is the only child of a wealthy widow; that is another matter altogether, for marrying one of those girls means that her wealth hangs in the balance. Even if she doesn't bring her entire fortune with her in the marriage, the dowry alone will be of considerable size, and the fact that she is the reincarnation of an evil spirit will lose its importance. The people have a saying that "Money can make even a ghost put his shoulder to the grindstone!" It would seem that they don't really believe in ghosts and feel that the reports of their existence are highly exaggerated.

And yet the monks beat their drums resoundingly as the river lanterns are released, urgently reciting their charmlike sutras in celebration of the ghosts' transmigration. They therefore give witness to the belief of the critical nature of this fleeting moment; it is an opportunity that cannot be missed, one in which each ghost – male or female – must quickly raise a river lantern on the palm of its hand in order to achieve reincarnation. After they have finished reciting the sutras the monks begin to play their reed organs, flutes, and panpipes again, producing beautiful sounds that are heard far and wide.

It is at this time that the river lanterns begin floating downstream in bunches. They drift slowly, calmly, and steadily, and there are no visible signs that there are ghosts in the river waiting to snatch them away. As the lanterns drift downstream they give off golden flashes of light that combine with the masses of spectators to give a sense of real activity. There are more river lanterns than can be counted, perhaps hundreds or even thousands. The children on the riverbank clap their hands, stomp their feet, and shout continuously in appreciative delight. The adults, on the other hand, are so completely absorbed in the sight that they utter not a sound and act as though they have been mesmerized by the light of the lanterns glistening on the river. The water glimmers under the rays of the lanterns, while moonlight dances on the surface. When in the history of man has there ever been such a magnificent spectacle!

The clamor continues until the moon is directly overhead and the evening star and its followers fill the sky, at which time the grand spectacle gradually begins to abate.

The river lanterns have begun their voyage several *li* upstream, and after a long, long while start passing in front of the people. They continue to drift for a long, long while before they have all passed by. During this process some are extinguished in the middle of their voyage, others are dashed against the riverbank where they are snagged in the wild grass growing there. Then, too, when the river lanterns get to the lower reaches children use poles to snatch them out of the water, and fishermen lift out a couple that drift near their boats, so that as time goes by the number of lanterns diminishes.

As they approach the lower reaches they have thinned out so much that they present a desolate and lonely sight. They drift to the farthest part of the river, which appears pitch black, and one after another they disappear.

As the river lanterns pass by, though many fall behind and many others sink below the surface, nonetheless one still does not have the feeling that they are disappearing on the palms of ghosts. As the river lanterns begin their voyage far upstream the people's hearts are light and gay, and they experience little emotion as the lanterns pass in front of them; it is only at the end, when the lanterns have drifted to the farthest point of the lower reaches, that an involuntary emptiness grips the hearts of the river-lantern watchers.

"Where do those river lanterns float to, after all?"

When things have reached this point most people pick themselves up and leave the riverbank to return to their homes. By then not only have the waters grown desolate, but the riverbank, too, is deserted and quiet. If you should then gaze far downstream, with each successive glance still another river lantern is extinguished, or perhaps two die out simultaneously, and at this time it truly looks as though they are being carried away on the palms of ghosts.

By the third watch the banks are completely deserted and the river is totally devoid of lanterns. The river waters are as calm as ever, though gusts of wind now and then raise slight ripples on the surface. The moon's rays do not strike the river as they do the ocean, where splinters of gold flash about on the surface; here the reflection of the moon sinks to the bottom of the river, making it seem as though a fisherman could simply reach out and lift it into his boat.

The southern bank of the river is lined with willow groves; the northern bank of the river is where the town of Hulan River is located. The people who have returned home after watching the river lanterns are probably all fast asleep, but the moon continues to cast its rays down onto the river.

III

The open-air opera is also performed on the bank of the river, and also in the autumn. If, for example, the autumn harvest is good, there will be an opera performance to thank the gods. If there is a summer drought, people wearing willow headdresses will call for rain; dozens of them will dash back and forth in the streets for days, singing and beating drums. These rain dancers are not permitted to wear shoes, so that the venerable Dragon King will take pity on them as their feet are scalded on the sun-drenched ground, and reward them with rain. Then if the rains do in fact come, there will be an opera performance in the autumn as fulfillment of the vows taken during the rain dance. All vows must be fulfilled, and since they included the offering of an opera, then that opera must be performed.

A performance lasts for three days.

A stage is put up on a sandbar alongside the river. It is erected on poles that are tied together and covered with an awning, so that it won't matter if it drizzles, and the stage will be protected from the sun's rays.

After the stage has been finished bleachers are erected on both sides, which include gallery seats. Sitting in the gallery seats is very desirable, for not only is it cool there, it also affords one the opportunity to look all around the area. But gallery seats are not easy to come by, as they are reserved for local officials and members of the gentry; most people seldom get the chance to use them, and since tickets are not sold, even money won't buy them.

The construction of the stage alone takes nearly a week. When the stage framework has been put in place the towns-people say: "The stage framework is up." Then when the awning is in place they say: "The stage awning is in place."

Once the stage is completed a row of bleacher seats is placed to the left and to the right of it, parallel and facing each other. They extend for a distance of perhaps fifty yards.

Seeing that the structure is nearly completed, the people go to fetch their families and call their friends. For example, when a young married woman who is visiting the home of her parents is about to return to her husband's home, her mother will see her just beyond the front gate, wave to her, and say: "When the opera is performed in the autumn I'll come and fetch you."

Then as the cart bearing her daughter moves off into the distance, the mother says again with tears in her eyes: "I'll come and fetch you when it's time to watch the opera."

And so the opera entails more than just the simple enter-tainment of watching a performance; it is an occasion to summon daughters and sons-in-law, a time of great festivity.

The daughter of a family to the east has grown up, and it is time for the son of a family to the west to take a wife; whereupon the matchmaker begins to make her calls on the two families. Arrangements are made for both sets of parents to look the children over below the opera stage on the first or second day of the performance. Sometimes these arrangements are made only with the boy's family, without telling the girl's, something known as "stealing a look." This way it doesn't matter whether or not the match is made, and it offers more freedom; for, after all, the girl is unaware of what is going on.

With this in mind, all the young maidens who go to watch the opera make themselves up as nicely as they can: they wear new clothes, apply rouge and powder to their faces, trim their bangs neatly, and comb their braids so that not a hair is out of place. Then they tie their braids with red bands at the top and green at the bottom, or perhaps with bands of pink and light blue. They carry themselves with the airs of honored guests, and as they nibble on melon seeds they hold their heads high and keep their eyes fixed straight ahead in a cultured and refined manner, as though they have become the daughters of highly respected families. Some are dressed in long robin's-egg-blue gowns, some in purplish blue, and others in silvery gray. Some of them have added borders to their gowns: there are robin's-egg-blue gowns with black borders, and there are pink gowns made of muslin adorned with dark blue borders. On their feet they wear shoes of blue satin or embroidered black satin. The shoes are embroidered with all manner of designs: butterflies, dragonflies, lotus flowers, peonies.

The girls carry embroidered hankies in their hands and wear long earrings, which the local people call "grain-tassel earrings." These grain-tassel earrings come in two types: one is made of gold and jadeite, the other of copper and glass. Girls from wealthy families wear gold ones, those from less-well-off families wear glass ones. At any rate, they are all attractive as they dangle beneath the girls' ears. Dazzling yellows and deep greens, set off by very correct smiles on their faces; who can all these respectable young ladies be?

Young married women also make themselves up and gather to meet their sisters of the neighborhood below the stage, where they examine and compare each other. So-and-so looks very comely, the curls of temple hair on so-and-so are shiny black; so-and-so's bracelet is the newest thing at the Futai Jewelry Shop, so-and-so's hair ornaments are dainty and lovely; the embroidery on so-and-so's dark purple satin shoes is exquisitely done.

The old women shy away from colorful clothes, though every one of them is neat as a pin. They carry long pipes in their hands and arrange their hair in buns atop their heads, looking very kindly and gentle.

Before the opera performances have even begun, the town of Hulan River is all a-bustle, as the people scurry about fetching the young married daughters and summoning sons-in-law; the children have a delightful little ditty they sing:

> Pull the long saw,
> Drag the long saw;
> By Grandpa's gate they sing an opera song.
> The daughters are brought,
> The sons-in-law too;
> Even the grandchildren all go along.

By then young nephews, third aunts, second aunts by marriage — the reunions all start taking place.

Every family performs the same tasks: they kill chickens, buy wine, greet visitors with smiles, and talk among themselves of family affairs. They discuss matters of interest deep into the night, wasting more lamp oil than anyone knows.

An old woman in such-and-such a village is mistreating her daughter-in-law. The old grandfather of such-and-such a family makes a scene whenever he drinks. And how about the girl who married into such-and-such a family just barely a year before giving birth to twins! Did you hear about so-and-so's thirteen-year-old son who has been betrothed to an eighteen-year-old girl? The people nearly talk the night away under the light of candles and lanterns amidst a warm and cheery atmosphere of intimacy.

In families where there are many daughters who have already married it sometimes happens that as many as two or three years pass without an opportunity for the sisters to be reunited, since they usually live far apart. Separated by rivers or mountains and encumbered with many children and household duties, it is fruitless for them to even think of calling on one another.

And so when their mother summons them all home at the same time, their meeting truly seems as though it follows a separation of decades. At their family reunion they are at a loss for words and terribly shy; wanting desperately to say something, they hold back, overcome by embarrassment the moment they begin to speak, and before long their faces are flushed. They greet each other with silence, their hearts torn between happiness and sadness. But after the time it takes to smoke a pipeful, when the blood that had rushed to their faces has receded and the dizzying effects of their meeting have abated, they finally manage a few short comments of little relevance, such as: "When did you arrive?" or: "Did you bring the children?" They dare not utter a single word regarding their separation of several long years.

On the surface they don't seem the least bit like sisters, since there isn't the slightest trace of an expression of affection; as they face each other it is impossible to determine their relationship. It looks as though they were complete strangers, that they had never met before, and were seeing one another for the first time today, so coolly formal do their attitudes seem. But this is only the exterior; a mutual understanding has long filled their hearts. For that

matter, as many as ten days or two weeks earlier their hearts
had already begun to stir, starting from the day they had
received their mother's letters. The letters had said that
she wanted to summon the sisters home to watch the opera,
and from that moment on each of them began deciding upon
the gifts she was going to take home to give her sisters.

It might be a pair of black velvet cloud-slippers that she
made with her own hands. Or perhaps in the town or village
where one of them is living there is a famous dyer's shop
that produces beautifully hued cotton goods, so she will
supply the shop with a couple of bolts of white cotton fabric
and instructions to dye them as delicately as possible. One
bolt is to have blue designs over a white background, the
other white designs on a blue background. The design on the
blue material is to be a little boy with bangs playing with a
gold coin, that on the white material is to be butterflies
frolicking among lotus flowers. One bolt will be given to
elder sister, the other to younger sister.

All these things are packed in a hamper and brought along,
then after a day or two, during a quiet evening, she will
gently remove them from the bottom of her hamper and
place her elder sister's gift in front of her, saying: "Why don't
you take this dyed cotton quilt cover back home with you!"

That is all she says, not at all the sort of thing one would
expect from someone giving a gift. Her way is quite different
from that of modern times, where a person gives some little
present and, afraid that the neighbors might miss the event,
shouts and carries on, boasting that it comes from a certain
mountain somewhere, or that it came straight from the
ocean. Even if it only came from a little stream somewhere,
the glories of that particular stream have to be sung — how un-
common and unique it is, not at all like your average stream.

These countryfolk with their muddling ways don't know
how to express what they feel, and so they say nothing, but
simply hand the thing over and are done with it.

The recipient of the gift says nothing either — not a single word of thanks — and merely takes it from her. Some will briefly decline to accept the gift, saying: "Why don't you just keep it for your own use!" Naturally the giver refuses to do so, at which time the gift is accepted.

Every young woman who returns to her mother's home to watch the opera brings a great many different items along with her — gifts for her parents, her brothers and their wives, nieces, nephews, and other members of the family. Whoever brings the most and can produce a little something for each of her elders and all of the young children is the one who is judged to be the warmest and most affectionate.

Talk of these things, however, must await the completion of the opera performances and the dismantling of the stage; then they gradually work their way into each family's conversations.

Every young woman who then returns to her husband's home from the home of her parents takes back with her a wealth of objects that have been given to her as gifts. There is an abundance of things to use and things to eat: salted meat that her mother had prepared with her own hands, fish that her elder sister had personally dried and cured, and the pickled drumstick of a wild goose that her brother had shot on a hunting trip in the mountains (this has been given to the young woman who had come home for the opera for her to take back for her father-in-law to enjoy with his wine).

With one thing and another to keep them busy on the night before their departure, the sisters don't even have a free moment to talk to each other, and when they finish there is a pile of packages of all sizes.

During the period of the opera performances, besides family reunions and gatherings of friends, there are many other happy events taking place, specifically the engagements of young couples and the announcements of their forthcoming weddings in March or April of the following year. After the drinking of the betrothal wine comes the exchanging of the "engagement gifts," which constitutes a legally binding commitment; once it has been completed, the girl is considered a daughter-in-law in the boy's family.

Families with marriageable children from neighboring villages also come to town for the opera, leaving the young boys and girls at home and making arrangements for the nuptials through a matchmaker. Sometimes during the drinking and festivities some families will casually promise their daughters to someone, and there are even those who betroth their unborn sons and daughters. This is called a "marriage made in the womb," and it generally only occurs between families of substantial means.

Both families are very wealthy: one operates the local distillery, the other is a big landowner from White Flag Village. One of the two families plants sorghum, the other distills wine. The distiller needs sorghum, and the sorghum farmer needs a distiller to buy his harvest; a distillery cannot get by without sorghum, and sorghum must have its distillery. By a happy coincidence, the wives of both families are pregnant, and so they arrange a "marriage made in the womb." It makes no difference who has a boy and who has a girl, for as long as there is one of each, they are proclaimed husband and wife. Now if both give birth to boys, there is no need to force the issue of their marriage, and the same holds true if both give birth to girls.

The drawbacks of these "marriages made in the womb," however, greatly outnumber the advantages. If along the way the fortunes of one of the families should decline — if the distillery should go out of business or the landowner lose his land — then the remaining family would be unwilling to gain a poverty-stricken daughter-in-law or lose its daughter to a family of no means. If it is the girl's family that has suffered reverses, then the matter is easily disposed of, for

if the marriage agreement is not honored, there is nothing
they can do about it. But in cases where the boy's family
has fallen on bad times, inasmuch as a boy must take a wife,
if the marriage is then canceled, the girl's reputation is
ruined; people will say that she "brought injury" to so-
and-so's family, and then would not marry into it. The
superstition surrounding these words "brought injury" is
that a certain family has been reduced to poverty owing to
the harshness of the girl's horoscope. From that time on it
will be extremely difficult to find a family that will accept
her as a daughter-in-law, and she will be labeled an "un-
wanted spinster." With this unhappy prospect before it, her
family will reluctantly allow the marriage to take place.
But as time goes on, her sisters-in-law will accuse her of being
a woman who cares only for luxury, and they will insult her
in every conceivable manner. Eventually even her husband
will grow to dislike her, and she will be mistreated by her
parents-in-law; unable to withstand so much abuse, this
unworldly young woman returns to her parents' home, but
there is nothing that can be done there either. The mother
who years before had been a party to the "marriage made
in the womb" will say to her: "This is all part of your 'fate,'
and you must accept it as best you can!"

The young women, bewildered, cannot understand why
they must suffer such a fate, and so tragedy is often the
result; some jump down wells, others hang themselves.

An old saying goes: "A battlefield is no place for a
woman." Actually, that's not a fair statement; those wells
are terribly deep, and if you were to casually ask a man
whether or not he would dare to jump down one, I'm afraid
the answer would be "no." But a young woman, on the
other hand, would certainly do so. Now while an appearance on a battlefield doesn't necessarily lead to death,
and in fact might even result in an official position later,
there's not much chance of someone emerging alive after

jumping down a well — most never do.

Then why is it that no words of praise for the courage of these women who jump down wells are included in the memorial arches for a chaste woman? That is because they have all been intentionally omitted by the compilers of such memorials, nearly all of whom are men, each with a wife at home. They are afraid that if they write such things, then one day when they beat their own wife, she too may jump down a well; if she did she would leave behind a brood of children, and what would these men do then? So with unanimity they avoid writing such things, and concern themselves only with "the refined, the cultured, and the filial. . . ."

These are some of the things that happen before the staging of the first opera. Once the performances actually begin, throngs of people swarm around the foot of the stage, pushing and shoving insufferably. The people who erect the stage certainly know what they are doing: they select a large level sandbar beside the river that is both smooth and clean, so that even if someone were to fall down his clothing wouldn't get the least bit soiled. The sandbar is about a half *li* in length.

The people are laughing and carrying on as they watch the opera performance, making such a loud commotion they invariably drown out the chorus of gongs and drums. On the stage someone dressed in red walks on as someone in green walks off, and this parade of people walking on and off is about all the spectators notice; naturally they are unable to tell you if the singing is of high quality or not, since they cannot even hear it. Those closer to the stage can see that the beardless actor's mouth is open; those farther away can't even tell clearly whether the actor on stage is a male or female. One might think it would be preferable to watch a puppet theater.

But supposing a puppeteer were to come around then

and begin singing; if you asked these people if they would prefer to watch him, their answer would be emphatically negative, and even those who are so far away they cannot even make out the edge of the stage, or, for that matter, those as much as two *li* distant, still would not choose to watch the puppet show. For even if all they do is take a little snooze beneath the big stage and then go home, what counts is that they have returned from a spot beneath the big opera stage, and not from some other place. Since there isn't much of anything else to see during the year, how could they lightly let this opera performance pass them by? And so whether they watch it or not, they must at least put in an appearance at the foot of the opera stage.

They come from the countryside, riding in great wagons with teams of horses, in carts pulled by old oxen, in fancily decorated carriages, and in small drays pulled by big mules. In a word, they arrive in whatever vehicles they happen to own, and those who don't raise horses or other beasts of burden hook up a young donkey to a carriage that they have decorated and come in it.

After they have arrived they leave their vehicles and their animals on the sandbar, where the horses feed on the grass and the mules go down to the river to drink. Awnings are put up over their carts, which then become little bleachers standing in a line some distance from the stage. The carts and wagons have brought entire families, from grandmothers to the wives of their grandsons — three generations of family — and have deposited them a considerable distance from the stage. They can hear nothing and can see only figures in red and green wearing strange hats and clothing as they run around in circles on the stage. Who can tell what they are doing up there on the stage? Some people attend all three days of the performances, yet cannot tell you the name of a single opera performed. They return to their villages and relate to others their experiences, and if by chance someone

should ask them what opera they are talking about, their
sole answer is a long, hard stare.

The children at the foot of the stage are even less aware
of what is going on. About all they know is that there is
someone with a beard and someone else with a painted face
up there, but they haven't the slightest idea what they are
doing; just a confusion of movements and a flurry of swords,
spears, clubs, and staffs. At any rate, there are peddlers
of rice pudding and candy balls beneath the stage, so the
children can always go and eat what they like. There are all
kinds of things like rice cakes, pan-fried buns, and fermented
bean curd, and since these things are not filling, they can
always sample a little of everything. Watermelons are sold
there, and muskmelons, and there are swarms of flies buzzing
to and fro.

The heavens reverberate with the clanging of gongs and
the beating of drums at the foot of the stage. Apparently
concerned that the people in the rear cannot hear them, the
actors shout their songs for all they are worth, but they could
never drown out the chorus of gongs and drums even if they
destroyed their vocal cords in the process. People beneath
the stage have long since forgotten that they are there to
watch the opera, as they talk interminably about this or that.
Men and women alike spend their time discussing domestic
affairs. Then there are the distant relatives who never see
each other throughout the year; meeting her today, how
could they not greet one another? Therefore maternal and
paternal aunties shout to each other amidst the crowds of
people gathered there. Suddenly an old woman sitting in the
bleachers beneath one of the awnings jumps to her feet and
shouts out: "Second Maternal Auntie, when did you get here?"

She is answered by the person she has called to. Now the
people in the gallery seats are relatively near the stage, close
enough to actually hear the singing, so it is generally less
noisy there. Young women — married and unmarried — sit

there nibbling melon seeds and sipping tea. People are naturally annoyed by the shouts of this old woman, but they dare not try to stop her, for the minute they asked her to speak a little more softly, she would begin cursing them: "This open-air opera isn't being performed just for your family, you know! If you want to hear some opera then invite the troupe of actors to come to your house to sing it!"

Then the other woman would chime in with: "Well, I'll be! I've never seen anything like this. Once they start watching the opera they don't even give a damn about their own kin. Why, a person can't even talk. . . ."

These are some of the nicer things; there are worse. Out of their mouths might come such comments as: "You husband-stealing slut . . . screw your grandmother! Never in my life have I heard a harsh or angry word from anyone, and now you expect me to let you tell me what to do . . . up your mother's. . . ."

If the abused party lets this pass without notice, the whole incident is soon forgotten, but if there is a reply, naturally it will not be one that is very pleasing to the ear. What ensues is a brawl between the two parties, with watermelon rinds and other objects flying back and forth.

Here we have people who have come to watch an opera performance, but who have unexpectedly begun putting on their own show beneath the stage. Like a swarm of bees, people rush over to watch this real-life, knock-down-drag-out performance. Several ruffians and good-for-nothings in the crowd shout their approval, causing all present to roar with laughter. If one of the combatants is a young woman, then those irksome ruffians, with their lewd comments, provoke her into more volatile and viciously abusive language.

Naturally the old woman has been guilty of shouting abuses at the other without any regard for propriety or reason, but after a while it is impossible to tell who is in the right and who is in the wrong.

Fortunately, the actors on the stage remain cool and collected, not wavering from their singing in the face of this disruption, so that in the end the slugfest and all its attendant commotion gradually die down.

Another activity at the foot of the stage is the flirting that goes on, primarily by people like the married woman from the bean-curd shop on Avenue South, or the wife of the miller who runs the grain mill. The miller's wife has her eye on one of the carters, or a bean-curd maker casts amorous looks at the daughter of a grain-shop owner. With some, furtive glances pass back and forth between both of them, but on other occasions one of the parties is eagerly attentive, while the other demonstrates total indifference. The latter situation usually involves one member of the upper class and one from a lower class, two people with a great disparity in family wealth.

Members of the gentry also have their flirtations as they sit in the gallery seats casting glances here and there. They cannot help but eye members of their own families — in-laws, cousins, and the rest — especially since every one of them is made up so beautifully and is so eye-catching.

Normally when members of the gentry call upon one another in the guest halls of their homes they absolutely will not allow themselves to ogle their host's daughter; this would be terribly ungentry-like behavior, not to mention immoral. And if one of these young girls were to tell her parents, they would immediately sever their relationship with the friend in question. Actually, a severed relationship isn't all that serious; what is important is that once this information has leaked out, the person's reputation is quite ruined, and since the gentry are supposed to be noble, how could they let their names be besmirched? How could they permit themselves to desire the daughter of a friend without respect to the difference in ages, like the lower classes do?

When members of the gentry come calling they are ushered into the guest hall, where they seat themselves very correctly, drink a little tea, and smoke a pipe. Well-mannered and ceremoniously courteous, they give one another the respect due a peer. The wife and children come out to pay their respects, treating the guest as their elder, and in such a situation the guest can inquire only about how many books the young master has read and how many more characters he has learned to write. He cannot speak more than a few words even to his friend's wife, to say nothing of the daughter; he cannot even raise his head to face her, let alone give her the once-over.

But here in the gallery seats it makes no difference, for if someone asks what he is doing, he can say he is just looking around to see if some of his friends are in any of the other rows. Besides, with all those people casting glances here and there, most likely no one is even paying attention. A look here and a look there, and even though he doesn't fall for any of his friends' daughters, he has an infatuation for a woman he has seen somewhere before. This woman is holding a small goosefeather fan over which she looks his way. She might be a married woman, but she is certainly young and pretty.

Logically, this particular member of the gentry ought to stand up right then and whistle to show how pleased he is, but the older Chinese gentry don't operate that way. They have a different way of acting; he just looks straight ahead, his eyes half-open in that style of his that shows the limitless affection he feels for the woman. But unhappily, she is so far away she probably cannot see him clearly, and his efforts may all be in vain.

Some of the young people beneath the stage refuse to heed the admonitions of their parents and the counsel of matchmakers, and pledge their lives to one another on their own, though these activities are generally restricted to cousins who are the sons and daughters or fairly respectable families. They vow on the spot to share their lives forever. For some of these young couples their parents' obstruction will produce a great many frustrations. But these frustrations will be beautiful ones, as talk of them will engender more interest than a reading of the romance *Dream of the Red Chamber*, and during the opera performances of years to come, the young girls' reminiscenses will be greatly enhanced by talk of such delightful things.

The countryfolk who have come to town in carts for the opera pitch camp on the sandbar beside the river. In the evening after the day's performance has ended, the townspeople return to their homes, leaving only those with their carts and horses to spend the night on the sandbar. The scene is reminiscent of a military bivouac with the ground beneath and the sky above. Some just stay over for the night and return home the next day, while others stay for all three nights, until the performances are concluded, before they drive their carts back to the country. Needless to say, the sandbar presents a fairly impressive sight at nighttime, as each family sits and drinks tea or chats among itself around a campfire, though, in point of fact, their number is rather too small — no more than twenty or thirty carts. Since the campfires they build aren't numerous enough to really light up the sky, there is a certain air of forlornness there. In the deep of night the river water turns especially cold, chilling the people sleeping on the riverbank. It is even worse for the carters and others who tend the animals, as they cannot sleep for fear that bandits may come and steal their horses, and must sit there waiting for the coming day. Sitting beneath paper lanterns in groups of twos and threes, they gamble until the first light of day appears, at which time they lead their horses down to the river to drink. There they are met by an old fisherman in a crab boat who says to them: "Yesterday's performance of *A Fisherman's Revenge* wasn't bad. I hear they're going to do *Fenhe Bay* today."

The fellow who has led his animal to the water knows nothing at all about opera. He listens only to the lapping noises of the drinking animals, having no response to any comments made to him.

IV

The festival at the Temple of the Immortal Matron, which falls on the eighteenth day of the fourth lunar month, is for spirits and ghosts, not people. This festival, which the local people call a "temple stroll," is attended by men and women of all ages, although most are young women.

The young women get up in the morning and begin combing their hair, bathing, and preparing themselves as soon as breakfast is over. Then after they have finished getting themselves ready, they arrange with neighbor girls to go and join the temple stroll. Some begin making themselves up the moment they get out of bed, even before breakfast, then leave the house as soon as they have eaten. In any event, on the day of the temple stroll there is a mad rush to get there early, so that before noon the temple grounds are already so crowded there is barely room to breathe.

Women who have lost their children in the crush stand there shouting, while the children who cannot find their mothers cry in the midst of all those people. Three-year-olds, five-year-olds, and even some two-year-olds who have just learned to walk are separated from their mothers in crowds.

Consequently there are policemen at the festival each year whose job is to locate such children and stand on the temple steps until their parents come to claim them. Since these children are always the more timorous ones, they wail loudly and pitifully until their faces are bathed in tears and sweat. Even twelve- and thirteen-year-olds get lost, and when one of them is asked where he lives, he is invariably stumped for an answer. Pointing first to the east, then to the west, he says that there is a small river running past his gate, which is called "Shrimp Canal" because it is full of tiny shrimp. It is possible that the place where the child lives is itself called "Shrimp Canal," a name that means nothing to the people who hear it. When asked how far from town this Shrimp Canal is, the child answers that it is about a meal's ride on horseback or three meals' ride in a cart. But this doesn't tell you how far from town the place is. Asked his family name, he answers that his grandfather is called Shi Er and his father, Shi Cheng, and no one dares pursue the matter any further. If he is asked whether or not he has eaten, he answers: "I've already had a nap." There's nothing anyone can do at this point, and it's best to just let him go; and so children of all ages gather at the temple gate under the watchful eyes of policemen, crying and shouting, and sounding like a pack of small animals.

The Temple of the Immortal Matron is on Avenue North, not far from the Temple of the Patriarch.

Even though the people who go to light incense at the temple are doing so to ask for sons and grandsons, and by rights should first light their incense in front of the Immortal Matron, still they believe that men are considered superior to women in the nether world, just as they are here, and they dare not upset the cosmic order. Consequently, they always go first to the Temple of the Patriarch, where they strike the gong and kowtow to the deity, as though they were kneeling there to report for duty; then and only then do they proceed to the Temple of the Immortal Matron.

In the Temple of the Patriarch there are more than ten clay images, and it is hard to tell just which one is the Patriarch, as they are all so imposing and stern, truly looking as though they rise above the world. The fingertips of some of the clay idols have been broken off, and they stand there with their fingerless hands raised in the air; some have had their eyes gouged out and look like blind people; some even have written characters scribbled all over their toes, characters with rather inelegant meanings that are not at all suited to deities. There are comments that say that the clay idol should take a wife or else it will be jealous when it sees the monks chasing after the little nuns. Actually, the characters themselves no longer remain, but this is what people say used to be written there.

Because of this the County Magistrate once sent down an order that the doors of all temples were to be closed and locked except on the first and fifteenth of each month, and no loiterers were to be allowed entrance.

This County Magistrate is a man particularly concerned with the Confucian concepts of humanity, justice, and morality. The story has it that his fifth concubine was taken from the nunnery, so he has always been convinced that no nun would ever try to tempt a monk. From earliest times nuns have been ranked together with monks, and inasmuch as the common people do not personally investigate the situation, they simply parrot what others before them have said. Take the County Magistrate's number five concubine, for example: she herself was a nun, and is it possible that she too had once been sought out by some monk? There isn't the slightest chance of that. And so the order was sent to close all temple doors.

The Temple of the Immortal Matron is generally more serene than the others. There are clay idols there too, mostly female, which are for the most part devoid of harsh, malignant stares. People are simply not frightened by them when they enter the main hall, since the idols look pretty much like common people. Obviously, these are the Matrons, and of course they are good and obedient females. Why, even the female ghosts are not paticularly malevolent; their hair is a little mussed up and that's about all. There isn't one that even barely resembles the clay idols in the Temple of the Patriarch, with their flaming eyes or tigerlike mouths.

Children are not the only ones who are frightened to tears when they walk into the Temple of the Patriarch; even a young man in his prime becomes very respectful when he enters, as if to show that even though he is in the prime of his life, if that clay idol were to take it into its head to walk over and begin fighting with him, the man would certainly come out on the short end. And so whoever kowtows in the Temple of the Patriarch, where the clay idols are so tall and powerful, does so with greater piety.

When they go to the Temple of the Immortal Matron the people also kowtow, though they have the feeling that there is nothing very spectacular about the Matron.

The people who cast the clay idols were men, and they fashioned the female figures with an obedient appearance, as though out of respect to women. The male figures they fashioned with a savage, malignant appearance, as though in condemnation of men's dispositions. That, however, is not the case. Throughout the world, no matter how fiercely savage, there has probably never been a single man who had flaming eyes. Take Occidentals, for instance: though their eyes are unlike those of the Chinese, it is simply that theirs are a limpid blue, somewhat resembling those of cats, but certainly not flaming. The race of people with flaming eyes has never appeared on the face of the earth. Then why have the people who cast the clay idols made them look that way? For the simple reason that a single glance will strike fear into someone, and not only will he kowtow, he will do so with absolute conviction. Upon completing his kowtows, when he rises and takes another look, there will never be the slightest regret; the thought that he has just prostrated himself before an ordinary or unremarkable individual would simply not occur to him. And why have the idol-makers cast the female figures with such obedient appearances? That is in order to tell everyone that obedience indicates a trusting nature, and that the trusting are easily taken advantage of; they are telling everyone to hurry and take advantage of them!

If someone is trusting, not only do members of the opposite sex take advantage of her, but even members of the same sex show no compassion. To illustrate: when a woman goes to worship at the Temple of the Immortal Matron all she does is ask for some sons and grandsons. Her prayers ended, she rises and leaves, and no manifestations of respect are apparent. She has the feeling that the Matrons of Sons and Grandsons is nothing but a common, ordinary woman who just happens to have a surplus of children.

Then when men hit their wives they can say: "The Immortal Matron is supposed to be in constant fear of being beaten by the Patriarch, so what makes a gossipy woman like you any different?"

It is obvious that for a man to beat a woman is a Heaven-ordained right, which also holds true for gods and demons alike. No wonder the idols in the Temple of the Immortal Matron have such obedient looks about them — this comes from having been beaten so often. It becomes apparent that obedience is not the exceptionally fine natural trait it has been thought to be, but rather the result of being beaten, or perhaps an invitation to receive beatings.

After they have worshiped at the two temples the people come out and crowd into the streets, where there are peddlers of all types of toys, most of which are suited for the smaller children. There are clay roosters with two red chicken feathers stuck on to make a tail, making the toys look better by far than the real thing. Anyone with children will be forced to buy one, especially since it will make a loud whistling noise when put to the mouth and blown.

After they have bought the clay roosters the children spy some little clay men with holes in their backs in which reeds can be inserted to make whistles. The sound they make is not very pleasing to the ear — almost like a cry of grievance — but the children like it, so their mothers have to buy them.

Of the remaining toys — the whistles, reed flutes, metal butterflies, and tumbler dolls — it is the tumbler dolls that are the most popular and the ones made with the greatest care. Every family buys one — bigger dolls for the well-to-do families, smaller ones for poorer families. The big ones are nearly two feet in height and the small ones can be as tiny as a duck's egg. But big or small, they are all very lively. They right themselves the moment they are pushed over, quickly and without fail. They are tested on the spot by every prospective buyer; occasionally, if a doll has been made by an inexperienced hand, the bottom will be too large and the doll will not fall over, while others will fall over and not right themselves. So before they buy the tumbler dolls, the people invariably reach out and push them all over together, then buy whichever one rights itself first. This process of knocking them down and watching them right themselves produces a great deal of hilarity among the children who surround the peddler's stand to laugh at the goings-on.

A tumbler doll is very attractive, so white and plump, and though it is called "the old man who won't fall down," this is just a name, and the toy looks nothing like an old man. In fact, it is a fat little child, and the ones that have been made with a little more care even have a few strands of hair that represent the child's hair. The ones with hair sell for ten coppers more than those without, and many of the children are adamant in wanting a doll with hair. Not wishing to make this additional expense, the child's mother offers to take it home and add a few hairs she can cut off the family dog. But the child insists on having one with hair already on it, so he picks one of them up and refuses to put it back. Seeing that there is nothing she can do, the mother buys it for him. The child carries the doll with him on the road back home, happy as can be, but by the time he arrives home he discovers that the tuft of hair has already fallen off somewhere along the way, and he begins to cry loudly. His mother quickly cuts a few hairs from the family dog and sticks them onto the doll, but the child cannot help but feel that this hair is not the real thing and doesn't look nearly as good as the original. Now the original hair may very well have been dog hair too, for that matter, and worse looking than what is on the doll now, but the child is not content with it, and is dejected for the rest of the day.

By the afternoon the festival is concluded, but the temple doors remain open, and there are still some people inside burning incense and worshiping the Buddha. Women who have no sons remain inside the Temple of the Immortal Matron to play some little tricks: they stick buttons onto the back of the Matron of Sons and Grandsons, tie red sashes around her feet, and hang earrings on her ears. They fit her with a pair of eyeglasses, then steal off with one of the clay infants that have been placed beside her, in the belief that they themselves will then produce sons the following year.

There are a great many peddlers of sashes at the gate to the Temple of the Immortal Matron, and the women flock to buy them, believing that this purchase will bring a son into the family. If an unmarried girl should inadvertently buy one she becomes the object of a great deal of raucous laughter.

Once the temple festival is over, each family is in possession of a tumbler doll, even those who live as far away from the city as eighteen *li*. When they get home they place the doll just inside the front door so that other people can see it at a glance and know that this family now has a tumbler doll of its very own. This is incontrovertible evidence that the family was not left behind during the time of the festival, but clearly had participated in the "stroll."

There is a local song that goes:

> Dear young woman, take your temple stroll.
> A graceful walk, a charming gait;
> And don't forget to buy a tumbler doll.

V

All these special occasions are designed for ghosts, certainly not for people. Although the people do get to watch some opera and take their temple strolls, these are really only the incidental benefits they receive.

The dance of the sorceress is all about ghosts; the great opera is sung for the benefit of the venerable Dragon King; the river lanterns, released on the fifteenth day of the seventh lunar month, are used by ghosts to light the road to transmigration by carrying them over their heads; the lighting of incense and kowtowing on the eighteenth day of the fourth lunar month is also to honor ghosts.

Only the harvest dances are performed for the benefit of the living and not for ghosts. These dances are performed on the fifteenth day of the new year, during the season of rest for those who work the land. They take advantage of the New Year's festivities to masquerade themselves, with men making themselves up as women and presenting a comical scene that delights everyone.

Lion dances, dragon-lantern dances, land-boat dances, and the like, also seem to be in honor of ghosts, though there are so many different kinds it is difficult to give a clear account of them all.

3

Granddad and Me

I

The town of Hulan River is where my granddad lived. When I was born Granddad was already past sixty, and by the time I was four or five he was approaching seventy.

The house where we lived had a large garden that was populated by insects of all types — bees, butterflies, dragonflies, and grasshoppers. There were white butterflies and yellow ones, but these varieties were quite small and not very pretty. The really attractive butterflies were the scarlet ones whose entire bodies were covered with a fine golden powder.

The dragonflies were gold in color, the grasshoppers green. The bees buzzed everywhere, their bodies covered with a fine layer of down, and when they landed on flowers their plump little round bodies appeared to be motionless tiny balls of fur.

The garden was bright and cheerful, deriving its freshness and beauty from all the reds and the greens. It had once been a fruit orchard that was planted because of Grandmother's fondness for fruit. But Grandmother had also been fond of raising goats, and they had stripped all the bark from her fruit trees, killing them. From the time of my earliest recollection the garden had only a single cherry tree and a single plum tree, and since neither bore much fruit, I was not very aware of their existence. When I was a child

I was conscious only of the garden's big elm tree. This tree, which was in the northwest corner of the garden, was the first to rustle in the wind and the first to give off clouds of mist when it rained. Then when the sun came out, the leaves of this big elm tree shone radiantly, sparkling just like the mother-of-pearl found on a sandbar.

Granddad spent most of the day in the rear garden, and I spent my time there with him. Granddad wore a large straw hat, I wore a small one; when Granddad planted flowers, so did I; and when Granddad pulled weeds, that's what I did too. When he planted cabbage seeds, I tagged along behind him filling in each of the little holes with my foot. But with my random and careless footwork, there was no way in the world I could have made a neat job of it. Some of the time not only did I fail to cover the seeds with soil, I even sent the seeds themselves flying with my foot.

The Chinese cabbages grew so quickly that sprouts began appearing within just a few days, and in no time at all they were ready to be picked and eaten.

When Granddad hoed the ground, so did I, but since I was too small to manage the long handle on my hoe, Granddad removed it and let me do my hoeing using only the head. Actually, there wasn't much hoeing involved in it, as I really just crawled along on the ground chopping and digging at will with the head of my hoe, not bothering to differentiate between the sprouts and the grass. Invariably I mistook leeks for weeds and pulled them all out together by their roots, leaving the foxtails, which I had mistaken for grain stalks, in the ground. When Granddad discovered that the plot of ground I had been hoeing was covered only with foxtails, he asked me: "What is all that?"

"Grain," I answered.

He started to laugh, and when he had finished he pulled up a foxtail and asked me: "Is this what you've been eating every day?"

"Yes."

Seeing that he was still laughing, I added: "If you don't believe me, I'll go inside and get some to show you."

So I ran inside and got a handful of grain from the bird-cage, which I threw to Granddad from a distance, saying: "Isn't this the same thing?"

Granddad called me over and explained to me patiently that the grain stalks have beards, while the foxtails have only clusters that look very much like real foxes' tails. But although Granddad was teaching me something new, I wasn't really paying any attention, and I only made a cursory acknowledgement of what he was saying. Then, raising my head, I spotted a ripe cucumber and ran over, picked it, and began to eat. But before I had finished, a large dragonfly darting past me caught my eye, so I threw down the cucumber and started chasing after it. But how could I ever expect to catch a dragonfly that flew that fast? The nice part about it was that I never really had any intention of catching it, and only got to my feet, ran a few steps, then started doing something else.

At such times I would pluck a pumpkin flower or catch a big green grasshopper and tie one of its legs with a piece of thread; after a while the leg might snap off, so there would be a leg dangling from the piece of thread, while the grasshopper from which it had come was nowhere to be found.

After I grew tired of playing I would run back over to where Granddad was and dash about noisily for a while. If he was watering the plants, I would snatch the watering gourd away from him and do it myself, though in a peculiar fashion: instead of sprinkling water on the vegetables themselves, I would splash the water upward with all my might and shout: "It's raining, it's raining!"

The sun was particularly strong in the garden and there was a very high sky above. The sun's rays beat down in all directions so brightly I could barely keep my eyes open; it was so bright that worms dared not bore up through the ground, and bats dared not emerge from their dark hiding places. Everything that was touched by the sunlight was healthy and beautiful, and when I smacked the trunk of the big elm tree with my hands, it resounded; when I shouted it seemed as though even the earthen wall standing opposite me was answering my shouts.

When the flowers bloomed it was as though they were awakening from a slumber. When the birds flew it was as though they were climbing up to the heavens. When the insects chirped it was as though they were talking to each other. All these things were alive. There was no limit to their abilities, and whatever they wanted to do, they had the power to do it. They did as they willed in complete freedom.

If the pumpkins felt like climbing up the trellis they did so, and if they felt like climbing up the side of the house they did so. If the cucumber plant wanted to bring forth an abortive flower it did so; if it wanted to bear a cucumber it did so; if it wanted none of these, then not a single cucumber nor a single flower appeared, and no one would question its decision. The cornstalks grew as tall as they wished, and if they felt like reaching up to the heavens, no one would give it a second thought. Butterflies flew wherever they desired; one moment there would be a pair of yellow butterflies flying over from the other side of the wall, the next moment a solitary white butterfly flying over from this side of the wall. Whose house had they just left? Whose house were they flying to? Even the sun didn't know the answers to such questions.

There was only the deep blue sky, lofty and far, far away.

But when white clouds drew near they looked like great etched silver ingots, and as they passed over Granddad's head they were so low they seemed about to press down and touch his straw hat.

When I had grown tired from all my playing I searched

for a cool, shady place near the house and went to sleep. I didn't need a pillow or a grass mat, but simply covered my face with my straw hat and fell asleep.

II

Granddad had smiling eyes and the hearty laugh of a child. He was a very tall man of robust health who liked to carry a cane when he walked. Never without a pipe in his mouth, whenever he met children he loved to tease them by saying: "Look at that sparrow up in the sky."

Then, when the child was looking skyward, he would snatch the child's cap off his head. Sometimes he stuck it up under his long gown, other times he hid it up his wide sleeve; then he would say: "The sparrow has flown away with your cap."

The children all knew this trick of Granddad's and were never fooled by it; they would wrap their arms around his legs and try to get their caps back by feeling around inside his sleeve or by opening up the inner lapel of his gown until they found what they were looking for.

Granddad often did this, and he always hid the caps in the same places — either up his sleeve or inside the lapel of his gown, and there wasn't a single child who didn't find his cap inside Granddad's clothing. It was as though he had made an agreement with the children: "Now I'll just put it in here and you try to find it."

I don't know how many times he did this, but it was a lot like an old woman who is forever telling the story of "Going Tiger Hunting on the Mountain" to the children; even if they have already heard it five hundred times, they still clap their hands and shout appreciatively each and every time. Whenever Granddad played this little trick both he and the children laughed loud and long, as though it were the very first time.

Other people who saw Granddad do this usually laughed too, but not in appreciation of his sleight-of-hand; rather they laughed because he used the same method each and every day to snatch away the children's caps, and this was a very comical thing as far as they were concerned.

Granddad wasn't much good at financial matters, and all the household affairs were handled by my grandmother. He simply passed his day relaxing to his heart's content, and I felt it was a good thing I had grown up — I was three — otherwise, how lonely he would have been. I could walk . . . I could run. When I was too tired to walk Granddad carried me, and then when I felt like walking again he pulled me along. Day in and day out, inside or out-of-doors, I never left his side; for the most part, Granddad was in the rear garden, and so that's where I was too.

When I was little I had no playmates to speak of, and I was my mother's first-born child. I can remember things from my very early childhood, including a time when I was three years old and my grandmother used a needle to prick my finger. I disliked her a great deal as result of this.

The windows in our house had paper stuck up on all four borders, with an inlay of glass in the center. Grandmother had an obsession with cleanliness, and the paper in the window of her room was always the cleanest in the house. Whenever anyone carried me into her room and put me down on the edge of the *kang,* I would dash over to the window beside the *kang* almost automatically, reach out to touch the white paper with the floral decoration in her window, and poke some small holes in it with my finger; if no one interfered, there would soon be a whole line of little holes, but if they did try to stop me, I would hurriedly poke one or two final holes before stopping. That paper was as tight as a drumhead, so it made a popping noise each time my finger poked through. The more holes I made, the more pleased I was with myself, and I was even happier when Grandmother came and tried to chase me away — I would laugh, clap my hands, and stomp my feet.

One day when Grandmother saw me coming she picked up a large needle and went around to the outside of the window to wait for me. The moment I poked my finger through, it began to hurt like the dickens, and I shouted out in pain. Grandmother had pricked my finger with the needle. From that time on I never forgot what she had done, and I disliked her because of it.

She sometimes gave me candy and shared her pork kidney with me when she prepared kidney and Sichuan fritillary for her cough, but after I had finished the kidney I still didn't like her.

Once, when her illness was at its worst and her days were numbered, I gave her a real scare. She was sitting by herself on the edge of the *kang* mixing some medicine in a kettle that rested on a charcoal brazier beside her. The room was so quiet I could hear the medicine bubbling in the kettle. Grandmother lived in two rooms, one inner and one outer, and by a happy coincidence, that day there was no one else in either the outer or the inner room — she was all alone. She didn't hear me open the door, so I rapped loudly with my fist on the wooden partition: Bang, bang! I heard her blurt out "Oh!" as the steel fire tongs crashed to the floor. When I looked inside, she saw me and began cursing at me. She looked like she was going to climb down and chase after me, so I ran off laughing.

Frightening Grandmother like that wasn't something I had done for revenge; I was just an ignorant little five-year-old, and I probably just thought it would be fun.

All day long Granddad was idle, as Grandmother was unwilling to give him any jobs to do. There was just one thing: on a casket on the floor there were some pewter ornaments, and Granddad regularly polished them. I'm not sure if he was given this assignment by her or if it was something he undertook to do on his own. But whenever he began to polish them, I grew unhappy, partly because this meant he couldn't take me out to play in the rear garden, and also because he would often be yelled at; Grandmother would scold him for being lazy and scold him for not doing a good job of polishing. And whenever she began to scold him, somehow or other even I got yelled at.

When Grandmother started to scold Granddad, I took him by the hand and started walking out with him. "Let's go out into the rear garden," I would say.

Maybe that's the reason Grandmother started scolding me too. She would curse at Granddad, calling him a "useless old bag of bones," and then call me a "useless little bag of bones."

I would lead Granddad out into the rear garden, and the minute we got there we were in a different world altogether. We were no longer in the confined and cramped environment of the room, but in a spacious world where we were at one with heaven and earth. The sky above and the ground below were vast, stretching far, far into the distance; try though we might, we could not touch the sky with our outstretched hands. And the earth around us was so luxuriant with growing things that we could not take it all in at a single glance, which made us feel that we were surrounded by a vast layer of fresh greenery.

As soon as I stepped into the rear garden I began aimlessly running to and fro. It may have looked as though I was running after something that had caught my eye, or that there was something just waiting for my arrival, but I actually seldom had any objective in mind at all; I simply felt that absolutely everything in the garden was so alive that I was powerless to keep my legs from jumping. When Granddad called to me to stop before I wore myself out, if I hadn't yet exhausted my energy I would have none of it, and, in fact, the more he called for me to stop, the worse I behaved.

I would sit down to rest only when I was too tired to even move, but my respites were very brief ones: I would sit down right in the middle of a vegetable bed, pick a cucumber, and eat it. Then after this brief rest I would be up and running again.

Obvious though it might have been that there was no fruit on the cherry tree, I would still climb up the tree to look for some cherries. The plum tree was already half dead, and had long since stopped bearing fruit, but still I went over to look for plums. As I searched for them I shouted out questions to Granddad: "Grandpa, why aren't there any cherries on the cherry tree?"

"There aren't any cherries because there are no flowers on the tree," Granddad would answer from afar.

"Why aren't there any flowers on the cherry tree?"

"There aren't any flowers on the tree because you have such a greedy mouth."

As soon as I heard this I knew he was teasing me, and I would virtually fly over to where he was standing, pretending I was mad at him. But when he raised his eyes to look at me, I could see that there was no trace of malice in the look he gave me, and I would break out laughing. I would laugh for the longest time before I could stop. Just where all this happiness came from, I simply couldn't say. I don't know how loud my laughter was during such hell-raising in the rear garden, but it seemed even to me to be earsplitting.

There was a rosebush in our rear garden that bloomed every June and stayed in bloom until July. Each blossom was as big as a soy-sauce plate, and they were in such great profusion that the entire bush was covered with them. The fragrance of the flowers attracted tremendous numbers of bees to the rosebush, around which they swarmed with a great buzzing noise. When I had tired of playing with everything else I would be reminded of this rosebush and its flowers, and I would pick a great many of them and put them into the overturned crown of my straw hat. There were two things that frightened me about picking the roses: first I was afraid that I might be stung by a bee, and second that I might prick my fingers on a thorn. One time I picked a large bunch of the flowers, which was no easy task for me, but then I found I didn't know what to do with them after having picked them. Suddenly a brilliant idea came to me: Wouldn't Granddad look terrific wearing these flowers!

He was kneeling on the ground picking weeds, so I began adorning him with flowers, and though he was aware that I was playing around with his hat, he didn't know for sure just what I was up to. I decorated his straw hat with a wreath of twenty or thirty bright red flowers, laughing all the while.

"The spring rains have been heavy this year," he said. "The flowers on that rosebush of ours are so fragrant you can smell them a couple of *li* away."

I was so convulsed with laughter when I heard him say this that I was barely able to continue sticking the flowers in, and even after I had finished, Granddad was still blissfully unaware of what was happening. He just kept pulling up the weeds from a little mound of earth. I ran off some distance and stood there, not daring to even look over to where he was in order to keep from laughing. I took the opportunity to go inside the house for something to eat, and before I returned to the garden, Granddad followed me into the house.

The moment he stepped inside, Grandmother noticed the bright red flowers that covered his head. She didn't say a word when she saw them, but just broke out laughing. My father and mother started to laugh too, though I was laughing the hardest of anyone and rolling around on the *kang*.

Then Granddad took off his hat, looked at it, and found that the source of the fragrance of the roses wasn't a result of heavy spring rains this year, but rather because his head was covered with a wreath of flowers. He put his hat down and laughed for a full ten minutes or more without stopping;

after a while he thought about it again and broke out laughing. Then just when he seemed to have forgotten the incident, I reminded him of it again: "Grandpa, the spring rains this year have sure been heavy."

With this reminder Granddad's laughter returned, and I started rolling around on the *kang* again.

This is how it went, day in and day out: Granddad, the garden, and me — the inseparable trio. I don't know how windy or rainy days affected Granddad, but I always felt extremely lonesome. With no place to go and nothing to do, such a day seemed to me to last several days.

Hard though I may have wished it otherwise, the rear garden was sealed off once every year. Following the autumn rains it would begin to languish; the flowers would yellow and fall, and it seemed that they would very soon wither and die, almost as though there were someone crushing and destroying them. None of them appeared as hardy as before — it was as though they were worn out and needed rest, and were thus putting their affairs in order before returning to the place from which they had come.

The big elm tree was also shedding its leaves, and on those occasions when Granddad and I sat beneath the tree, its leaves fell upon my face. Soon the rear garden was blanketed with the fallen leaves.

Before too long heavy snows would begin to fall, burying the garden. The rear door leading into the garden was sealed with a thick layer of mud, and frost and icicles hung from it throughout the winter.

There were five rooms in our house, two for my grandparents and two for my parents. My grandparents occupied the rooms to the west, my parents the ones to the east. The five rooms of the Main house were arranged in a line, the middle one being the kitchen; the rooms all had glass windows, dark green walls, and tile roofs.

My grandparents had an outer and an inner room. The former was furnished with a large oblong chest, a rectangular table, and an armchair. There was a red cushion on the armchair, a vermilion vase atop the oblong chest, and a desk clock on the rectangular table. Hat stands were placed on either side of the clock, though instead of being used for hats, they were decorated with a number of peacock feathers. As a child I was intrigued by those peacock feathers; I used to say that there were gold-colored eyes on them, and I was forever wanting to play with them. But Grandmother refused to let me touch them — Grandmother had an obsession with cleanliness.

The desk clock atop the oblong chest was a strange-looking timepiece on which was painted the very lifelike figure of a young maiden dressed in ancient costume. Whenever I was in Grandmother's room alone, this young maiden glowered at me, and I told Granddad about this several times; but he always said: "She is just a painted figure; she can't stare at you."

But I was convinced that she could, and I told him that as far as I was concerned her eyeballs moved.

The large oblong chest in Grandmother's room was also decorated from one end to the other with carved human figures, each of them wearing ancient costume — wide-sleeved gowns, officials' caps, and peacock feathers. The chest was virtually covered with the figures — there must have been twenty or thirty of them; some were drinking wine, others were eating, and still others were in the act of bowing.

I was forever trying to get a closer look at the figures, but Grandmother wouldn't let me get within arm's length of the chest, saying to me as I stood off at a distance: "Don't you dare touch it with your filthy hands!"

On the wall of Grandmother's inner room hung a strange, strange clock that had two metal cornhusks suspended by chains beneath it. The metal cornhusks were a lot bigger than real ones, and looked to be so heavy that you could kill a person if you hit him with one. The inside of the clock was even stranger and more curious; there was a figure of a little blue-eyed girl inside, and every second those eyes of hers moved in concert with the ticking noise of the clock.

The differences between that little girl with her yellow hair and blue eyes and me were too great, and even though Granddad told me that it was the figure of a *maozi ren* or "hairy one," I wouldn't accept the notion that she was supposed to be a real person. Every time I looked at that wall clock I stared at it so long I began to look dazed. I thought to myself: "Doesn't that *maozi ren* do anything else but stay inside that clock? Won't she ever come down and play?"

In the slang of Hulan River, Caucasian foreigners were called *maozi ren.* When I was four or five I had yet to see my first *maozi ren,* and I thought this girl was called "hairy one" because she had such curly hair.

There were a lot of other things besides these in Grandmother's room, but since none of them really interested me in those days, I can only remember these few items.

In my mother's rooms there were none of these kinds of unusual curios; there were only commonplace things like a gold-bordered wardrobe and a variety of hat stands and flower vases — nothing remarkable enough to linger in my memory.

In addition to these five rooms — four serving as living quarters plus a kitchen — there were two incredibly small and dark rooms in the rear of the house, one for my grandparents and one for my parents. These rooms were filled with things of all kinds, since they served as storerooms. Earthen jugs and pitchers, chests and wardrobes, baskets and hampers — besides the things that belonged to our family, there were objects that other people had left there for safekeeping.

It was so dark inside the rooms that I could see only if I carried a lantern in with me. The air inside these rat- and cobweb-infested rooms was pretty bad, and there was always a sort of medicinal odor that assailed my nose. I loved playing in those storerooms, since any chest that I opened was invariably filled with a number of good-looking things like colorful silk thread, strips of silk of all colors, perfume satchels, waistband pouches, trouser legs, detachable over-sleeves, and embroidered collars, all of them antique-looking, their colors blending together beautifully. Often I would also find jadeite earrings or rings in the chests, and when I did I was so insistent about wanting one to play with that Mother would usually toss one over to me.

Then there were the drawers in a desk that yielded up even more interesting items: copper rings, a wooden knife, bamboo measuring sticks, and the white material we called Guanyin powder. These were all things I had never seen anywhere else, and the best part was that these drawers were never locked. So I opened them pretty much whenever I felt like it, digging out whatever was inside without being the slightest bit selective. Holding the wooden knife in my left hand and some Guanyin powder in my right, I chopped here and daubed there. Then I came across a little saw, and I began destroying things right and left with it, sawing on objects like chair legs and the edges of our *kangs*. I even ruined my little wooden knife by sawing on it. I carried these things with me whether I was eating or sleeping. At meals I used my little saw to cut open steamed buns, and when I dreamed at night I would shout out: "Where did my little saw go?"

The storerooms became in a way the scenes of my explorations. Often, when Mother was not in her room, I would take the opportunity to open the door and go inside. There was a window at the rear of the storeroom through which a little light filtered in during the afternoons. I used to take advantage of this light to open the drawers, all of which

I eventually rummaged through completely, until there was nothing new to be found inside them. I would go through them again until I lost interest, then emerge from the room. In the end I even dug out a lump of resin and a little piece of string, at which time I had picked all five desk drawers absolutely clean.

In addition to these drawers there were some baskets and trunks, but I didn't have the nerve to touch them, since they were all so dark and covered with who knows how much dust and how many layers of cobwebs that I never even gave a thought to touching them.

I remember that once when I went to the farthest and darkest recess of this unlighted room, my foot bumped into something with a thud. I picked it up and carried it over to the light, where I discovered that it was a lantern. I scraped off some of the dust with my finger, revealing that it was made of red glass. The chances are that when I was one or two years old I had seen this lantern before, but by the time I had reached four or five I no longer recognized it and didn't really know what to call this thing I was holding in my hand. I carried it out with me to ask Granddad what it was. After he had cleaned it all up for me he stuck a piece of candle inside. I was so delighted with it that I carried it all around the room with me, and, in fact, ran around with it in my hand for several days until I finally dropped it, smashing it to smithereens.

Once I also bumped into a piece of wood in the unlighted room. The top part of the wood had carvings on it and was very rough to the touch. I took it outside and began sawing on it with my little saw, until Granddad spotted me: "That's an engraving block for printing currency certificates," he said.

I had no idea what a currency certificate was, so he smeared a little ink on it and printed one to show me. I could only see that there were a few human figures on it, plus some motley designs and some written characters.

"When we operated the distillery we used this to make the currency certificates we issued," he told me. "This one is for a thousand coppers; we also had them for five hundred and one hundred." He printed up a bunch of them for me, and even printed some using red ink.

I also found and tried on a tasseled hat worn during the Qing dynasty, and I fanned myself with a great big goose-feather fan that had been around for many years. During my rummaging I came across a little *sharen*, which was a medicine for stomach ailments. Mother took some, and I took some right along with her.

Before too long I had brought all these ancient relics out into the open; some had been put there for safekeeping by my grandmother, while others had been stored by aunts of mine who had married and left home. They had lain in that storeroom for years, touched by no one. Some of the things were falling apart, and others were infested by bugs, owing to the fact that they had long been neglected by their owners. It was as though they no longer existed on the face of the earth. Suddenly here they all were, right in front of everyone's eyes, and the memories of these things came rushing back to them with a start.

Each time I brought out some new item, Grandmother would say to me: "This goes back a lot of years! Your eldest aunt played with this when she was living at home."

If Granddad saw something he might say: "Your second aunt used this when she was living at home," or: "This was your eldest aunt's fan; those embroidered shoes belonged to your third aunt. . . ." Everything had a history of its own. The problem was, I didn't know who my third aunt and my eldest aunt were. Perhaps I had seen them when I was one or two years old, but I had forgotten them by the time I was four or five.

My grandmother had three daughters, though by the time I was old enough to know about such things, they had all

married and left home. Obviously, for some twenty or thirty
years there had been no children around, and now there was
only one — me. Actually, I had a younger brother, but at
the time he was no more than a year old, so he didn't count.
All these things had been put away in the house years before
and left untouched. The people led their lives, looking
neither ahead nor behind; that which was in their past was
forgotten, while they held out no great hope for the future.
They simply passed their days in their stolid fashion, uncom-
plainingly accepting the lot handed down to them by their
ancestors.

My birth had proved a source of inestimable joy to my
Granddad, and as I grew up I was the apple of his eye.
As for me, I felt that all I needed in this world was Granddad,
and with him by my side I had nothing to fear. Even the
cold attitude of my father, my mother's mean words and
nasty looks, and the incident in which my Grandmother
pricked my finger with a needle faded into insignificance.
And if that weren't enough, there was also the rear garden!
And even though the garden was sealed off by ice and snow
some of the time, I had discovered the storerooms. Just
about everything conceivable could be found inside, and the
treasures they held were often things I had never imagined
could even exist. I was struck by the thought of how many,
many things there must be in this world! And all of them
fun and unique.

For example, once I dug up a package of dye — Chinese
dark green — and although it gave off a gold sheen when I
looked at it, the moment I dabbed some on my fingernail,
the fingernail turned green; then when I rubbed a little on
my arm, the spot appeared a leafy green. It was both highly
attractive and highly confusing, and I was secretly delighted
to think that I might have stumbled onto a real treasure.

I came across a chunk of Guanyin powder. When I rubbed
this powder on the door, a white streak appeared on it, and

when I rubbed it across the window, it left a white streak there too. This was very strange to me; probably what Granddad used when he wrote was black ink, I thought, and what I had here was white ink.

I also discovered a round piece of glass that Granddad called a "magnifying glass." Holding it under the sun, I found that it could light the tobacco in his pipe.

How happy things like this could make me, as each and every one of them underwent some kind of change. Someone might call a certain thing a piece of scrap metal, but who was to say it might not prove useful? To illustrate: once I picked up a square piece of metal that had a small hole on the top, into which Granddad placed a hazelnut, cracked it, then gave it to me to eat. Breaking the hazelnut open in that hole was unbelievably faster than using his teeth to open it. Besides, Granddad was an old man, and most of his teeth weren't much good anyway.

Every day I moved objects out of that dark room, and every day there was something new. I would carry out a load of things and play with them till I broke or grew tired of them, then go and get some more. All of this caused a lot of sighing on the part of my grandparents. They told me how old a certain thing was, that it had been in our home before my third aunt was even born. Then they told me how old something else was, that it had been brought to our home when my great-grandfather's inheritance was divided up. Then there was this thing or that, given to us by someone whose family had by this time completely died off without a trace, and yet this object was still around.

I remember the wicker bracelet that I used to play with; Grandmother told me that she had worn this bracelet, and that one summer she was riding to her mother's home in a small carriage, carrying my eldest aunt in her arms, when she encountered some bandits on the road. They took her gold earrings from her, but not this bracelet. Had it been made of gold or silver, there was the danger it too would have been taken by them.

After hearing this story I asked her: "Where is my eldest aunt now?"

Granddad chuckled as Grandmother answered me: "Your eldest aunt's children are all older than you."

So this incident had happened some forty years earlier; no wonder I wasn't aware of it! Yet here I was, wearing that very same wicker bracelet, so I raised my arm and twirled it in the air, which made it look like some kind of windmill as it slithered up my arm — you see, the bracelet was too big and my arm too thin.

Grandmother often observed me moving the things from the past out of the room and scolded me: "There's nothing you won't play with, child! You'll never amount to anything."

Though this was what she was saying, still she seemed to gain some satisfaction from the reminiscences this opportunity to see these objects from her past in broad daylight afforded her. Consequently, her scolding wasn't particularly harsh at all, and naturally I paid no heed, but went right on picking up whatever I pleased.

As a result, these things in our house that had not seen the light of day for the longest time reappeared only because I had brought them out. Afterwards they either wound up broken or discarded, until they all finally ceased to exist.

This was how I passed the first winter that I can remember. Although I didn't actually feel lonely, it could never be as much fun as playing in the rear garden. But then, children forget easily and can make the best of any situation.

IV

The following summer we planted a lot of leeks in the rear garden because Grandmother liked to eat dumplings stuffed with leeks. But by the time the leeks began to appear, Grandmother had become seriously ill and could not eat them, and since no one else in the family ate leeks, they were left neglected in the garden.

Owing to the seriousness of Grandmother's illness, the house was all a-bustle; my eldest aunt and my second aunt both came.

Second Aunt came in a carriage owned by her husband's family and pulled by a donkey with a bell around its neck that tinkled loudly as it stood beneath the window.

First out of the carriage was a child who hopped down onto the ground. This child, who was my second aunt's son, was a little taller than I. His nickname was Little Orchid, and Granddad told me to call him Orchid Brother. I don't remember what else happened, and I only recall that before long I was leading him out into the rear garden. I told him that this was a rosebush, this was called a foxtail, and the cherry tree no longer bore any fruit.

I didn't know if he had ever seen me before, but I was sure I had never laid eyes on him. As I was leading him over to look at the plum tree in the southeast corner, he said to me as we approached it: "This tree died the year before last."

He surprised me when he said this. How did he know that this tree had died? I began to experience pangs of jealousy, as I felt that this garden belonged to me and Granddad, and that other people had no right to know anything about it.

"Then you've been to our home before?" I asked him.

He answered that he had.

This made me even angrier; why wasn't I informed that he had been to our home before?

"When were you here?"

He said it had been the year before last, and that he had brought me a little stuffed monkey. "Don't you remember? After you grabbed the stuffed monkey and ran off, you fell down and started to bawl!"

Hard as I tried, I couldn't remember the incident. But at any rate, considering that he had given me a stuffed monkey and was nice to me, I could no longer be angry at him.

From then on we played together every day. He was eight years old — three years my senior — and he told me he was studying in a school. He had even brought a few books along with him, which he took out and showed me in the evenings beneath the light of a kerosene lamp. The words for "people," "scissors," and "house" were printed inside, and since there were illustrations for all of them, I was confident I could read the words the moment I saw them, so I said: "This is read *jiandao,* for 'scissors,' and this is read *fangzi* for 'house.'"

"No," he corrected me, "this is the single character *jian,* and this is *fang.*"

I pulled the book over and looked closely. Sure enough, there was only one character given for each, not two; I had been going by the illustrations, and so I was wrong. I also had a box of flash cards with illustrations on one side and the characters on the other, so I brought them out and showed them to him.

From that time on we played together all day long, every day. I was no longer aware of the state of Grandmother's illness, although I noticed that a few days before she died they put a set of new clothes on her, as though she were going visiting. They said they were afraid that if she died there wouldn't be enough time to dress her in new clothing.

Owing to the seriousness of Grandmother's illness, the house was all a-bustle, with many relatives coming to call, all of them busily doing one thing or another. Some were noisily tearing out strips and patches of white cloth; off to the side others were sewing these patches together; while still others were filling small jars with rice and sealing the mouths with red cloth. Someone else went out into the rear garden to set up a fire for frying wheat cakes.

"What are those?" I asked.

"These are cakes to ward off dogs."

She told me there are eighteen check stations in the nether world, and when you reach the station of the canines, the dogs there will come up to try and bite you. But if you throw out some of those cakes, the dogs will eat them instead of attacking. It seemed to me that she was just talking to hear herself talk, so I didn't pay any attention to what she was saying.

The more people who came to our house, the lonelier I got. I would walk into a room to ask about this or that, but it was all beyond my comprehension. Even Granddad seemed to have forgotten me. Once, after catching an especially large grasshopper in the rear garden, which I took in to show him, he said without even looking: "That's fine, that's just fine. Now you go out and play in the garden, all right?"

On days when Orchid Brother wasn't with me, I just played in the rear garden all alone.

V

Grandmother was now dead, and everyone else had already been to the services at the Dragon King Temple and returned; as for me, I was still playing in the rear garden.

A light rain started to fall there, so I decided to go inside and get my straw hat. As I walked by the pickling vat (at our house the pickling vat was located in the rear garden), I noticed a couple of drops of water land noisily on the lid, and it occurred to me that since the lid was so large, it would keep the rain off me a lot better than my straw hat. So I flipped it over onto the ground, where is rolled around a bit, just as the rain started falling heavily. With a great deal of difficulty I managed to find a way to squeeze myself under the lid, which was really too big for me to handle — it was almost as tall as I was.

I stood up and walked a few steps with it on my head, but I couldn't see a thing; it was so heavy it made walking very difficult. I had no idea where my steps were taking me, and all I noticed was the pitter-patter of rain above my head. Then I looked down at my feet and discovered that I was standing in a patch of foxtails and leeks. When I found a spot thick with leek plants I sat down and was immediately pinned to the ground by the lid, which now must have looked like a little roofed cottage. This was a lot better than standing, because I no longer had to carry the lid on my head — it was now supported by the patch of ground where the leeks were growing. But inside it was so pitch dark I couldn't see a thing.

Meanwhile, all the noises I heard seemed to be coming from far away. The big tree was rustling in the wind and rain, but it sounded as though it had been moved over into someone else's compound. The leeks had been planted at the base of the north wall, and I was sitting on the leeks. Since the north wall was a long way from the house, the noises of activity inside the house seemed to be coming to me from a great distance.

I listened very carefully for a while, but, unable to distinguish any of the sounds, I just kept sitting there inside that little cottage of mine. What a great little cottage it was, safe from the wind and the rain. When I stood up I walked off supporting my roof on my head, which made me feel as carefree as can be. Actually, it was quite heavy and made walking very difficult.

I felt my way along, propping up the lid of the vat as I walked over to the back door of the house with the idea of showing Granddad what I was carrying on my head. The threshold of our back door was quite high off the ground, and since the vat lid was so big and heavy, I couldn't step

over it. I didn't even have the strength to lift my legs. But
with a great deal of effort I was finally able to pull them
over with my hands, and I had more or less stepped across.
Having entered the house, I still didn't know which way to
go to find Granddad, so I shouted at the top of my voice.
But before the sound had died out my father gave me a kick
that sent me sprawling, almost knocking me into the wood
fire burning in the stove. The vat lid had crashed to the
ground, where it was rolling around.

After being helped to my feet, I looked around: something was very wrong here — everyone was dressed in white
clothing. Another look, and I could see that Grandmother
was sleeping, but not on her *kang;* she was laid out on top of
a long piece of wood.

From that day on Grandmother was dead.

VI

Following Grandmother's death a continuous stream of
relatives came to our house. Some of them brought incense
and paper money with them, went over and wailed beside
the corpse for a moment, then left to return home. Some
came with bundles of all sizes and stayed over with us.

While trumpets blared by the main gate, a mourning tent
was erected in the courtyard; wailing sounds filled the air
throughout the whole noisy affair, which lasted for more
days than I could count. Buddhist monks and Taoist priests
were brought over, and the commotion of all that eating,
drinking, talking, and laughing lasted late into the night.

It was fun for me too, and I was happy then, especially
since now I had some little playmates, where before I had
had none. Altogether there were four or five of them, some
elder than I, some younger. We climbed the tree and clam-
bered up onto the walls, and nearly climbed up onto the roof

of the house. They took me to catch pigeons on top of the small gate, and moved the ladder over under the house eaves so that we could catch some sparrows. Spacious as my rear garden was, it was no longer big enough to hold me.

I went with them over to the edge of the well and looked down inside. I had never seen just how deep that well was. When I shouted into it, someone down inside answered me; then I threw down a rock, and the noise it made when it hit the bottom came from far away. They also took me over to a grain storeroom and to a grain mill, and on occasion they even took me out onto the street. I had left the confines of my home, and not under the supervision of anyone in the family. I had never gone so far before.

The fact that there were bigger places than my own rear garden had never occurred to me, and as I stood there at the side of the street I was not so much looking at all the activity or at the people, animals, and carts, but wondering if someday I could travel as far as this all by myself.

One day they took me to the south bank of the river, which wasn't all that far from my house — probably less than a *li* — but since it was the first time I had ever gone there, it seemed to me that it was a long way off, and I worked up a sweat getting there. On our way we passed a loess pit and a military barracks with soldiers standing guard at the entrance. The courtyard in front of the barracks building looked much too large to me, larger than it had any right to be. The courtyard in our house was already big enough, so how could their courtyard be so much bigger? It was so big it made me uncomfortable, and even after we had passed by I kept turning my head back to look at it.

Then we passed a house on the road where the people had placed some potted plants along the top of the wall. This didn't seem like such a good idea to me, because someone might come along and steal them when no one was looking.

I also saw a small Western-style house that was ten times

better looking than my own house. If you had asked me what was so good about it, I couldn't have told you, but to my eyes it seemed new from top to bottom and not all worn-down like our house. I had traveled no more than half a *li* or so, but I had already seen an awful lot, which fortified my belief that the south bank of the river must still be a long way off.

"Are we there yet?"

"Just about, we're almost there," they answered.

And just as they had promised, as soon as we rounded the corner of the barracks wall the river came into view. This was the first time I had ever seen the river, and I wondered where its waters came from and how many years they had flowed here. It seemed enormous; I scooped up some dirt along the bank and threw it into the river without dirtying the water even a tiny bit. There were a few boats on the river heading in either direction, some of which were being rowed over to the apparently deserted opposite shore, which was lined with willow trees. I looked off even farther, but I didn't know what places I was seeing, since there weren't any people or houses or roads over there, and no sounds to be heard. I wondered whether someday I could go over to that deserted place myself and take a look around.

Beyond the rear garden at my house there was a wide street; beyond the street there was a wide river; beyond the river there was a willow grove; beyond the willow grove there were places even farther away, deserted places where there was nothing to be seen and no sounds to be heard. What else might there be beyond these places? The more I pondered this, the more any answers eluded me.

Leaving aside all those things that I was seeing for the first time in my life, even the courtyards and potted plants were different: we had a courtyard and potted plants at my house too, but the barracks courtyard was so much bigger than ours, and at our house we put the potted plants in the rear garden, while others put theirs on the tops of walls. It was obvious that there was a lot I didn't know.

And so Grandmother died, while I actually got smarter.

VII

After Grandmother died I began to study poetry with Granddad. Now that Granddad's room was empty, I caused a big scene by demanding to sleep in there with him.

I recited poems in the mornings and in the evenings, and I even recited them when I woke up in the middle of the night. I would recite for a little while until I was drowsy, then go back to sleep. Granddad taught me the verses in the *Thousand Poet Classic,* though instead of using a book, we relied on his memory. He would recite a line and then I would recite it after him.

Granddad would recite:

I left home young, I return an old man . . .

Then I would recite:

I left home young, I return an old man . . .

I couldn't have told you what the words meant, but they sounded good when I said them, so I shouted them out gleefully along with Granddad, though I was always louder than he was.

Whenever I recited poems I could be heard in every room in the house, and since Granddad was afraid I would injure my voice with all that shouting, he often said to me: "You're going to blow the roof right off the house!"

I would smile at this joke of his for a moment, but before long I was shouting again.

In the evening I shouted as always, until Mother scared me by saying if I kept it up she would spank me. Even Granddad said: "No one recites poetry like you do; that isn't 'reciting' poetry, it's just a lot of screaming."

But there was no way I could change my habit of

screaming, and if I couldn't shout, what was the use in reciting them anyway? Whenever Granddad started to teach me a new poem, if I didn't like the way it sounded, right away I said: "I'm not going to learn that one."

Then he would choose another one, and if it didn't please me, I'd say no to it too.

> I slept in spring not conscious of the dawn,
> But heard the gay birds chattering round and round.
> I remember, there was a storm at night;
> I know not how many blossoms fell to the ground.

I really liked this poem, and whenever I got to the second line, "But heard the gay birds chattering "round and round," the words "round and round" pleased me no end. I really thought this had a nice ring to it, especially the words "round and round."

There was another poem, "Flower Shadows," which I liked even better:

> Layer upon layer they cover the steps;
> The servant, summoned often, still cannot sweep them away.
> Taken from sight with the setting of the sun,
> The moon brings them back at the close of day.

But instead of "The servant, summoned often, still cannot sweep them away," I always said, "Serving some off the sill cannot sweep them away."

The more I recited it the better it sounded to me, and my interest grew with each recitation. Whenever we had company in our home Granddad had me recite my poems, and this is the one I liked doing the most. I don't know if the guests understood what I was saying, but they nodded their heads and complimented me.

VIII

Just memorizing a lot of poems without any understanding

of their meaning wasn't the long-range plan, and after I had memorized dozens of them, Granddad explained to me what they meant.

> I left home young, I return an old man;
> The speech is the same, though my hair is thin.

"This is about someone who left home to go out into the world when he was young and returned when he was an old man," Granddad explained. "'The speech is the same, though my hair is thin' means that the accent of his hometown remains the same even though his beard has all turned white."

"Why did he leave home when he was young?" I asked. "Where was he going?"

"Well, it would be just like your Grandpa here leaving home when he was about your age, then returning as old as he is now. Who would know him after all that time? 'The children see me, not knowing who I am / They smile and ask: "Stranger, where do you come from?"' You see, he is met by the children, who call out to him: 'Say, where have you come from, white-bearded old man?'"

I didn't like what I was hearing, so I quickly asked Granddad: "Will I be leaving home? Won't even you recognize me when I come home with a long white beard, Grandpa?"

My heart was filled with foreboding, but Granddad laughed and said: "Do you think your Grandpa will still be around when you get old?"

After he said this he could see I was still unhappy, so he quickly added: "You won't be leaving home . . . how could you leave home? Now, hurry up and recite another poem! Let's hear 'I slept in spring not conscious of the dawn'!"

As soon as I began reciting "I slept in spring not conscious of the dawn" out came the shouts again, and my contentment returned. I couldn't have been happier, and everything else was forgotten.

But from then on I made sure that every new poem was explained to me first, and I also made sure that the ones I had already learned were explained. It seemed like my habit of shouting and screaming had changed a little for the better.

> Two yellow orioles sing in the green willows;
> A line of egrets climb into the blue sky.

At first I like this poem a great deal, because I mistook the word for "orioles" as the word for "pears," and pears were one of my very favorite fruits. But after Granddad explained that this poem was about a couple of birds, I completely lost interest in it.

> This time last year behind this gate
>   her face and the blossoms glowed in the peach trees.
> Now the face is no more; only the blossoms
>   are still smiling in the spring breeze.

I didn't understand this poem either when Granddad recited it for me, but I liked it anyway. That was because peach blossoms were mentioned in it. After all, don't peach blossoms bloom just before the fruit appears? And aren't peaches delicious to eat?

So each time I finished reciting this poem I quickly asked Granddad: "Will there be any flowers on our cherry tree this year?"

IX

Next to reciting poetry, my favorite activity was eating.

I recall that the family who lived to the east of the main gate raised pigs, and there was always a bunch of little pigs following behind the sow. One day one of the little pigs fell down the well, and although someone fished it out with a dirt-carrying basket, it was already dead by the time they got it up. A lot of people had gathered around the sides of the well to see what all the commotion was about, and Granddad and I were there to join in the excitement.

As soon as they had gotten the little pig out of the well,

Granddad said he wanted it. He carried it home, where he packed it in yellow clay, then stuck it into the stove and cooked it. When it was done he gave it to me. I stood beside the *kang* with the whole pig lying there in front of my eyes, then when Granddad split it open, oil oozed out. It was so fragrant — I had never had anything that smelled as good in my whole life, and I had never eaten anything that tasted so delicious.

The next time it was a duck that fell down the well; Granddad also packed it in yellow clay and cooked it for me. I helped him do the cooking — that is, I helped him with the yellow clay, yelling and shouting all the while, just like a cheerleader rooting him on.

The duck tasted even better than the pig because there wasn't much fat on it, and so duck became my favorite food.

Granddad sat beside me watching as I ate, but he wouldn't take any for himself until after I had finished. He said that I had small teeth, which made it harder to bite, so he wanted me to eat the tenderest portions first, then he would eat whatever was left.

Granddad sort of nodded his head with each swallow I took and made lighthearted comments like: "What a greedy little thing you are," or "This little thing sure eats fast."

My hands were dripping with oil, which I rubbed on my lapels as I ate. Granddad said without a trace of anger: "Quickly, add a little salt and some leeks; you shouldn't eat that without anything else, or before you know it you'll have an upset stomach. . . ." So saying, he picked up a pinch of salt and put it on the piece of duck meat I was holding. I opened my mouth and stuffed the whole thing in.

The more Granddad praised my appetite, the more I ate. Starting to worry that I might eat too much, he finally told me to stop, and I put it down. I knew for sure that I couldn't eat another bite, but still I said: "Even a whole duck isn't enough for me!"

From that time on I thought a great deal about eating duck, but the longest time went by without another duck falling into the well. On one occasion I saw a flock of them in the vicinity of the well, so I picked up a stick and tried to drive them into it. But they just scattered and ran round and round the mouth of the well making loud quacking noises, and still none of them fell in. I yelled out to the kids nearby that were watching all the fun: "Give me a hand here!"

While we were shouting and running around, Granddad hurried over and asked:

"What's going on here?"

"I'm driving the ducks over to the well so one of 'em will fall in. Then we can fish it out and cook and eat it."

"There's no need to do that. Grandpa will catch one for you and take it home and cook it."

But instead of listening to him, I kept chasing after the ducks. He stepped in front of me and brought me to a stop, then picked me up in his arms and wiped the sweat off me as he said: "You come home with me now. I'll get a duck and cook it for you."

I thought to myself: You can't catch a duck unless it's fallen into the well, so does he expect one of them to just walk over and let itself be packed in yellow clay and cooked? I struggled to get down out of Granddad's arms as I yelled: "I want one that's fallen down the well! I want one that's fallen down the well!"

Granddad could barely hold me.

4

The Compound

I

By the time summer arrived the mugwort had grown as high as an adult's waist and was over my head; if the yellow dog ran in amidst it, you couldn't see a trace of him. The mugwort rustled in the night winds, and since it virtually covered the courtyard, the rustling noise was especially loud as big clumps moved noisily with each gust. When it rained, clouds of mist rose from the tips of the stalks, and even if the rainfall was actually a light one, it seemed to be quite heavy to anyone who was looking at the mugwort. During light drizzles the mugwort took on a hazy, indistinct appearance, as though covered by a layer of fog or an overcast sky. The scene was one of a frosty morning where everything is blurred under a pall of rising vapor.

The courtyard turned dreary with the coming of the winds and rain, and even on a clear day with the sun shining brightly in the sky the courtyard remained dreary-looking. There were no dazzling or eye-catching decorations there, nor a trace of any man-made objects. Everything just followed its own nature: if it wanted to grow this way, it grew this way; if it wanted to grow that way, it grew that way. A natural, primitive scene would have been maintained if only it had been left alone, but something was wrong here. What sort of scenery was this? Off to the east there was a pile of rotten

wood, while off to the west the ground was covered with
discarded firewood; to the left of the gate a layer of old
bricks, to the right a pile of clay drying in the sun.

The clay had been used by the cook to put up the kitchen
stove, and he had just dumped the remainder beside the gate.
If someone had asked him whether or not the leftover clay
could serve any purpose, I doubt that he could have come up
with any, and he had probably just forgotten all about it.

I hadn't the slightest idea what the old bricks were for, as
they had been there for a long time, buffeted by the wind,
baked by the sun, and drenched by the rain. But since bricks
are impervious to water, it really didn't matter that they
got rained on. As a result, no one gave them a moment's
thought, and just let them get rained on. In fact, there was
no reason to bother about them. if it happened that the
stove or the opening beneath one of the *kangs* was in need of
repair, they could still be used for the job. There they were,
right in front of you — all you had to do was reach out and
pick them up, and what could be handier than that? At any
rate, the stove seldom needed fixing, and the openings of
the *kangs* were well put together. I don't know where they
found such competent workmen, but the *kang* openings held
up for at least a year; if they were repaired in September,
by the middle of the following year they were still holding
up, and then when September rolled around again a plasterer
and a bricklayer were called, who used a knife to remove and
replace the bricks one at a time. And so that pile of bricks
by the side of the gate served little purpose the year round.
It remained there year after year, though it most likely grew
smaller as time went on, with this family taking one to use
as a base for a flower pot and that family taking one for
something or other. If the reverse had been true — that the
pile had grown bigger as time went on — things would have
been in a sad state, for eventually they would have blocked
the entire gate.

But, in fact, the pile did grow smaller. With no interference by man, the natural course of events would see to it that the pile would completely disappear within two or three years. At the time, however, it was still there in front of us, soaking up the sun just like the pile of clay nearby; the two piles kept each other company.

Additionally, there were also the splintered remains of a large vat that had been tossed over by the base of the wall, and an earthen jar with a chipped and broken mouth that rested on the ground alongside it. The jar had been put out there empty, but was now half-filled with rainwater; if you picked it up in your hand by the lip and shook it, you could see a tiny world of living creatures swimming around. Looking a little like fish and a little like insects, they were actually neither, and I could not tell just what they were. Looking at the big vat that was already splintered and standing there very precariously, threatening to topple over, you could see that there was nothing at all inside it. Actually, I shouldn't be saying "inside," since it was split wide open, and there was no longer any "inside" or "outside" to speak of; let's just call it a "vat pedestal." This vat pedestal, on top of which there was nothing, was delightfully smooth and shiny, and it even made a resounding noise when I slapped it with my hand. When I was young I liked to move it from one spot to another, for I was always fascinated by what I found: beneath the vat pedestal were swarms of sowbugs. When I spotted them I ran away in fright, but after running off some distance I would stop, turn back, and take a long look, watching the sowbugs scurry around for a moment before they crawled back under the vat pedestal.

Then why wasn't this vat pedestal thrown away? Probably it had been left there for the purpose of raising sowbugs.

Opposite the vat pedestal stood an overturned hog trough. I don't know how many years this hog trough had lain there upside down, but it was already rotting away. The bottom was covered with dark colored mushrooms, small ones that didn't look as though they were edible, and I never could figure out what they were growing there for. A rusty old steel plow was lying in the grass beside the trough.

Strange as it may sound, everything at our house seemed to come in twos; there were only pairs, no single items: The bricks lying in the sun had the clay to keep them company, the broken jar was matched up with the splintered vat, and the hog trough was accompanied by the steel plow. It was as though they were paired or mated to each other. Not only that, each couple brought new life into the world. There were, for example, the fishlike creatures in the jar, the sowbugs beneath the vat, the mushrooms that grew on the hog trough, and so on.

I don't know why, but the steel plow didn't look as though any new life was associated with it; meanwhile, it was falling apart and covered with rust. Nothing was born of it, nothing grew from it — it just lay there turning rusty. If you touched it with your finger, flakes fell to the ground, and although it was made of steel, it had by this time deteriorated so much that it looked as though it were made of clay that was on the verge of crumbling to pieces. When viewed alongside its mate, the wooden trough, there was absolutely no comparison — it was covered with shame. If this plow had been a person it would doubtless have wept and wailed loudly: "I'm made of better stuff than the rest of you, so why has my condition weakened to its present state?"

Not only was it deteriorating and rusting, but when it rained, the rusty pigment that covered it began to run, spreading with the rain water over to its companion, the hog trough, the bottom half of which had already been stained the color of rust. The fingers of murky water spread farther and farther away, staining the ground they touched the color of rusty yellow.

II

My home was a dreary one.

Just inside the front gate, along the eastern wall of the covered gateway, were three dilapidated old rooms, and along the western wall were three more. With the covered gateway in the middle, they gave the appearance of seven rooms standing in a line. From the outside they seemed very imposing with their tall roofs and sturdy frames of thick, solid wood. The posts were so thick that a child could not wrap his arms around one. All the buildings were roofed with tiles, and the ridges were adorned with tile decorations that were a delight to behold when the sun glinted off them. Each end of the house ridge was finished off with a pigeon, which was probably also made of tile. They remained there all year long, never moving. From the outside these buildings didn't look half bad.

But to my eyes there was an emptiness about them.

Our family used the three buildings to the west to store grain — there wasn't all that much grain kept in them, but there were hordes of rats. Holes had been chewed through the granary floors by the rats, whole families of which were eating the grain. And while down below it was being consumed by rats, up above it was being eaten by sparrows. A rank, moldy odor filled the rooms. The broken windows had been boarded up; the dilapidated doors shook on their hinges when they were opened.

The three buildings along the eastern wall beside the covered gateway were rented out to a family of hog farmers. Inside and out, there were nothing but "hogs" — grown hogs and newborn hogs, hog troughs and hogfeed. The only people who came and went there were hog dealers; the buildings, the people, everything was permeated with a horrible stench.

Come to speak of it, that family didn't raise all that many

hogs, perhaps eight or ten. Every day at dusk people far and near could hear the sounds of their hogcalls as they banged on the troughs and the tops of the sties. They would shout a few times, then stop; their voices rose and fell, and in the solemn evening air it sounded like they were complaining of the loneliness of their lives.

There were, in addition to these seven rooms standing in a row, six more dilapidated buildings — three run-down huts and three milling sheds.

The three milling sheds were rented out to the family of hog farmers, since they were located right next to the sties.

The three run-down huts, which were in the southwest corner of the compound, had run off by themselves a long way from everything else, and were standing all alone, squalid-looking and leaning to one side or the other.

The roofs of these buildings were covered with lichens, and from a distance appeared as an eye-catching patch of green. When it rained, mushrooms grew on the roofs, which the people climbed up to pick, like they were foraging for mushrooms on a mountain. There was always a bumper crop. Rooftops that produced mushrooms were a rare sight indeed, and of the thirty or so buildings my family owned, none of the others could boast this distinction. So whenever the people who lived there took their baskets up onto the roof to pick mushrooms, everyone in the compound would begin to comment enviously: "Those mushrooms are certainly nice and fresh, so much better than the dried ones we have. If you killed a young chicken and fried it along with them, it would be simply delicious!"

"Fried bean curd and mushrooms — my, wouldn't that be tasty!"

"Even a baby chick isn't as tender as rain-fed mushrooms."

"If you fried chicken with some of those mushrooms, everyone would eat the mushrooms and leave the chicken."

"If you cooked some noodles with those mushrooms,

everyone would drink the soup and forget the noodles."

"It would be quite a feat if someone could even remember his name while he was eating those mushrooms."

"If you steamed them and added some sliced ginger, you could eat at least eight bowls of steamed rice along with them."

"It'd be a mistake to treat something like those mushrooms lightly, because they're an unexpected windfall!"

The envious people who shared the compound hated themselves for not having had the good fortune to live in those huts, and if they had known that the crop of mushrooms went with the buildings, they would have insisted they be rented to them. Whoever heard of such luck — renting a house with mushrooms thrown into the bargain! They just stood there sighing and commiserating with one another.

Then, of course, what glory came to the person who was standing on the roof picking mushrooms under the scrutiny of all those eyes! So he picked them very slowly, and a job that should have taken no longer than the time it takes to smoke a pipeful was stretched out to perhaps half the time it takes to eat a meal. Not only that, he purposefully picked several of the larger ones and threw them down, saying as he did so: "Just look at those, will you! Have you ever in your life seen cleaner mushrooms than those? There isn't another rooftop around that has mushrooms like these."

The people down below had no way in the world of knowing just how big the rest of the mushrooms on the roof were, so they had to assume that they were all the size of the ones thrown down, which increased their astonishment no end. They hastily bent over, picked them up, and carried them home; then at dinnertime, when the bean-curd peddler came around, they splurged several coins on a little piece of bean curd and cooked it up with the mushrooms.

But, owing to his feelings of pride, the fellow on top of

the house has forgotten that there are several bad spots on the roof, some of which have even sprung holes, and in a careless moment he puts his foot completely through the roof. He pulls his foot back up through the hole only to discover that his shoe is missing.

The shoe has fallen from the ceiling staight down into a pot in which water is being boiled, and so his shoe is cooked in the pot of boiling water. The people sifting bean flour alongside the pot are both intrigued and amused by the sight of a shoe bobbing around in the boiling water; a murky substance oozes from the sole of the shoe, turning all the bean noodles that have already been sifted a yellowish color. But still they don't fish the shoe out of the pot, their explanation being that the bean noodles are to be sold anyway, and aren't intended for their own consumption.

The roof over this house could produce mushrooms, but it couldn't keep out the rain, and each time it rained, the whole room filled up like a jar of water. Everything in the room was wet to the touch.

Fortunately, the people who lived there were all coarse individuals. There was a child with a crooked nose and staring eyes whose nickname was Iron Child. He held an iron shovel in his hands all day long, which he used to chop things in a long trough. But what exactly was he chopping? When you first entered the place you couldn't see clearly because of the clouds of steam that filled the room and prevented you from discerning what anyone was doing there. Only when you had a chance to look more closely could you see that he was chopping potatoes. The trough was filled with potatoes.

This particular hut was rented out to people who made noodles out of bean flour. They were a coarse lot who could not afford to wear good shoes or socks and owned no decent bedding. There wasn't much difference between them and pigs, so that living in this type of building was very appropriate — if they had lived in a nice home they would probably have turned it into a pigsty in no time. Then, of course, their diet was enhanced by the addition of mushrooms every time it rained.

When the people who lived in this bean-flour mill had mushrooms to eat, they always mixed them with the bean flour they milled: they had fried mushrooms and bean flour, stewed mushrooms and bean flour, and boiled mushrooms and bean flour. When there was no soup they called it "fried," when there was soup they called it "boiled," and when there was slightly less soup they called it "stewed."

Often, after making such a meal, they brought a large bowlful over to give to Granddad. He would wait for the boy with the crooked nose and staring eyes to leave, then say: "We can't eat this; if there were something unclean in it, we could die of food poisoning."

But no one in the bean-flour mill ever died of food poisoning, and as a matter of fact, they spent the day singing as they sifted the bean flour.

A rack several feet tall had been erected in front of the bean-flour mill, from which shiny lengths of bean noodles hung like cascading waterfalls. All the time the people were hanging out the noodles they were singing to themselves, and after the noodles had dried in the sun, they gathered them in, still singing as they worked. Their songs were not an expression of the joys of their work; rather they were like sounds of someone laughing with tears in his eyes.

Stoically they accepted their hardships: "You say that the life I live is a pitiable one; well, that's all right with me. In your eyes I am in mortal danger, but my life gives me satisfaction. And if I were not satisfied, what then? Isn't life made up more of pain than pleasure anyway?"

The songs that emerged from that bean-flour mill were like a red flower blooming atop a wall — the brighter and lovelier it was, the more desolate the feeling it evoked.

> On the fifteenth day of the very first month
> Lanterns are hung by one and all;
> While others' husbands are reunited at home,
> Meng Jiangnü's spouse labors on the Great Wall.

On clear days, as the bean noodles were being hung out to dry, this song could always be heard. Inasmuch as the hut was located in the southwest corner, the sounds of the singing were more distant than others. Once in a while someone imitating a woman singing "Nighttime Yearnings" could be heard.

The hut they lived in was certainly beyond repair. Every time there was a heavy rain a new support had to be placed on the northern side of the building, and eventually there were as many as seven or eight such struts, but still the house leaned farther and farther to the north every day. The lean grew more and more pronounced until it frightened me just to look at it. I could imagine its collapsing to the ground just at the moment I was passing by and pinning me beneath it. No question about it, the hut was in sad shape: the windows, which had originally been square, had become twisted out of shape by the lean of the building. The door-frame was so awry that you couldn't close the door, and the tie beams above the wall seemed on the verge of crashing to the ground; having broken loose they seemed about to leap out of the building. The central beam of the roof ridge moved a little farther north each day, since the tenons had already broken loose from the mortices, and there was nothing left to control it. It was now moving as a free agent. As for the smaller beams that had been nailed to the ridge-pole of the building, those that were able to keep up with it just followed along this northward journey as a river follows its course; those that couldn't keep up simply wrested their nails loose and sagged downwards, hanging precariously over the heads of the people inside the bean-flour mill. They didn't come falling down because the other ends were anchored down by the outside eaves, so they just sagged and creaked.

I just had to go inside the mill and see how the people sifted the bean flour, but I didn't dare survey the scene around me too closely, for fear that the beams would fall in on top of me.

When winds arose, the entire building creaked and groaned; the beams, the timbers, the doors, the windows — everything strained and moaned.

The rains, too, caused the building to creak, and in the nighttime, even if there was no wind or rain, there were still creaking noises. As night deepened and people noises died out, the creatures of the night began their chorus; how then could this building, whose nature it was to creak, be expected to keep silent?

In fact, its creaking noises could be heard above all else. The other sounds, though audible, were much less discernible, and not very reliable. Perhaps the people's ears were playing tricks on them, and the sounds were not there at all, for these were not the noises that one expected to hear, unlike the sounds of animate creatures like cats, dogs, and insects.

On more than one occasion someone heard a building crying out in the night; he would wonder just whose house it was that could cry out like that, making the plaintive sounds of a living creature, and so very loud. It invariably awakened whoever was sleeping inside. But the person who had been awakened merely turned over and said: "The house is on the move again."

It truly seemed as though he were talking about a living thing, and that the building was betaking itself to a new site. Now, since the building was off to a new location, wouldn't you think that the person sleeping inside would get out of bed? But no, he just rolled over and went back to sleep.

The people who lived in this hut felt no sense of danger regarding the possibility of its collapsing around them; they treated the building with such trust and confidence that one might suppose there was a blood relationship between them. It was as though even if the building did collapse someday, it would not fall on their heads, and even on the outside chance that it did, their lives would be spared — there was absolutely no danger of losing one's life. I don't know the origin of this extreme self-assurance, but perhaps the people who lived there were made not of flesh and bones, but of iron. Either that or they were like a suicide squad who placed little value on their own lives. Otherwise, how could they be so brave as to scoff at death?

On second thought, it may be inaccurate to say that they scoffed at death, for on those occasions when the pole from which one of them was taking down strips of bean noodles that were drying in the sun crashed to the ground, that person was frightened speechless.

The noodles are dashed into small pieces, but he has escaped being hit, and as he scoops up the noodles, he can't take his eyes off the pole; after reflecting for a moment, he comments: "If it hadn't. . . ."

The more he thinks, the more bizarre it seems to him — how could he have missed getting hit, while the noodles were shattered into pieces? He picks up the pole and puts it back in place, then stands off a bit and sizes it up, experiencing an ever-increasing apprehension. "Aiya! If that had fallen on top of my head . . .!" But that is too alarming a prospect to imagine, and as he rubs his head he is aware of just how fortunate he has been. He vows to be more careful next time.

The truth of the matter is, the pole isn't as thick as the house's roof beams, but the mere sight of it gives him a scare. From then on, each time he hangs the bean noodles out to dry he shies away from that pole to the point of refusing to even walk by it, keeping a wary eye on it at all times. He forgets the incident only after the passage of many days.

During thunderstorms the people inside always doused their lights, for according to them, fire is thunder and lightning's mortal enemy, and they were afraid of being struck. Whenever they crossed the river they first threw two copper coins into the water, for legend has it that the rapacious river spirit often causes people to drown. But if copper coins are thrown in, he is appeased and will spare them.

All of this goes to prove that the people who lived in this creaky hut were just as timorous as anyone else and, like others, spent their days on this earth in mortal fear. That being the case, why weren't they afraid of the prospect of their house's collapsing on top of them?

According to Old Zhao the steamed-bun peddler: "That teetering building is exactly the one they want!"

According to the boy with the crooked nose and staring eyes who lived in the mill itself: "This is only a place to live; you don't have to look for the perfection you would in choosing a wife."

According to the two young gentry youths from the Zhou family who shared our compound: "You couldn't find a more fitting place for coarse people like that to live in."

And according to Second Uncle You: "They're only interested in the cheapest place they can find. Since there are good houses all over the town of Hulan, you wonder why they don't just move, don't you? Well, a good house would cost them money, not like this place of ours. Here they can live for only ten or twenty catties of dry noodles a year, and that's it — why, it's the same as free rent. If your Second Uncle had no family, he'd look for a place just like that to live in."

Perhaps there was some truth in what Second Uncle You said.

It had long been Granddad's plan to tear that building down, but several times the tenants had come en masse to persuade him not to, and thus it remained standing. As for the questions of whether or not the building would someday collapse, and whether it would bring good fortune or ill to those inside, that was considered by everyone something too far in the future to warrant any thought.

III

The compound in which we lived was a dreary one.

The occupants were some bean-flour sifters who lived on one side and some hog farmers who lived on the other. There was also a miller who lived in one of the side rooms belonging to the hog farmers. This miller would strike his wooden clappers at night, the whole night through. Among the family of hog farmers there were several individuals with time on their hands and little to do, who often got together to sing their Shaanxi opera to the accompaniment of a two-stringed violin. On clear days the bean-flour sifter in the southwest corner of our compound liked to sing "Night-time Yearnings."

Now, although they played their two-stringed violins, struck wooden clappers, and sang this song, one must not be misled into believing that these were indications of prosperity or progress; it was certainly not that they could see a bright future ahead of them, nor even that they entertained any hopes for a bright future — it meant none of these things. They could see nothing that could be considered bright, nor could they have recognized it for what it was even if they had. They were like a blind man standing in the sun who, though unable to see the sun, can nonetheless feel the warmth on his head.

These people were like that: they did not know where the

brightness was, but they were fully aware of the cold that enveloped their bodies. It was their struggling to break free from this cold that brought them to grief. Ushered into this world by their mothers without any real expectations, they could only hope to eat their fill and dress warmly enough. But they were forever hungry and cold.

Foully the affairs came; fairly they were accepted. Not in the course of their lifetimes did affairs ever come fairly.

The sounds of wooden clappers being struck at night in the mill shed often increased in intensity as the night deepened, and the more vigorously they were struck, the more desolate the sound. That was because they were the lone sounds in the night — there were no others to accompany them.

IV

The compound in which we lived was a dreary one.

A carter and his family lived in one of the siderooms attached to the bean-flour mill. The dance of the sorceress was frequently performed for this family's benefit, so there often arose from that place the sounds of drumbeats and chants. The sound of drums generally lasted late into the night, accompanied by talk of fairies and ghosts, and the ritual of dialogue between the sorceress and her assistant; they were mournful, distant sounds that confused one's sense of time. The old woman of this family was sick the year round, and the dance of the sorceress was performed for her benefit.

This family was more blessed than any other in the compound, with its three generations living together. Their family traditions were the best defined and the neatest: they treated one another with respect, there was mutual understanding and good feelings among the siblings, and a great deal of love existed between parent and child. There was no one in the family who was an idler or who had time on his hands. No similarity existed between them and the people who lived in the bean-flour mill or the mill shed, the ones who spent so much of their time singing or weeping as the feeling moved them. No, their home was forever quiet and tranquil. Not counting, of course, the dance of the sorceress.

The grandmother in the family — the old woman who was always sick — had two sons, each of whom was a carter. Both of the sons had wives: the elder son's wife was a plump woman in her fifties; the younger son's wife a slim woman in her forties. In addition, the old woman had two grandsons: the elder grandson belonged to the woman's younger son, while the second grandson belonged to her elder son.

As a consequence, there was some small degree of disharmony insofar as relations between the two daughters-in-law were concerned, although it was not all that apparent, and perhaps only the two of them were aware of it. The wife of the elder son felt that the wife of the younger son treated her with less obedience and respect than might be called for, an attitude whose origin she suspected was the fact that her sister-in-law's son was older than her own. The younger daughter-in-law, on the other hand, felt that her sister-in-law was trying to ride herd over her, inasmuch as her son was too young to have a wife. To her, this meant that the elder woman was upset that she herself had no daughter-in-law to control.

With two sons and two grandsons, the old woman was unreservedly pleased with her life. How could the family fail to prosper with such an equitable arrangement for the distribution of family chores?

One need look no further than the operation of the big cart; there was enough combined strength here to handle it completely, and who else could boast of a cart handled by four men of the same family? Everyone — from the one holding the whip to those seated in the rear of the cart — was named Hu, so no outsider was needed. And whatever the occasional domestic conflict that might arise, they presented themselves to the outside world as a close-knit family. For this reason the old woman had an optimistic view of life though she was constantly ill, and even that could be put out of her mind with the performing of the sorceress' dance. She felt that even if she should die, she would do so with her mind at peace and free of misgivings. But for the moment, there was still life in her body, which meant that she could continue to watch the labors of her sons with her own two eyes.

Her daughters-in-law also treated her quite well, seeing to her every need on a regular basis, and spending whatever was necessary to engage the sorceress to do her dance.

Each time the sorceress danced for her, the old woman reclined on her *kang,* her head resting on a pillow; straining into an upright position, she would say to the women and girls who had gathered to watch what was going on: "The arrangements this time were made by my elder daughter-in-law," or "The arrangements this time were made by my younger daughter-in-law." Saying this always gave her feeling of pride and satisfaction, so she said it over and over until she no longer had the strength to sit up. Since she was afflicted with paralysis, she would quickly call for her daughters-in-law to come and help her lie down, an effort that would leave her momentarily gasping for breath.

Among those who had gathered to watch the excitement, not a single one failed to comment on the kindliness of the old woman and the filial behavior of her daughters-in-law. And so people came from far and near each time the sorceress visited her, from the east and west compounds and all the neighboring streets. The one thing they could not do was reserve a place, so the early arrivals sat on benches and on the edge of the *kang,* while those who came later had to stand.

At such times the Hu family briefly enjoyed a position of leadership in the community owing to the filial conduct of its members, who served as models for other women. Men, as well as women, made comments: "Providence has smiled on old Hu's family, and one day wealth will come to them as well."

"Of the three factors — proper time, auspicious site and harmonious relations — harmonious relations are the most important. If the relations are harmonious, even if the time is not proper or if the site is inauspicious, it's still all right."

"You wait and see — today they are a family of carters, but in another five years, if they aren't a-second-class family, they'll be at least a third-class one."

Second Uncle You's comment was: "You mark my word; before too many years have passed, they will own a stableful of donkeys and horses. Don't be fooled by the fact that they only own a single cart now."

There were no new developments in the disharmonious relationship between the two daughters-in-law, though it never completely worked itself out either.

The wife of the elder grandson, a red-faced young woman, was both capable and obedient. She was neither too fat nor too thin, neither tall nor short, and when she spoke her voice was neither loud nor soft. She was a woman perfectly suited to this family. When the cart returned home she led the horse over to the well to drink, and before the horse and cart left the compound, she fed the animal. To look at her you wouldn't have thought she was made for this type of rough life, but when she worked she seemed no frailer than anyone else, and in this respect suffered little in comparison even with the men.

After she had finished her duties outside the house she began her domestic chores, all of which she handled quite capably. Whether it was needlework, mending or what have you, she managed everything just as you would expect it to be managed. And though there were no silks or satins in their house to work with, still the coarse materials had to be sewn with fine, even stitches.

Then, as New Year's approached, no matter how busy she might be, she nonetheless found time to make pairs of embroidered shoes for the old grandmother, her mother-in-law, and her aunt. Although she had to do without dainty shoe tops, even if she had only a piece of plain blue cloth to work with, the needlework still had to be delicately done. Since she had no silk, she had to use cotton thread instead, but she still managed to make the color combination fresh and crisp. The pair she made for her husband's grandmother were embroidered with large pink lotus petals, those for her aunt were festooned with peonies, and the pair for her mother-in-law were decorated with elegantly simple green-leafed orchids.

Whenever this young woman returned to her mother's home, she was asked how things were at the home of her husband. Her response was that everything was just fine, that the family was destined someday to make its fortune. She told of her uncle's cautious and attentive nature, and of how hard-working and capable of enduring hardship her father-in-law was. "The grandmother," she said, "is a good woman, as is her aunt; in fact, there isn't a person in the family who is anything but good." Everything was just as she would have wished it, and families like that are not easy for a woman to find. Granted that her husband sometimes beat her, but, as she said: "What man doesn't beat his wife?" And so this did nothing to lessen her complete satisfaction with the way things had turned out.

When the grandmother was presented with the finished embroidered shoes, the fine workmanship caused her to experience a sense of guilt in her treatment of this wife of her grandson. She felt that with her ability to do such fine needlework, it was an insult to have her spend each day

slopping the hogs and kicking the dogs. The old grandmother reached out and took the shoes from her, but, not
knowing what she should say, she held them gently in her
hands and nodded her head with a smile on her ashen face.

We have thus seen how good a woman the wife of the elder
grandson was. As for the second grandson, even though a
wife had already been selected for him, he was still too young
for the marriage to take place.

The fact that this girl had not yet been brought into the
family was the cause of the ill feelings between the two
daughters-in-law. The girl's prospective mother-in-law pro-
posed that she be brought over as a child-bride, while the
younger daughter-in-law objected, since the girl was too
young to do anything but eat, and what good would that
do them? They argued over this matter for some time without ever resolving the issue; it was always: "Wait till the
next time we have the sorceress over for the old woman and
we'll ask her opinion."

V

My home was a dreary one.

Roosters crowed before the sun was up, and the sound of
the wooden clappers from the mill continued even after
daybreak. Once the sky turned light, flocks of crows appeared in the sky. I slept beside Granddad, and as soon as he
woke up, I asked him to recite some poems; and so he began:

> I slept in spring not conscious of the dawn,
> But heard the gay birds chattering round and round.
> I remember, there was a storm at night;
> I know not how many blossoms fell to the ground.

"Someone sleeping on a spring morning slowly awakens to
the new day, and the first thing he hears is the sound of birds
all around. His thoughts return to the rainstorm of the night

before, but he doesn't know how many fallen flowers are on the ground today."

Each reading of a poem was followed by an explanation, for this is what I had demanded.

As Granddad was explaining the poem to me, our family cook had already got up. I could hear him coughing as he carried the water bucket out to the well to fetch some water. Our well was a long way from the rooms where we slept. It was too far for us to be able to hear the sound of the well rope being pulled up during the day, but in the early morning the sound came through loud and clear.

Even after the old cook had fetched his water, the others in the house were still asleep. Then came the sounds of the old cook scraping the pot. After he had scraped the pot clean he boiled some water for us to wash our faces, and still no one else was out of bed. Granddad and I continued to recite poems until the sun rose in the sky.

"Let's get up." Granddad said to me.

"Just one more poem."

"One more and then we've got to get up."

So we did one more, and when we had finished, I stalled by saying that that one didn't count, and I wanted to do one more.

Every morning we carried on like that. Once the door was opened, out we went into the garden, which by then was already flooded with light. The sun baked down on us as it climbed overhead. Granddad walked over to the chicken coop to let the chickens out, so that's where I went too; Granddad went over to the duck pen to let the ducks out, and I followed right behind him. I tagged along behind him with the big yellow dog following on my heels. I was hopping and jumping; the big yellow dog was wagging his tail.

The dog's head was the size of a small washbasin. He was a large dog, and round, and I was forever trying to ride him as I would a horse, though Granddad wouldn't allow it.

Nonetheless, the big yellow dog liked me, and I loved him.

The chickens and the ducks came out of their coops, shook out their feathers, and began to run around the yard, cackling and quacking noisily. Granddad scattered some kernels of bright red sorghum on the ground, and then the golden kernels of some other grains. Immediately the air was filled with the pecking sounds of chickens as they ate the feed on the ground.

After the chickens had been fed we looked up at the sky to see that the sun had climbed pretty high. Granddad and I returned to the house, where we set up a small table, and he ate a bowl of rice porridge with sugar sprinkled on top. But I didn't eat. I wanted some baked corn, so he led me back out into the rear garden; then, walking on the dew-covered ground, he went over to the clump of corn stalks and pulled off an ear of corn for me. Our shoes and socks were soaked through by the time he had broken off the ear of corn.

Granddad told the cook to bake the corn for me, but by the time it was ready I had already eaten two bowls or more of sugared rice porridge. I took the corn from him, ate a few kernels, and complained that it wasn't any good – you see, I was by then already full. So what I did was take the corn out into the garden to feed Big Yellow. "Big Yellow" was the dog's name.

From out on the street beyond the wall came the voices of all the different peddlers: There was the bean-curd peddler, the steamed-bun peddler, and vegetable peddlers.

A vegetable peddler was calling out the things he had to sell – eggplants, cucumbers, various legumes, and scallions. After he had passed by with his basket of produce, another followed; but instead of eggplants and cucumbers, this one had celery, leeks, and cabbage.

There was a good deal of noise and commotion out on the street, though our house remained quiet.

The mugwort-covered courtyard was the hiding place of

hordes of chirping insects, as well as all sorts of discarded objects.

One would assume that my house was quiet because the day had just begun. But the truth of the matter was that there were a great many buildings, a large compound, and very few people living there. For that matter, even at high noon my house was still placid.

Each autumn, smartweed flowers covered the tops of the mugwort, bringing forth great numbers of dragonflies and butterflies that darted back and forth atop the dreary stretch of mugwort. But instead of bringing a look of luxuriance to the area, as one would expect, their presence increased the sense of gloom and loneliness.

5

The Child-bride

I

Except for the time I spent playing in our rear garden, accompanied by Granddad, I was left to my own devices to find amusement. Sometimes I pitched a makeshift tent all by myself beneath the eaves, then after playing for a while fell asleep there.

We had removable windows in our house that, when taken down, would stand up only if they were propped up against a wall, making a nice little lean-to. This I called my "little chamber." I often took naps in my little chamber.

Our entire compound was cover mugwort, over which swarms of dragonflies flew, attracted by the fragrance of the red smartweed flowers. I amused myself by catching dragonflies until I grew tired of it, after which I lay down in the mugwort and went to sleep.

Clumps of wild berries grew among the mugwort, looking like mountain grapes, and delicious to eat. I foraged for wild berries to eat among the mugwort, and when I grew weary of that I lay down beside the wild-berry bushes and went to sleep. The dense mugwort served as a kind of mattress for me as I lay atop it, and I also enjoyed the shade the tall grass offered.

One day just before suppertime, as the sun was setting in the west, I lay dreaming on my bed of mugwort. I must not have been sleeping all that soundly, for I thought I could hear a lot of people talking somewhere nearby. They were chatting and laughing with real gusto, but I couldn't quite make out just what was happening. I could only sense that they were standing off in the southwest corner, either inside the compound or just beyond it — whether it was actually inside the compound or not, I simply couldn't tell — and out there somewhere there was quite a bit of excitement. I lay there half awake for a while, and the noise eventually died out; most likely I had fallen asleep again.

After I woke up I went into the house, where I was given the news by our old cook: "The Hu family's child-bride arrived, and you weren't even aware of it. Hurry up and eat so you can go have a look at her!"

The old cook was busier than usual that day; he was carrying a platter of sliced cucumbers into Granddad's room with both hands, and his brief but animated conversation with me nearly caused him to drop the plate to the floor. As it was, the cucumber slices slid off the platter onto the floor.

I walked into Granddad's room, where I found him sitting alone at the supper table with all the dishes laid out before him. There was no one else there to eat with him; Mother and Father hadn't come to supper, nor had Second Uncle You. Granddad saw me come in and asked: "How does the child-bride look?"

He apparently thought I had just come from taking a look at her. I told him I didn't know, that I had just come in after eating wild berries amidst the mugwort.

"Your mother and the others have all gone to look at the child-bride over at old Hu's house — you know, the one where the sorceress is always doing her dance." When he finished speaking, Granddad called out to the old cook to hurry up with the plate of cucumbers.

The cucumbers, lying in vinegar sauce and topped by hot-pepper oil, were an eye-catching mixture of greens and reds.

I suspect that he had had to slice another plateful, since I had seen the original one scattered on the kitchen floor. The moment the cucumber dish arrived, Granddad said: "Hurry up and eat, so we can go have a look at the child-bride."

The old cook stood off to the side, wiping his sweaty face with his apron. Every time he spoke he blinked his eyes and spurted saliva from his mouth.

"There certainly are a lot of people going over to see the child-bride!" he said. "Even the second wife of the grain shop owner took her kids and went over. Little Pockface from the compound behind us is over there too, and several members of old Yang's family from the west compound who climbed over the wall to get there." He said he had seen all this as he was drawing water from the well.

Exhilarated by this news of his, I said: "Grandpa, I'm not hungry. I want to go see the child-bride."

But Granddad insisted that I eat before he would take me over, though I was in such a hurry I didn't eat a very good supper. I had never in my life seen a child-bride, whom I imagined to be beautiful beyond words! The more I dwelled upon it, the more I was convinced that she must indeed be beautiful, and the more excited I grew, the stronger was my conviction that she could not but be a rare beauty. Otherwise, why was everyone so eager to see her? Otherwise, why would even Mother miss her supper?

I grew more and more fidgety, since I was sure that the best part of the show was already over. Now if I left right away, at the very least I would be able to see something worthwhile, but I was afraid I would be too late if I waited much longer. So I pressed Granddad: "Hurry, hurry up and eat, Grandpa, please hurry."

The old cook was still standing off to the side talking a blue streak, while Granddad asked him a question every once in a while. I could see that the cook was interrupting Granddad's meal, but even though I tried to get him to stop talking, he ignored me. He kept on chuckling and laughing until finally I got down from my chair and literally pushed him from the room.

Granddad still hadn't finished when Third Granny from old Zhou's house came over to report that their rooster kept running over to our house, and that she had come to fetch it. But instead of leaving after she had her rooster, she came up to the window and notified Granddad: "The little child-bride has already arrived at old Hu's. Aren't you going over to see her? There are lots of people over there getting an eyeful, and I plan to go over after supper."

Granddad told her that he was going over after supper too, but I didn't think he'd ever finish his meal. First he asked for some more hot-pepper oil, then he wanted some salt. I could see that I wasn't the only one who was growing impatient — the old cook could barely contain himself; his brow was sweating profusely and his eyes were blinking continuously.

The moment Granddad put his rice bowl down, I began dragging him along with me over to the southwest corner of the wall without even letting him light up his pipe. As we hurried along, I experienced feelings of regret every time I saw someone coming back from watching all the fun. Why had I waited for Granddad anyway? Why hadn't I run over there by myself a long time ago? The recollection that I had heard some excitement coming from over here while I was lying in the mugwort added to my displeasure. Really, the more I thought about it, the stronger my regrets grew. This affair had already taken up half the afternoon, and I just knew that the good part was over, and that I was too late. Coming now was a waste of time — there wouldn't be anything left to see. Why hadn't I rushed over to take a look the second I heard all that talking and laughing while I was lying in the grass? My regrets grew so strong that I was getting mad at myself, and just as I had feared, when we drew up next to old Hu's window, there wasn't a sound coming from inside. I was so mad I nearly cried.

When we actually walked in the door, it wasn't at all as I had been led to expect. Mother, Third Granny Zhou, and several people I didn't know were all there, and everything was contrary to what I had imagined; there was nothing worth seeing here. Where was the child-bride? I couldn't spot her anywhere until the others pointed and nodded, then I saw her. This was no bride, it was just a young girl! I lost all interest the moment I saw her, and I started pulling Granddad toward the door.

"Let's go home, Grandpa."

The next morning I saw her when she came out to draw some water to wash up. Her long black hair was combed into a thick braid; unlike most young girls, whose braids hung down to about their waists, hers came down almost to her knees. Her complexion was dark and she had a hearty laugh.

After the people in the compound had all taken a look at the child-bride of old Hu's family they agreed that apparently there was nothing wrong with her, except that she seemed a little too proud-spirited and didn't look or act much like a child-bride.

Third Granny Zhou said: "She hasn't the least bit of shyness when she's with people."

Old Mrs. Yang from the next compound agreed: "She isn't even a tiny bit shy. Her very first day at her mother-in-law's house she ate three bowls of rice!"

Then Third Granny Zhou said: "Gracious! I've never seen the likes of it. Even if she weren't a child-bride, but someone who came to the house already married to the boy, she'd still have to get to know what the people are like her first couple of days in the home. Gracious! She's such a big girl, she must be well into her teens!"

"I hear she's fourteen!"

"How could a fourteen-year-old be that tall? She must be lying about her age!"

"Not necessarily. Some people develop early."

"But how are they going to handle their sleeping arrangements?"

"You've got a good point there, since there are three generations of family and only three small *kang.*"

This last response to Third Granny Zhou came from old Mrs. Yang, as she leaned over the top of the wall.

As for my family, Mother was also of the opinion that the girl was not at all like a child-bride should be.

Our old cook said: "I've never seen the likes of her, with such a proud bearing and eyes that look right at you."

To which Second Uncle You added: "What's this world coming to when a child-bride doesn't look anything like a child-bride ought to?"

Only Granddad had nothing to say on the subject, so I asked him: "What do you think of that child-bride?"

"She's quite all right," he said.

So I felt she was quite all right too.

Every day she led their horse to the well to drink, and I saw her on many of these occasions. No one properly introduced us, but she smiled when she saw me, and I smiled back and asked her how old she was.

"Twelve," she replied.

I told her she must be wrong: "You're fourteen — everybody says so."

"They think I'm too tall," she said, "and they're afraid people will laugh if they know I'm only twelve, so they told me to say I'm fourteen."

I couldn't figure out how being very tall would cause people to laugh.

"Why don't you come over and play in the grass with me." I asked her.

"No," she said, "they won't allow it."

II

Before many days had passed, the people in that family began to beat the child-bride. They beat her so severely that her cries could be heard far away, and since none of the other families in the entire compound had any children, cries or shouts were seldom heard there.

As a result, this became *the* topic of conversation throughout the neighborhood. The consensus was that she had deserved a beating right from the start, for whoever heard of a child-bride with no trace of shyness, one who sat up straight as a rod wherever she was, and who walked with a brisk, carefree step!

Her mother-in-law, having led the family horse up to the well to drink one day, said to Third Granny Zhou: "We've got to be harsh with her right from the start. You mark my words, I'm going to have to beat her when I go back to the house. This little child-bride of ours is really a handful! I've never seen the likes of her. If I pinch her on the thigh, she turns around and bites me, or else she says she's going home to her mother."

From then on the sounds of crying filled our compound daily — loud, bitter cries accompanied by shouts.

Granddad went over to old Hu's house several times to try to dissuade them from beating her, since she was just a young girl who didn't know much, and if there were problems in her behavior, he recommended trying to educate her. But as time went on the beatings grew even more severe, day and night, and even when I woke up in the middle of the night to recite my poems with Granddad I could hear the sounds of crying and shouting coming from the southwest corner of the compound.

"That's the child-bride crying, isn't it?" I would ask Granddad.

To keep me from being frightened, he would answer: "No,

it's someone outside the compound."

"What could they be crying about in the middle of the night?" I would ask him.

"Don't concern yourself about that," he would say, "and just keep reciting your poems."

I got up very early, and just as I was reciting, "I slept in spring, not conscious of the dawn," the crying sounds from the southwest corner started in again. This continued for the longest time, and only when winter arrived did the sounds of her crying finally come to an end.

III

The sounds of weeping had been replaced by those of the sorceress, who came to the southwest corner every night to do her dance. The staccato beats of a drum resounded in the air, as the sorceress first chanted a line, and was then answered by her assistant. Since it was nighttime, the words they sang came through loud and clear, and I soon memorized every line.

There were things like: "Little spirit flower," and "May the Genie let her 'come forth.'" Just about every day the sorceress chanted these kinds of things.

Right after I got up in the mornings I started to minic her chants: "Little spirit flower, may the Genie let her 'come forth. . . .'" Then I went *bong-bong, bang-bang,* imitating the sounds of the drumbeat.

"Little spirit flower" meant the young girl; the "Genie" was supposed to be a fox spirit; to "come forth" meant to become a sorceress.

The sorceress performed her dances for nearly the whole winter, until she finally succeeded in causing the child-bride to fall ill. The child-bride soon had an unhealthy look about her, but even though her complexion was no longer as dark as it had been when she first arrived that summer, she retained her hearty laugh.

When Granddad took me over with him to visit her family, the child-bride even came over and filled his pipe for him. When she looked at me she smiled, but on the sly, as though she were afraid her mother-in-law would see her. She didn't speak to me.

She still wore her hair in a thick braid, but her mother-in-law told us she was ill and that the sorceress had been engaged to drive the evil spirits away. As Granddad was leaving their house, the mother-in-law walked out with him, saying in a low voice: "I'm afraid this child-bride isn't going to make it; she's being claimed by a genie who is determined to have her 'come forth.'"

Granddad would have liked to ask them to move, but here in Hulan there is a custom that the time for moving in the spring is March and in the autumn, September. Once March or September has passed, it is no longer the time for moving.

Each time we were startled out of our sleep in the middle of the night by the sorceress' dance, Granddad would say: "I'm going to ask them to move next March."

I heard him say this on any number of occasions. Whenever I imitated the shouts and cries of the sorceress and chanted "Little spirit flower," Granddad said the same thing — he'd ask them to move next March.

IV

But during the interim the commotion emanating from the southwest corner of our compound grew in intensity. They invited one sorceress and quite a few assistants, and the beat of drums resounded the day long. It was said that if they allowed the little child-bride to "come forth," her life would be in peril, so they invited many assistants in order to wrest her from the sorceress' clutches.

Whereupon many people volunteered their opinions to the family, for who would not come to the rescue of someone facing death? Every person of conscience and good will extended a helping hand; he would offer a special potion, she would share her magical charms.

Some advocated making a straw figure for the girl, to be burned in the big pit to the south.

Some advocated going to the ornament shop and having them make a paper figure called a "proxy doll," which could then be burned as her substitute.

Some advocated painting a hideous face on the girl, then inviting the sorceress over, with the expectation that when the sorceress saw her she would find her too ugly and reject her as a disciple; that way she would not have to "come forth."

But Third Granny Zhou advocated that she be made to eat a whole, unplucked rooster — feathers, feet, and all — on a given star-filled night, then be covered with a quilt. She should be made to sweat it out until cockcrow of the following morning before allowing her to emerge from under the quilt. For after she ate a whole rooster and sweated profusely, a rooster would forever exist in her soul, and spirits, ghosts, genies, and the like would not dare try and possess her body. Legend has it that ghosts are afraid of roosters.

Third Granny Zhou told of her own great-grandmother, who had fallen under the power of a genie and was in the throes of this agony for a full three years, on the verge of death. Eventually she was cured by this very method, and was never again ill for the rest of her life. Whenever she was having a bad dream during the night, one that would nearly frighten her to death, the rooster in her soul would come to her rescue by crowing and waking her from her nightmare. She was not ill another day in her life and, strange as it sounds, even her death was extraordinary. She died at the age of eighty-two, and even at that advanced age she was still able to do embroidery work. At the time she was busy embroidering a child's apron for her grandson, and after sitting on a wooden stool and embroidering for a while she felt tired, so she leaned back against the door and dozed off. She died in her sleep.

Someone asked Third Granny Zhou: "Were you there to see it?"

"I certainly was," she replied. "Just listen: for three days and nights after she died she could not be laid out, and eventually there was nothing to do but make a special coffin and seat her inside it. Her cheeks were still pink, just as though she were still alive."

"Did you see that too?" someone else asked.

"Gracious! That's a strange question to be asking," she answered. "With all the tales of things that have happened in this world, how many can a person witness in one lifetime? How else can we know about things unless we are told?" She appeared somewhat put out by the question.

And then there was old Mrs. Yang from the west compound, who also had a tonic: She said you needed two ounces of bitters and half a catty of pork, both of which had to be finely chopped and cured over a piece of tile, then pounded into powder and divided into five portions. Each portion was to be wrapped in red paper, then taken individually. This potion's specialty was curing convulsions and a drifting soul.

Her prescription was simple enough, even though the child-bride's illness was neither convulsions nor a drifting soul, and there seemed to be some disparity between the disease and the cure. But then what harm could it do to give it a try — after all, it only called for two ounces of bitters and half a catty of pork. Besides, here in Hulan there was often some cheap pork available. And even though the pork was said to be infected and not entirely dependable, this was, after all, a matter of curing an illness, not eating a meal, so what difference could it make?

"Go ahead and buy half a catty of pork and see how it works on her."

"Anyway, even if it doesn't cure her, it certainly can't do any harm," a bystander said approvingly.

"We've got to try," her mother-in-law said, "because where there's life there's hope!"

And so the child-bride began her cure by eating half a catty of pork and two ounces of bitters.

This prescription was personally prepared for her by her mother-in-law, but the slicing of the pork was the job of the wife of the elder grandson. The pork was all dark and discolored, but there was a portion of bright red meat in the center, which the wife of the elder grandson secretly held back. She figured that it had been four or five months since her husband's grandmother had eaten any meat, so she used this piece of pork she had secretly held back to make a large bowl of meat-and-flour soup for the old woman.

"Where in the world did this meat come from?" the grandmother asked her.

"Why don't you just eat and enjoy it as a treat your grandson's wife prepared especially for you."

Meanwhile, the child-bride's mother-in-law was curing the medicine on a piece of tile over the fire in the stove, saying as she did so: "What I have here is half a catty of pork, not a fraction less."

The pork smelled better and better as it was being cured, its odor eventually attracting a kitten that came over to snatch a piece. But when the kitten stretched out a paw to take it, the child-bride's mother-in-law reached over and gave it a swat with her hand.

"So you think you can get your paws on this, do you! You greedy little thing, this is someone's medicine — a full half catty of pork — so what makes you think you deserve a bite? If I gave you a piece, there wouldn't be enough medicine to work the cure. Then the responsibility for the girl's death would be yours; don't you know any better! There is exactly half a catty of meat here — no more, no less."

After the prescription was prepared it was pulverized and given to the child-bride together with water. Two portions were to be taken each day. She managed all right on the first day, but on the morning of the second, when the people who had prescribed the remedies came over, there were still three portions lying on the altar where the kitchen god was placed.

Someone present questioned the wisdom of eating bitters, for they were, after all, a cold ingredient, and if someone like her, who experienced night sweats, ate bitters, her vital energy would be driven out; now how could a person get by after her vital energy has been driven out?

"She can't take that!" someone else agreed. "Within two days after she's eaten it she will have passed on to the nether world."

"What'll we do now?" the child-bride's mother-in-law exclaimed.

In an apprehensive voice, the man asked her: "Has she already taken some?"

Just as the mother-in-law of the child-bride opened her mouth to answer, the clever wife of the elder grandson cut her short: "No, she hasn't — not yet," she said.

"Well, since she hasn't taken any yet," the man replied, "then there's nothing to worry about. The Hu family is certainly blessed; your lucky star is watching over you, for just now you came awfully close to throwing away a human life!" Then he offered a potion of his own, which according to him, was actually not a potion at all, but simply a cure-all that the proprietor of the Li Yongchun Pharmacy on Road Two East often prescribed. The medicine was so effective that a hundred uses resulted in a hundred cures, and it worked for everyone — man, woman, young, and old — every single time. It didn't even matter what the symptoms were — headaches, aching feet, stomachaches, visceral disorders, falls, broken bones, cuts, boils, carbuncles, rashes — whatever the illness, it disappeared with one application of this remedy.

What was this remedy? The more the people heard of the great results it produced, the more eager they were to learn just what it was.

"If an elderly person takes it," he said, "his dimming eyesight will be restored to what it was during his youth.

"If a young man takes it his strength will be great enough to move Mount Tai.

"If a woman takes it her complexion will be the color of peach blossoms without the aid of rouge or powder.

"If a child takes it, an eight-year-old can draw a bow, a nine-year-old can shoot an arrow, and a twelve-year-old will become a *zhuangyuan,* first on the list at the official examinations."

When he began talking, everyone in old Hu's family was absolutely amazed and awed, but toward the end his discourse somehow lost its effect on them. After all, the men in old Hu's family had always been carters, and there had never been a *zhuangyuan* among them.

The wife of the elder grandson asked the crowd of onlookers to move away a bit, then she walked over to the make-up chest and took out an eyebrow pencil. "Won't you please hurry and write down the ingredients of this prescription for us," she said, "so that we can go to the pharmacy right away and get some of that remedy?"

Now the person who was telling them about this prescription had at one time been the cook at the Li Yongchun Pharmacy, but had not worked there for some three years,

ever since the woman with whom he had been having an
affair had run out on him, taking with her the little savings he
had managed to accumulate over half a lifetime. He had been
in such a rage over this that he had developed a touch of
insanity. But even though he was slightly mad, he had not
completely forgotten the names of the medicines he had
committed to memory during his employment at "Li Yongchun." Since he was illiterate he gave a verbal listing of the
ingredients:

"Two-tenths of an ounce of plantain, two-tenths of an
ounce of honeywort, two-tenths of an ounce of fresh reh-
mannia, two-tenths of an ounce of Tibetan safflower,
two-tenths of an ounce of Sichuan fritillary, two-tenths of an
ounce of atractylis, two-tenths of an ounce of Siberian milk-
wort, two-tenths of an ounce of the euphorbia spurge. . . ."

At this point he seemed unable to recall the remaining
ingredients, and nervous beads of perspiration began to dot
his forehead. So he blurted out: ". . . and two catties of
brown sugar . . . ," thereby completing his prescription.

Once finished, he began asking the people around him for
some wine: "Do you have any wine here? Give me a couple
of bowlfuls."

Everyone in Hulan River knew this slightly mad fellow
well; everyone, that is, but the members of old Hu's family.
Having moved here from somewhere else, they were taken in
by him — hook, line, and sinker. Since they had no wine
in the house, they gave him twenty coppers to go out and
buy his own. As for the remedy he had prescribed, it was absolutely unreliable, merely a product of his wild imagination.

The child-bride grew more seriously ill with each passing
day and, according to her family, often sat bolt upright as
she slept during the night. The sight of another person
threw a terrible fright into her, and her eyes were invariably
brimming with tears. It seemed inevitable that this child-
bride was fated to "come forth," and if she were not allowed

to do so, there seemed little hope that she would ever be well again.

Once the news of her plight began spreading throughout the area, all of the people living nearby came forth with their suggestions; how, they said, could we not come to the rescue of someone at death's door? Some believed that she should simply be allowed to "come forth," and let that be the end of it. Others were of the opposite opinion, for if someone of such tender years were to "come forth," what hope was there for her ever living a normal life?

Her mother-in-law adamantly refused to let her "come forth": "Now don't any of you get the wrong idea that I'm opposed to letting her 'come forth' only because of the money I spent when I arranged for the engagement. Like the rest of you, I feel that if someone so young were to 'come forth,' she would never be able to live a normal life."

Everyone promptly agreed that it would be best not to allow her to "come forth," so they turned their collective energies to finding the right prescription or engaging the right sorceress, each extolling the virtues of his own plan.

Finally there came a soothsayer.

This soothsayer told them he had come unhesitatingly from the countryside a great distance away as soon as the news reached him that old Hu's family had recently brought a child-bride into their home, one who had fallen ill shortly after her arrival and remained so even after being seen by many eminent physicians and mystics. He had made the trip into town expressly to have a look for himself, for if he could perform some service that might spare her life, then the trip would have been worth making. Everyone was quite moved by this speech of his. He was invited into the house, where he was asked to sit on the grandmother's *kang,* was given tea, and offered a pipeful of tobacco.

The wife of the elder grandson was the first to approach him: "This younger sister of ours is actually only twelve years old, but since she is so tall, she tells everyone she is fourteen. She's a cheerful, sociable girl who up to now was never sick a day in her life. But ever since she came to our house she has grown thinner and paler every day. Recently she lost her appetite for food and drink, and she even sleeps with her eyes open, as she is easily startled. We've given her every imaginable remedy and have burned incense of every kind for her benefit, but nothing has worked. . . ."

Before she had finished, the girl's mother-in-law interrupted her: "I've never abused her all the time she's been in my home. Where else will you find another family that has not abused its child-bride by giving her beatings and tongue-lashings all day long? Now I may have beaten her a little, but just to get her started off on the right foot, and I only did that for a little over a month. Maybe I beat her pretty hard sometimes, but how else was I expected to make a well-mannered girl out of her? Believe me, I didn't enjoy beating her so hard, what with all her screaming and carrying on. But I was doing it for her own good, because if I didn't beat her hard, she'd never be good for anything.

"There were a few times when I strung her up from the rafters and had her uncle give her a few hard lashes with a leather whip, and since he got a little carried away, she usually passed out. But it only lasted for about the time it takes to smoke a pipeful, and then we always managed to revive her by dousing her face with cold water. We did give her some pretty hard beatings that turned her body all black and blue and occasionally drew some blood, but we always broke open some eggs right away and rubbed the egg whites on the spots. The swellings, which were never too bad, always went down in ten days or a couple of weeks.

"She's such a stubborn child; the moment I began to beat her she threatened to return to her home. So I asked her: 'Just where do you think your home is? What is this, if not your home?' But she refused to give in. She said she wanted

to go to her *own* home. And this made me madder than ever.
You know how people are when they get mad — nothing else
seems to matter — so I took a redhot flatiron and branded
the soles of her feet. Maybe I beat her soul right out of her
body, or maybe I just scared it away — I don't know which —
but from then on, whenever she said she wanted to go home,
instead of beating her, all I had to do was threaten to chain
her up if she even tried, and she would start screaming with
fright. When the Great Genie saw this he said she should be
allowed to 'come forth.'

"It costs a lot of money to bring a girl into a family as a
child-bride. Figure it out for yourself: the engagement was
arranged when she was eight years old, at which time we had
to hand over eight ounces of silver. After that there was the
money we spent for her trousseau, and finally we had all
the expenses of bringing her here by train from far-off
Liaoyang. Then once she got here, it was a steady series of
exorcists, incense, and one potion after another. If she had
gotten better as time went on, then everything would have
been fine, but nothing seemed to work. Who knows eventually. . . what the outcome will be . . .?"

The soothsayer, who had come unhesitatingly from so far
away, was a most proper and serious man who showed the
signs of much travel. He wore a long blue gown under a short
lined coat, while on his head he wore a cap with earflaps.
He was a man whom others treated with the respect due a
master the moment they saw him.

Accordingly, the grandmother said: "Please draw a lot
quickly for my second grandson's child-bride and tell us what
her fate will be."

The soothsayer could tell at first glance that this family
was a sincere and honest one, so he removed his leather cap
with the earflaps. The moment he took off his cap everyone
could see that his hair was combed into a topknot and that
he was wearing Taoist headwear. They knew at once that

this was no ordinary run-of-the-mill individual. Before anyone could even utter the questions they wanted to ask, he volunteered the information that he was a Taoist priest from such-and-such a mountain, and that he had come down to make a pilgrimage to the sacred Mount Tai in Shandong. But how could he have foreseen that midway on his journey he would have to cut his trip short for lack of traveling expenses? He had drifted to the Hulan River area, where he had been for no less than half a year.

Someone asked him why, if he was a Taoist, he wasn't wearing Taoist garb.

"There's something you people ought to know," he replied. "Each of the 360 trades in this world of ours has its share of miseries. The police around here are really mean; the minute they see someone dressed as a Taoist, they start in with a detailed interrogation, and since they are disbelievers of the Taoist creed who won't listen to reason, they are all too ready to take one of us into custody."

This man had an alias — the Wayfaring Immortal — and people far and near knew of whom you were speaking when you mentioned his name. Whatever the disease or discomfort, whether the signs were good or evil, life and death was settled for all time with the drawing of one of his lots. He told them that he had learned his divining powers from the head priest of the Taoists, Zhang Tianshi himself.

He did not have many divining lots — four in all — which he took out of the pocket of his gown one at a time. The first lot he brought forth was wrapped in red paper, as was the second; in fact, all four were wrapped in red paper. He informed everyone that there were no words written on his divining lots, nor were there any images; inside each there was only a packet of medicinal powder — one red, one green, one blue, and one yellow. The yellow one foretold the wealth of gold, the red one foretold ruddy-cheeked old age. Now if the green one were drawn, things could take a turn for the worse, for it represented the devil's fire. The blue one was not very good either, for it meant the cold face of death, and Zhang Tianshi himself had said that the cold face of death must come to meet Yama, the king of the nether world, whether the person be dead or alive.

Once the soothsayer had finished reciting his chants he called for someone in the afflicted person's family to reach out and draw a lot. The child-bride's mother-in-law figured this to be an easy, uncomplicated task, so she decided to quickly choose one and get some idea of whether it was the girl's fate to live or die. But she had overlooked something, for the moment she reached her hand out, the Wayfaring Immortal said: "Each drawing of a lot will cost you one hundred coppers. If you choose the blue one and are unhappy with it, you can choose another . . . one hundred coppers for each one. . . ."

Suddenly the child-bride's mother-in-law understood everything: this lot-drawing wasn't free after all, and at a hundred coppers apiece, it was no longer a laughing matter. For ten coppers she could buy twenty cakes of bean curd. Now if she bought one cake every three days, then with twenty cakes — since two threes are six — that would be enough bean curd for sixty days. But if one cake were bought only every ten days — that's three cakes a month — then there would be enough bean curd in the house for half a year. Continuing along this line of reasoning, she wondered who would be so extravagant as to eat a cake of bean curd every three days. According to her, a cake a month was enough for everyone to have a taste every now and then, in which case twenty cakes of bean curd — one each month — would be sufficient for twenty months, or a year and a half plus two months.

Or let's say rather than buying bean curd, she were to buy and raise a plump little pig. If she conscientiously fed it for five or six months until it was nice and fat, just think how much money that could bring in! And if she raised it for a whole year, then we're talking about twenty thousand coppers . . .

Or if she didn't buy a pig, but spent the money instead on chickens, a hundred coppers could buy ten or so chickens. After the first year the chickens would become egg layers, and everyone knows how much an egg is worth! Or if she didn't sell the eggs, but traded one of them for vegetables to feed the entire family — all three generations — for a whole day . . . not to mention the fact that each egg laid meant one more chicken, and by keeping the cycle going they could have an unlimited supply of chickens and an unlimited supply of eggs. Wouldn't they then make their fortune!

But her thoughts weren't really so grandiose; it would be sufficient if everyone had enough to eat and enough clothes to wear. If, by living frugally, she could manage to put a little something aside in her lifetime, that would be enough for her. For even though she had a real love for money, if she had been given the opportunity to actually make a fortune, she definitely would not have had the nerve to do so. The numbers she was contemplating were greater than she could count, more than she could ever remember. With chickens laying eggs and eggs producing more chickens in an unbroken cycle, wouldn't the situation soon have developed where there were as many chickens as there are ants? There would be so many they would cloud her vision, and clouded vision produces headaches.

This mother-in-law of the child-bride had raised chickens in the past; in fact, it was exactly a hundred coppers' worth — no more, no less. To her the ideal number to raise was a hundred coppers' worth. For one hundred coppers she was able to buy twelve little chicks, a number she considered just right. If there were more, she was afraid she might lose some, but if there were fewer, then they wouldn't have been worth a hundred coppers.

When she was buying these newly hatched chicks she picked them up one at a time to take a close look, rejecting one after the other. She rejected all those with black claws, those with spotted wings, and those with marks on the tops of their heads. She said that her mother had become an expert at choosing chickens after raising them for a lifetime. She had raised them year after year, and although she never kept too many, she was never short of household necessities during her lifetime, managing to trade eggs the year round for anything she needed. As a result, she really knew her chickens — which of them would be short-lived and which could be expected to live a long time — spotting the good ones unerringly every time. She could even tell at a glance which of them would lay large eggs and which of them would lay small ones.

As she was buying the chicks she constantly reprimanded herself for not having had the foresight to learn more about chickens from her mother in years past. Ai! Young people somehow never have an eye for the future! She was moved to sighing as she bought the chicks; having picked them out with a great deal of thought, she had done her very best in selecting. The chicken seller had over two hundred chicks for sale, every single one of which she picked over, but whether the ones she finally chose were the best of the lot was something of which she herself was never able to be absolutely sure.

She raised chickens with a great deal of care. She was forever concerned lest they be eaten by cats or bitten by rats, and whenever they dozed during the day she chased the flies away, fearing that the flies might wake them up; she wanted them to get plenty of sleep, for she was concerned that they got too little. If one of them had a mosquito bite on its leg, the moment she discovered it she immediately mixed an ointment of mugwort and water and rubbed it on the bite. According to her, if she didn't rub the ointment on right away, then if the chick later turned out to be a rooster, its growth would be stunted, and if it turned out to be a hen, it would lay small eggs. A small egg could be traded for two cakes of bean curd, while a large one would bring in three. That's what can happen to a hen. As for a rooster, they eventually wind up on the dinner table, and since everyone prefers fat ones, the stunted ones are difficult to sell.

Once her chickens had grown a bit and were ready to leave the house and go out into the courtyard and look for their own food, she put some dye on the top of each of their heads — six red and six green.

In order to determine where she should place the dye she first took a look at her neighbors' chickens to see where they had dyed theirs, after which she was able to make up her mind. Her neighbors had put the dye on the tips of the chickens' wings, so she put hers on the tops of their heads. If her neighbors had dyed the tops of their chickens' heads, she would have dyed the bellies of hers. According to her, people shouldn't dye their chickens in the same place, because then you couldn't tell them apart. Your chickens would run over to my house and mine would run over to your house, and there would be nothing but confusion.

The little dyed chickens were extremely eye-catching with their red or green heads, looking like they were wearing little colored caps. It was as though instead of raising a brood of chicks, she was raising a brood of children.

This mother-in-law of the child-bride had even said during her chicken-raising days: "Chickens have to be pampered a lot more than children. When someone raises children don't they just leave them to fend for themselves and grow up the best they can? There are always mosquito bites, bedbug bites, and what have you, so that there is hardly a child anywhere who doesn't carry scars on his body. Children who don't have some will be hard ones to raise — they won't live long."

According to her, she didn't raise many children of her own — in fact, only the one son — but even with the small number to care for, she didn't pamper him. By now he already had more than twenty such scars on his body.

"If you don't believe me," she would say, "I'll have him take off his clothes and let everyone see for himself . . . he has scars all over his body — one as big as the mouth of a rice bowl. Really, I've never pampered my child. Not counting those from his own falls and spills, some of the scars come from the beatings I gave him with an axe-handle. Raising a child isn't anything like raising chickens or ducks. If you raise a chicken carelessly, then it won't lay any eggs; a large egg is worth three cakes of bean curd, a small one is worth two, and that's nothing to laught at, is it? It certainly isn't!"

Once her son stepped on a chick and killed it; she beat him for three solid days and nights.

"Why shouldn't I have beaten him? Each chick is worth three cakes of bean curd — chicks come from chicken eggs, you know! In order to get a chicken, you have to have a chicken's egg — half an egg isn't enough, is it? Not only half an egg, but even an egg that's almost whole, but not quite, won't do either. Bad eggs won't do, nor will old eggs. One chicken requires one egg, and if a chicken isn't the same as three cakes of bean curd, what is it? Just think how great a sin it would be to knowingly put three cakes of bean curd on the ground and squash them with your foot! So how could I have not beaten him? The more I thought about it, the angrier I got; every time I thought about it I hit him, day or night, for three whole days. Eventually he fell ill from the beatings and woke up crying in the middle of the night. But I didn't let the matter overly concern me; I just beat on the door frame with the rice ladle to call his spirit back, and he got better on his own."

It had been several years since she had raised chickens, and in the time that had passed since making the engagement arrangements for this child-bride she had spent all the little savings she had managed to put aside. Not only that, she had had to spend money every year for gifts and other expenses, so that things had been particularly tight these past few years. So she begrudgingly had to forego raising a few chickens.

Now here was this Wayfaring Immortal sitting across from her asking one hundred coppers for each lot drawn. If he hadn't mentioned money, but had just let her go ahead and draw a lot, then asked for money afterwards, it would have been like she was drawing a lot for nothing. But no, the soothsayer had to mention the hundred coppers *before* he would let her draw a lot. So the child-bride's mother-in-law had a vision of all her money flying off into the distance — a hundred coppers every time she reached out her hand or opened her mouth. If this wasn't throwing money out the window, what was it? Without a sound or a trace it simply disappeared. It wouldn't even be the same as crossing a river and throwing money into the water, for at least when you do that there is the splashing sound and the ripples that spread out. Not a single thing could come from doing it this way — it was the very same thing as losing money when your mind is elsewhere, or meeting up with a robber who takes your money from you.

The child-bride's mother-in-law was nearly moved to tears by the anger welling up in her heart. As these thoughts occupied her, she felt that this was not so much drawing lots as it was paying some kind of tax. Accordingly, she drew back her outstretched hand, quickly ran over to the wash basin, and washed her hands. This was no laughing matter — it was money, a hundred coppers' worth! After washing her hands she went over and knelt before the kitchen god to offer up a prayer, after which she finally drew her lot.

Her first drawing produced the green one, and green wasn't very good — it represented the devil's fire. So she drew again, but this one was even worse — in fact, it was the worst of all; she had drawn the one in which blue medicinal powder was wrapped, the one that meant that the person would have to come face to face with Yama, whether dead or alive.

When the child-bride's mother-in-law saw that both of her choices had been bad ones, by rights she should have burst into tears. But that's not what she did. Ever since the child-bride had fallen seriously ill, the woman had heard every conceivable comment regarding the prospects of living or dying. In addition, they had engaged fox fairies and sorceresses any number of times with all of their chants and witchery, and she had seen a great deal of the affairs of this world in all that time. She seemed to live under the impression that although it is nice to be alive, she wouldn't be particularly grieved to die either, for she suspected that the meeting with Yama would not be taking place for the time being.

She then asked the Wayfaring Immortal whether, since both lots she had drawn were bad ones, there was some way to negate their power.

"Bring me a brush and some ink," was his answer.

Since there were no brushes in their home, the wife of the elder grandson ran over to the grain shop next to the main gate of the compound to borrow one.

The proprietress of the grain shop asked her in a heavy Shandong accent: "What's happening over at your place?"

"We're curing our younger sister-in-law's illness," the wife of the elder grandson answered.

"Your younger sister-in-law's illness is a serious one. Has she improved at all lately?"

Now the elder grandson's wife had planned to just get an inkstone and a writing brush and run back home with them, but since the woman had voiced her concern, it would have been impolite to just ignore her, and so she was gone long enough to smoke several pipefuls before heading back home.

By the time she finally came back with the inkstone, the Wayfaring Immortal had already torn some red paper into strips. He took up the writing brush and wrote one large character on each of the four strips of red paper. Since the strips were no more than half an inch in width and an inch in length, the large characters looked as though they were about to fly off the edges.

As for the four characters that he wrote, inasmuch as no one in the family knew how to read — even the scrolls hanging on either side of the kitchen god altar had been written by someone at their request — they all seemed to them to be identical, like children of the same mother. For all they knew, they might have been the very same character. The elder grandson's wife looked at them but didn't know what they said, and the grandmother looked at them without recognizing them either. But even though they couldn't read them, they felt certain that they couldn't have bad meanings, for otherwise, how could they be expected to effectively keep someone from having to come face to face with Yama? And so each of them nodded her head approvingly.

The Wayfaring Immortal then ordered them to bring him some paste. Now paste was something they went without the whole year long, as it was so terribly expensive — a single catty of flour cost over a hundred coppers — so when they had to repair shoes they settled for kernels of cooked millet.

The wife of the elder grandson went to the kitchen and scooped a gob of millet off the rice pot. The Wayfaring Immortal spread some of the gooey substance onto the strips of red paper, then lifted the tattered lined jacket off the head of the child-bride and told her to hold out her hands, sticking one of the strips onto each palm. Then he had her remove her stockings, after which he stuck a strip onto the sole of each foot.

When the Wayfaring Immortal noticed the large white scars on the soles of her feet he reckoned they must be from the brandings the mother-in-law had been talking about a short time before. But he feigned ignorance and asked: "What sort of malady did she have here on the soles of her feet?"

The child-bride's mother-in-law quickly reminded him: "Didn't I just say that I'd branded her with a flatiron? This girl refused to admit the error of her ways. She walked like she was on the top of the world and soon forgot all the beatings I gave her, so I had to brand her. Fortunately, it wasn't all that serious — after all, young people's skin is so resilient — and after being confined to bed for ten days or a couple of weeks she was just fine."

The Wayfaring Immortal mulled this over for a moment, then decided to throw a scare into the woman by saying that although he had stuck paper strips onto the scarred soles of her feet, he was afraid they might not hold; nothing, he continued, escaped Yama's attention, and these distinctive scars might just stick in his mind, which could make their plans go awry.

When he had spoken his piece, the Wayfaring Immortal looked to see if he had succeeded in frightening them or not; deciding that he had fallen somewhat short, he continued in an even graver tone: "If these scars aren't gotten rid of, Yama will be able to find her within a period of three days, and the moment he finds her he will snatch her away, even though she still be alive. The last lot you drew a while ago was infallible, so these red stickers are absolutely useless."

The Wayfaring Immortal never imagined that this chilling prospect still would not have noticeably frightened any of them, from the grandmother down to the grandson's wife, and so he continued: "Not only will Yama snatch the child-bride away, he will likewise come after her mother-in-law to seek retribution. For what is branding the soles of someone's feet, if not a form of torture? A woman who tortures her prospective daughter-in-law shall be consigned to a vat of boiling oil, and since the child-bride of the Hu family has been tortured by her prospective mother-in-law. . . ."

His voice grew louder as he went along, until he was on the verge of shouting; it was as though he were a gallant crusader attacking injustice — his demeanor had changed in the short time he had been there. When he reached this point there wasn't a single member of the Hu family — young or old — who was not gripped by fear. Trembling from head to toe, they felt as though an evil demon of some sort had infiltrated their household. The mother-in-law was more frightened than any of the others; mumbling incoherently about the ghastly prospects that were reaching her ears, she refused to believe that anyone on the face of the earth could ever torture her own daughter-in-law. She quickly fell to her knees and, with tears streaming down her face, said to the Wayfaring Immortal: "This is all a result of a lifetime of accumulating no virtures, and my sins are being visited upon my children. I implore the Wayfaring Immortal to break this terrible spell in good faith, to use his divine methods to snatch my daughter-in-law from the jaws of death!"

The Wayfaring Immortal changed his tune at once, saying that he had an infallible means of keeping the daughter-in-law from coming face to face with Yama — a guaranteed method. It was extremely simple: the child-bride need only remove her stockings once again; he would then make a mark with his brush over the scars, making them invisible to Yama. So the stockings were quickly removed, and he made his mark on the soles of her feet, chanting as he did so. Viewed as an extremely simple act by those who witnessed it, nonetheless, it cost the Wayfaring Immortal such great effort that beads of perspiration dotted his forehead. He performed the act with a deliberate gnashing of teeth, wrinkled brows, and staring eyes, as though making these marks had been no easy matter for him, that it had been every bit as trying as scaling a mountain of knives. Then, having made his mark, he tallied up his fee: two hundred coppers for the two drawn lots; four strips of red paper stuck onto the palms of her hands and soles of her feet, at fifty coppers apiece — half the normal rate — which amounted to two hundred coppers; and, finally, the two marks he had made (the usual rate was a hundred coppers per mark, but he had cut his fee in half for them), at fifty apiece, making another hundred coppers. Two hundred plus two hundred, and another hundred, made a total of five hundred coppers.

Accepting his fee of five hundred coppers, the Wayfaring Immortal departed the scene in high spirits.

Just before the mother-in-law of the child-bride had drawn the first lot, her heart was gripped by an excruciating pain as she learned that each one would cost her a hundred coppers. Thoughts of how she could have put that money to work raising chickens or raising hogs had crossed her mind. But now that the five hundred coppers had been handed over, she thought no longer about raising chickens or raising hogs. For she figured that when the episode had reached this point she had no choice but to hand it over. The lots had been drawn, the characters written, and it would have been out of the question to withhold payment. What else was one expected to do when affairs had reached this point? Even if it had been a thousand coppers instead of five hundred, what else could she do but hand it over?

And so, with a sense of resignation she handed over the five hundred coppers, which was part of the earnings from the sale of a quarter peck of soybeans that she herself had foraged in the fields in the autumn. She had sold the beans for a total of less than a thousand coppers. Foraging soybeans in the field was no easy task for these people, since after the landlord's harvesting there were precious few beans left on the surface of that vast plot of land. And yet there were hordes of poor people — children, women, old ladies — engaged in the same task, with the result that competition for each bean was fierce. A grand total of a quarter peck of beans had required two or three solid weeks of foraging in the field on her knees, until her back ached and her legs were sore. Ai! Because of those few beans the mother-in-law of the child-bride had had to make a visit to the Li Yongchun Pharmacy to buy two ounces of safflower. This she had been forced to do because the sharp point of a bean plant had pricked her under a fingernail while she was crawling along the ground looking for beans. She hadn't given it any thought at the time, but had merely removed the thorn from her finger and gone on about her business. Since she was there to forage beans, forage is what she would do. But for some unknown reason, after a night's sleep she woke up to find her finger swollen to the size of a small eggplant.

Even this swelling didn't concern her much, since she wasn't royalty and thus not used to being pampered. Besides, for those whose lives are at Heaven's mercy, who hasn't occasionally experienced Heaven's wrath? But after being discommoded over this for several days, until she could no longer sleep at night for the searing pain, she finally bought the two ounces of safflower.

Buying this safflower is something she should have done at the very outset. Urged to do so by the grandmother, she chose not to; prompted by the wife of the elder grandson to buy some, still she refused. Her own son, out of a sense of filial responsibility, tried to force the issue with his mother, demanding that he be allowed to go and buy some for her. He was rewarded for his troubles by a blow on the head from the bowl of her pipe, which raised a lump the size of an egg.

"You little scamp, are you trying to bring the family to ruin? Your mother isn't even in her grave, and already you're acting like the head of the family! You little devil, now let's see if you've got the nerve to bring up the subject of buying safflower again. We'll see if this big brat of mine has the nerve!" All the while she was cursing she was hitting him with the bowl of her pipe.

But in fact she eventually did buy some, most likely due to the urgency of her neighbors' advice; for if she didn't buy a little safflower, it wouldn't look good at all. Everyone would be gossiping about the wife of the elder son of the Hu family: Any money she accumulated throughout the year would disappear, they would say, as though it had fallen through a crack in the earth the moment it touched her hand; once it had come to her there was no chance it would ever reappear. Now this was not the sort of talk that did a family any good. Besides, after selling the beans she had picked for a price of nearly a thousand coppers, if it was necessary to part with twenty or thirty for a little safflower, then it should be done. All she had to do was grind her teeth once, then go and buy two ounces of safflower and rub it on.

But even though she gave it some serious thought, she still could not make up her mind to go ahead. She put it off for several days, never quite able to bring herself to "grind her teeth."

Ultimately, however, she did buy some. She chose a day when her condition was at its most serious — not only was her finger affected, but the whole hand had begun to swell. A finger that had originally puffed up to the size of a small eggplant was now as big as a small melon, and even the palm of her hand was so huge and puffy it looked like a winnowing basket. For years she had bemoaned the fact that she was too thin, saying that people who were too thin had less than their share of happiness. This was especially true for those with skinny arms and legs, which was an obvious sign of a lack of blessings, and even more so for those with bony hands; looking like a pair of claws, they were a sure indication of ill-fortune.

Now she had a plump hand, but it wasn't a very comfortable way of getting it. Not only that, she had come down with a fever, her eyes and mouth felt dry, and her face was flushed; experiencing hot and cold flashes all over her body, she commented: "Is this hand going to bring me to grief? This hand of mine...."

She said the same thing over and over from the moment she got up in the morning. She could no longer even move this hand, which had grown to the size of a winnowing basket. As though it were the head of a cat or a small child, she put it beside her on the pillow as she lay down.

"I'm afraid this hand of mine is going to bring me to grief!" This she said as her son walked up alongside her; from the tone of her voice he got the impression that this time she was prepared to buy some safflower. So he ran at once to see his grandmother to discuss the purchase of safflower for his mother.

Since their home was arranged with two *kangs* opposite each other — one facing north and one facing south — even though they carried on the discussion in hushed tones, his mother could hear what they were saying. Yet she pretended that she could not hear, so that no one could later accuse her of having been in on the decision to buy the safflower, or say that the idea had originated with her; it most assuredly wasn't she who had asked them to go and buy safflower!

Grandmother and grandson discussed the matter by the northern *kang* for a while, then the grandson said he would ask his mother for some money.

"Go and buy it with my money," his grandmother counseled. "We can talk about paying it back once your mother is well."

She intentionally raised her voice slightly as she said this, evidently wanting to make sure that her elder son's wife had heard her. She had; for that matter, she had heard every word they had spoken. Yet she lay there without moving, not letting on that she was listening.

After the safflower had been purchased and brought home, the son sat down beside his mother and said: "Ma, let me rub on some of this safflower tonic."

His mother turned her head on the pillow to face him, looking as though she had been caught completely unawares by the news that some safflower had been bought. "Well!" she exclaimed. "So this little rascal has bought some safflower for me, has he? . . ." But this time she refrained from hitting him with the bowl of her pipe. Instead she calmly put her puffy hand out and let him smear the safflower mixture all over it.

She wondered whether they had bought twenty coppers' worth of safflower, or thirty. If it was twenty, then they had gotten plenty for their money, but if they had paid thirty, then it was a bit too expensive. Now if she had gone to buy it herself, she most certainly wouldn't have bought so much; after all, wasn't it only some safflower! Safflower was merely something red, and who could say whether or not it had any medicinal qualities, or if it was anything more than a placebo?

These thoughts occupied her for a while, until the coolness of the tonic on her hand, the fragrant aroma of the heated mixture, and the strong medicinal aroma of the safflower combined to make her feel drowsy. She was feeling a good deal more comfortable now, and the moment she closed her eyes she began to dream.

She dreamed that she had bought two cakes of bean curd — big, white ones. Where had she gotten the money to buy it? It had been paid for with money left over after buying the safflower, for in her dream it was she who had bought the safflower, and she had not bought thirty coppers' worth, nor even twenty — she had spent only ten. Figuring it all up in her dreams, not only could she eat two cakes of bean curd that very day, but could eat two more anytime she felt like it! For she had spent only ten of thirty coppers on the safflower.

And yet she had just handed over five hundred coppers to the Wayfaring Immortal. Seen through her eyes, just think how much bean curd she could have bought with that much money! But these thoughts did not occur to her now. On the one hand, there was her prospective daughter-in-law, whose illness had involved them all inextricably and had already been a big drain on their finances; on the other hand, there was the Wayfaring Immortal with his savage powers, who had just accused her of torturing the child-bride. Giving him the money and letting him get the hell out of there had been the best way to handle it after all.

Having a sick individual in the house certainly exposes a person to all sorts of unpleasantness. The child-bride's mother-in-law thought about the whole matter, this unexpected calamity that kept growing and growing in her mind. She felt terribly put upon and wronged: wanting to vent her anger, there was no one to rail at; feeling like crying, she found herself unable to; wanting to strike out at someone, there was no one within reach.

Of course there was always the young child-bride, but she could not withstand another beating. Now if she had just then arrived at their house, then of course her mother-in-law could have grabbed hold of her, administered a beating, and let the chips fall where they may. Or if the mother-in-law had broken a rice bowl, she could have taken hold of the young child-bride and given her a beating; if she had lost a needle, again she could have taken hold of the young child-bride and given her a beating; or if she had taken a fall, tearing a hole in the knee of her unlined trousers, once again she could have taken hold of the young child-bride and given her a beating. Whatever the situation, when things were not going well with her, her reaction was to hit someone. Who would that someone be? Who could she get away with hitting? Who else but the young child-bride?

She couldn't hit anyone whose mother was nearby, and she didn't really have the heart to hit her own son hard. She could hit the cat, but was afraid she might never see it again, or she could hit the dog, but was afraid it might run away from home. If she hit one of the pigs, it might lose a few pounds of weight, and if she hit one of the chickens, it might stop laying eggs. The only one she could hit with impunity was the young child-bride. She wouldn't disappear from sight or run away; she didn't lay eggs; and, unlike a pig, if she lost a few pounds it wouldn't make any difference, since she was never weighed anyway. But as soon as this prospective daughter-in-law of hers started getting beaten, she lost her appetite. Now a lost appetite is nothing to be too concerned about, since she could always drink a little water left over from boiling rice; after all, whatever rice-water was left over was always fed to the pigs.

But these times of personal glory were now all in the past, and it didn't look as though such days of freedom would return for her in the foreseeable future. Not only was beating out of the question now, she couldn't even administer much of a tongue-lashing to her anymore. All of the woman's worries were now subordinated to her fear of the girl's dying. Her heart was constantly in the grip of a dark terror: her prospective daughter-in-law simply mustn't die on her!

As a result, she mustered her self-control to overcome all of her personal difficulties, grinding her teeth with determination, fighting back her tears, and restraining herself from cursing and beating. She would not allow herself to cry, even though she experienced countless sorrows and griefs, often simultaneously. She thought that perhaps the reason she was burdened with the girl in this life was because she herself had done nothing good in a previous one. Otherwise, how could it have reached the point that she wasn't even fated to have a child-bride in her family?

She couldn't recall ever doing anything evil in her life; with a kindly look on her face and a heart brimming with benevolence, she had always given way before others, allowing herself to get the worst of all matters. Granted that she had not abstained from eating meat and had neglected to chant her sutras, still she had fasted on the first and fifteenth days of each lunar month ever since she was a child. And granted that she had often been remiss in going to the temple to worship and light incense, still she had never once stayed home from the temple festival on the eighteenth day of the fourth lunar month, at which time she always lit incense at the Temple of the Immortal Matron and performed her three kowtows at the Temple of the Patriarch. Every year, without fail, she had done what was expected, burning incense and performing her kowtows. Granted, too, that she had not learned to read when she was young and did not know characters, nonetheless she was able to recite the Diamond Sutra and had memorized the prayer to the kitchen god. And granted that she had never performed such charitable acts as mending a road or repairing a bridge, yet she always gave her leftover soup and uneaten rice to beggars who came around over New Year's or other holidays. Finally granted that she had not lived a particularly frugal life, still she had never eaten a single cake of bean curd more than she should have. She could live with herself, for she had a clear conscience. Why then, in Heaven's name, had the seeds of disaster been planted in *her* body, of all people? The more she puzzled over this, the less sense it made.

"Things have turned out this way in my present life because I never performed any good deeds in a former one." When her thoughts reached this juncture, she let them go no further; since matters had already reached this point, what good could come of a lot of hasty thoughts and ideas? So she convinced herself that she must fight back her tears, bite down hard on her teeth, and simply part with that modest sum of money she had so diligently put aside after raising hogs and performing other menial tasks. It was a matter of ten coppers here, ten more there; fifty for this, a hundred more for that.

One neighbor advised the burning of incense and paper

money, another prescribed a rare remedy to be taken. She had tried them all: remedies, herbal medicines, sorceresses, exorcists, incense, and divining boards; and although she had spent untold sums of money, nothing seemed to have produced much in the way of results.

The young child-bride talked in her sleep at night and ran a fever during the day. During the night as she slept she talked only of returning to her home. In the eyes of the girl's mother-in-law the words "return home" were the most disquieting of all, for she imagined that the girl might be a reincarnated daughter of hell who was being summoned home by the Queen of Hell herself. And so she sent for a reader of dreams, whose explanation was just as she had feared: "return home" did, in fact, mean going to the nether world.

Thus, whenever the young child-bride dreamed of being beaten by her mother-in-law, or of being bound and strung up from the rafters of the house, or of being branded on the soles of her feet, or even of having her fingertips pricked with a needle, she began to wail and scream, shouting that she wanted to "return home." And the moment her mother-in-law heard her scream that she wanted to return home she reached out and pinched her on the leg. As the days went by, and one pinch followed another, the young child-bride's thighs became a welt of black and blue bruises, making her look like a spotted deer.

Now the woman's intentions were completely honorable: fearing that the girl would really be returning to the nether world, she wanted to quickly rouse her from her sleep. But the young child-bride, heavy with slumber, always imagined that she was actually being beaten by her mother-in-law, and as a result, she would begin to scream more loudly, roll over on the *kang,* and jump to the ground, where she thrashed around uncontrollably. At such times her strength was astonishing and her shouts fearfully loud, further strengthening her mother-in-law's conviction that she was seeing ghosts and being visited by devils.

The certainty that this child was possessed by a demon was felt not only by the mother-in-law — the whole family believed it to be true. Hearing what was going on, who could not believe? Shattering the late-night calm with her shouts of returning home, she then jumped to the floor upon being awakened, her eyes staring, her mouth agape; wailing and shouting, she was more powerful than an ox, her shouts like those of a pig being slaughtered.

Who could doubt it, especially when the girl's mother-in-law added the information that her eyeballs had turned green, like two little demon fires, and that her screams were more like an animal's roar than the cries of a human being?

And so the talk spread, until there was no one in the neighborhood who doubted. As a result, there were several people of good conscience who felt pity for this young girl who had unquestionably been seized by a demon. Where was there a child who had never had a mother, a person who was not born of flesh and blood? All people cared for their elders and educated their young . . . the people's natural compassions were greatly aroused. This family's auntie knew of a rare cure, that family's auntie was privy to a miraculous remedy.

And so it went : sorceresses, exorcists, incense, divining boards; there was a constant clamor at the home of the Hu family. It became the main attraction throughout the area, and anyone who didn't come to watch the dance of the sorceress or the rites of the exorcist was considered a fool. So many kinds of sorceress' dances were performed for the Hu family that it was a historic time — never had there been such activity. This record-breaking episode had ushered in a new age of sorceress-dancing, and if a person failed to see it for himself, his ears and eyes would henceforth be forever closed.

But these festivities went unrecorded since the town was without a local newspaper. If a person were to suffer paralysis of half his body, or a palsy, or a disease that kept him permanently bedridden, it was considered nothing less than the misfortune of a lifetime, and he was pitied by all. Such a person was feared to be forever cut off from the rest of the world, for he had been unable to personally witness such a momentous occasion.

This place, Hulan River, was much too closed off from the outside world, and there wasn't much culture to speak of. Nonetheless, the local officials and gentry were in the main satisfied, and a Hanlin Scholar of the Qing dynasty had been asked to pen a lyric about the place, which went:

> Natural forests along the Hulan,
> Since antiquity the source of remarkable timber.*

This lyric had been set to a melody imported from the Eastern Sea [Japan] and was sung by all of the elementary school children. Actually there was more to the song than just these two lines, but it was considered quite good enough just to sing the two. By good I mean that they were sufficient to instill feelings of complacence in anyone who heard them. To illustrate: during the Qingming Festival, when trees were planted at the gravesites of ancestors, the children from many of the elementary schools lined up and made a procession through the town, singing this melody as they passed by. When the citizenry along the route heard their singing they felt that Hulan River must be a truly magnificent place, and they spoke of it as "this Hulan River of ours." Even the child who collected animal droppings for fertilizer would talk of "this Hulan River of ours" as he walked along with his dung rake. I could never figure out,

* There is a pun here: the word for timber (*cai*) is homophonous with and sometimes used for the word meaning "talent/ability." Here the literal meaning is secondary.

though, just what Hulan River had ever done for him. Maybe the dung rake he carried was Hulan River's gift to him.

This place, Hulan River, may very well have been blessed with marvelous "timber," but it was still too closed off — it couldn't even support a newspaper. And so the curious tales and strange events that happened here went unrecorded, simply carried away on the wind.

The dance of the sorceress at the home of the Hu family was quite a novel event, as was the bath that the child-bride was given in a large vat in full view of everyone. As news of these unusual spectacles spread, people came in droves to get an eyeful. As for the paralyzed and the palsied, while no one gave much thought to the tragedy of their physical incapacitation, the fact that they were thus incapable of personally witnessing the public bathing given to the Hu's child-bride was, in their eyes, the calamity of a lifetime.

V

Dusk was ushered in by the beating of drums at the Hu house. All was in readiness: the vat, the boiling water, and the rooster. The rooster had been caught and brought forward, the water heated to a running boil, and the vat placed there ready for use.

People came in an unbroken stream to watch the activities, and Granddad and I came with the others. I went up to the dark-skinned child-bride with the hearty laugh as she lay on the *kang* and gave her a marble and a little platter. Commenting that it was a pretty little platter, she held it up in front of her eyes to look more closely at it. Then she said that the marble would be fun to play with as she flipped it with her finger. Seeing that her mother-in-law was not there beside us, she sat up with the idea that she would play with the marble on the *kang*. But before she even had a chance to begin, her mother-in-law entered and said: "You sure don't know what's good for you! What are you up to now?" She walked up alongside her and covered her up again with the tattered coat so that no part of her head — not even her face — was exposed.

I asked Granddad why the woman wouldn't let her play. "She's sick."

"No, she isn't, she's just fine." Then I climbed up onto the *kang* and removed the coat from her head.

The moment her face was visible I could see that her eyes were wide open. She asked whether or not her mother-in-law was gone, and when I answered that she was, she sat up again. But no sooner had she sat up than her mother-in-law reappeared, and once again she covered the girl up, saying: "Don't you even care that people will laugh at you? You're sick enough that we've had to invite sorceresses and exorcists over. Who ever heard of such a thing — sitting up any old time you feel like it!"

After saying this very quietly to the girl, the mother-in-law then turned to the gathered crowd and commented: "She has to be prevented from being in a draft, because even a slight one will cause her illness to take a turn for the worse."

As the clamor spawned by all this entertainment grew and grew, the young child-bride said to me: "You wait and see; they're going to give me a bath soon." She said it as though she were talking about someone else.

Before long, just as she had predicted, the bathing began, accompanied by a chorus of screams and shouts. The sorceress started beating her drum and ordered that the girl be stripped naked in full view of the crowd. But she resisted their efforts to take her clothes off, forcing her mother-in-law to wrap her arms tightly around her and ask for several people's assistance to come forward and rip the clothes off her body.

Now although the girl was twelve years old, she looked

more like a girl of fifteen or sixteen, so when her body was exposed, the young girls and married women looking on all blushed.

The young child-bride was quickly carried over and placed inside the vat, which was brim full of hot water — scalding hot water. Once inside, she began to scream and thrash around as though her very life depended upon it, while several people stood around the vat scooping up the hot water and pouring it over her head. Before long her face had turned beet-red, and she ceased her struggles; standing quietly in the vat, she no longer attempted to jump out, probably sensing that it would be useless to even try. The vat was so large that when she stood up inside only her head cleared the top.

I watched for the longest time, and eventually she stopped moving altogether; she neither cried nor smiled. Her sweat-covered face was flushed — it was the color of a sheet of red paper. I turned and commented to Granddad: "The young child-bride isn't yelling any more." Then I looked back toward the big vat to discover that the young child-bride had vanished. She had collapsed inside the big vat.

At that moment the crowd witnessing the excitement yelled in panic, thinking that the girl had died, and they rushed forward to rescue her, while those of a more compassionate nature began to weep.

A few moments earlier, when the young child-bride was clearly still alive and begging for help, not a single person had gone to rescue her from the hot water. But now that she was oblivious to everything and no longer seeking help, a few people decided to come to her aid. She was dragged out of the big vat and doused with cold water. A moment before, when she had lost consciousness, the crowd watching all the excitement had been moved to exquisite compassion. Even the woman who had been shouting, "Use hot water! Pour hot water over her!" was pained by the turn of events. How could she not be pained? Here was a sprightly young child whose life had suddenly come to an end.

The young child-bride was laid out on the *kang,* her whole body as hot as cinders. A neighbor woman reached out and touched her body, then another woman did the same. They both exclaimed: "Gracious, her body's as hot as cinders!"

Someone said that the water had been too hot, while someone else said that they shouldn't have poured it over her head, that anyone would lose consciousness in such scalding water.

While this discussion was going on, the mother-in-law rushed over and covered the girl with the tattered coat, exclaiming: "Doesn't this girl have any modesty at all, laying here without a stitch of clothing on!"

This was the same young child-bride who had fought having her clothing taken off out of a sense of modesty, but had been stripped on the orders of her mother-in-law. Now here she was, oblivious to everything, with no feelings at all, and her mother-in-law was protecting her chastity.

The sorceress beat some tattoos on her drum, as the assistant spoke several times to her, and the onlookers cast glances among themselves. None could say how this episode would end, whether the young child-bride was dead or alive, but whatever the outcome, they knew they hadn't wasted their time in coming. They had seen some eye-opening incidents, and were a little wiser in the ways of the world — that alone made it all worthwhile.

As some of the onlookers were beginning to feel weary, they asked others whether or not the final act of these rites had drawn to a close, adding that they were ready to go home and go to bed. Seeing that everything was lost if the crowd broke up, the sorceress gathered her energies to make sure she kept her audience. She beat a violent tattoo on her drum and sprayed several mouthfuls of wine into the child-bride's face. Then she extracted a silver needle from her waistband, with which she pricked the girl's fingertip. Before long the young child-bride came to.

The sorceress then informed the people that three baths were required — there were still two to go. This comment injected new life into the crowd: the weary were given a second wind, renewed vigor came to those wanting to go home to bed. No fewer than thirty people were gathered there to watch the excitement; a new sparkle in their eyes, they were a hundred times more spirited than before. Let's see what happens! If she lost consciousness after one bathing, what's going to happen when she takes a second? The possible outcome of yet a third bath was beyond their imagination. As a result, great mysteries crowded the minds of the onlookers.

As anticipated, the moment the young child-bride was carried out to the large vat and dumped into the scalding water, her eerie screams began anew. All the time she was shouting she was holding on to the rim of the vat, trying desperately to pull herself out. Meanwhile, as some people continued to douse her with water, others pushed her head down, keeping her under control until once again she passed out and collapsed in the vat.

As she was fished out this time, she was spurting water from her mouth. Just as before, among the onlookers there was no one of conscience who remained unmoved by the plight of this young girl. Women from neighboring families came forward to do whatever they could to aid her. They crowded around to see whether or not she was still alive. If there was still a spark of life, then they need not worry about rescuing her. But if she was breathing her last, then they must hurriedly douse her with cool water. If there was still life in her, she would come around on her own, but if her life was ebbing away, then they would have to do something quickly in order to bring her to. If they didn't they would surely lose her.

VI

The young child-bride was bathed three times that evening in scalding water, and each time she passed out. The commotion lasted until very late at night, when finally the crowd dispersed and the sorceress returned home to go to bed. The onlookers, too, returned to their homes to retire.

On this winter night the moon and stars filled the sky, ice and snow covered the ground. Snow swirled and gathered at the base of the wall, winds beat against the window sills. Chickens were asleep in their roosts, dogs slumbered in their dens, and pigs holed up in their pens. All of Hulan River was asleep.

There were only the distant sounds of a barking dog, perhaps in White Flag Village, or possibly a wild dog in the willow grove on the southern bank of the Hulan River. Whatever the case, the sound was coming from a great distance away and belonged to those affairs that occurred outside the town of Hulan River. The whole town of Hulan River was fast asleep.

There was no longer any hint of the dancing and drum-beating of the sorceress from the previous evening, and it was as though the shouts and cries of the young child-bride had never happened, for not a single trace of all of this remained. Every household was pitch dark, its occupants all sound asleep. The child-bride's mother-in-law snored as she slept.

Since the third watch had already been struck, the fourth watch was nearly upon them.

VII

The young child-bride slept as though in a trance the whole day following, as well as the day after and the day after that. Her eyes were neither completely open nor completely closed; small slits remained, through which the whites of her eyes were visible.

When members of her family saw how she lay there, they all said that she had undergone a great struggle, but that her true soul still had a grip on her body, and if so, then she would recover. This was the opinion not just of her family, but of the neighbors as well. As a result, not only did they feel no anxiety over her condition — neither eating nor drinking, and always in a sort of half-consciousness — but on the contrary, they felt it was something over which they should rejoice. She lay in a stupor for four or five days, which were four or five happy days for her family; then for six or seven days, which were six or seven happy days for her family. During this period not a single potion was used, not a single type of herbal medication was put to the test.

But after six or seven days had passed and she remained in a coma, neither eating nor drinking, giving no indication that she was on the road to recovery, the sorceress was called back. But this time she said nothing about effecting a cure, for it had now reached the point where there was no alternative but for the girl to "come forth," to become a sorceress herself.

The family then decided to apply the true methods of exorcism, so they went to the ornaments shop, where they had a paper image of her made, which they dressed in cotton clothing made especially for it (the cotton clothes were to make the image even more lifelike). Cosmetics were applied to the face and a colorful hankie attached to its hand; the result was a delight to behold — dressed completely in colorful clothes, it looked just like a maiden of seventeen or eighteen years. The image was carried by people down to the big pit on the south bank of the river, where it was burned.

This procedure is called burning a "proxy doll," and according to legend, when this "proxy doll" is burned, it takes the place of someone's real body, sparing that person's life.

On the day the "proxy doll" was burned , the child-bride's mother-in-law showed proof of her devotion by engaging a few musicians, who filed in behind the people hired to carry the image. The procession made its way to the big southern pit to the accompaniment of the musicians' tooting and clanging. It would have been accurate to call the procession a boisterous affair, with the trumpets blaring the same tune over and over again. But it would have been no less accurate to call it a mournful affair, for with the paper figure going in front and three or four musicians bringing up the rear, it looked like something between a funeral procession and a temple excursion.

There weren't many people who came out onto the street to watch all the commotion, since the weather was so cold. A few folks did stick out their heads or venture out to take a look, but as soon as it was clear that there wasn't much worth seeing they closed up their gates and went back inside. Therefore the paper figure was burned in the big pit in a mournful ceremony with little fanfare.

The child-bride's mother-in-law experienced pangs of regret as she burned the figure, for had she known beforehand that there weren't going to be many people looking on, she could have dispensed with dressing the figure in real clothing. She felt like going down into the pit to retrieve the clothing, but it was already too late, so she just stood there and watched it burn. She had spent a total of more than a thousand coppers for that set of clothes, and as she watched it burn, it was as though she were watching more than a thousand coppers go up in smoke. There was both regret and anger in her heart. She had by then completely forgotten that this was a "proxy doll" for her prospective daughter-in-law. Her original plan had been to intone a prayerful chant during the ceremony, but it slipped her mind completely until she was on her way back home, at which time it occurred to her that she had probably burned the "proxy doll" for nothing. Whether or not it would prove effective was now anybody's guess!

VIII

Later we heard that the child-bride's braid had fallen off one night as she slept. It had simply fallen off beside her pillow, and no one was quite sure how that could have happened.

The mother-in-law was firmly convinced that the child bride was some kind of demon, and the detached braid was kept around and shown to everyone who dropped by. It was obvious to anyone who saw it that it had been snipped off with scissors, but the mother-in-law insisted that such was not the case. She stuck to her story that it had simply fallen off by itself one night while the girl slept.

Eventually, as this curious news made the rounds throughout the neighborhood and outlying areas, not only did the members of her family express their unwillingness to have a demon among them, even the people in the same compound felt that it was a terrible situation. At night, while closing their doors and windows, the people commented: "The Hu family's child-bride is a demon for sure!"

The cook at our house was a real gossip, who was forever telling Granddad one thing or another about the Hu family's child-bride. Now there was something new to report: the girl's braid had fallen off.

"No it didn't," I retorted. "Someone cut it off with a pair of scissors."

But as far as the old cook was concerned, I was too young to know what was going on, so to ridicule me, he put his finger over my mouth and said: "What do you know? That young child-bride is a demon!"

"No she isn't. I asked her in secret how her hair had fallen off, and she had a grin on her face when she said she didn't know!"

"A nice child like that," Granddad interjected, "and they're going to kill her."

A few days later the old cook reported: "The Hu family is going to arrange a divorce; they're going to divorce away that little demon."

Granddad didn't hold the people in the Hu family in very high esteem. "Come March I'm going to have them move," he said. "First they nearly kill someone else's child, then they just abandon her."

IX

Before March rolled around, however, that dark-complexioned young child-bride with the hearty laugh died. Early one morning the elder son of the Hu family — the carter with the sickly face and big eyes — came to our house. When he saw Granddad he brought his hands together in front of his chest and bowed deeply.

Granddad asked him what had happened.

"We would like you to donate a small plot of ground to bury our young child-bride."

"When did she die?" Granddad asked.

"I was out with my cart and didn't get home till daybreak," he replied. "They say she died during the night."

Granddad agreed to his request, telling him to bury her on a piece of ground on the outskirts of town. He summoned Second Uncle You and told him to accompany them to the place. Just as Second Uncle You was about to leave, he was joined by the old cook. I said I wanted to go along too and watch them, but Granddad absolutely would not allow it: "You and I will stay home and trap some sparrows for us to eat...."

And so I didn't go along, though I couldn't take my mind off the whole affair. I waited and waited for Second Uncle You and the old cook to return so I could hear how things had gone, but they didn't come right back. It was after one o'clock when they finally returned, having first stopped over somewhere to have some wine and some lunch. They returned with the old cook in the lead, followed by Second Uncle You, the two of them looking like a couple of fat ducks; moving hardly at all, they walked slowly and with great complacence.

The old cook, who was in front, was red-eyed and his lips were glistening with oil. Second Uncle You, who was behind him, was flushed from his ears all the way down to the thick tendon below his neck. When they entered Granddad's room, one of them said: "The wine and food weren't half bad. . . ."

". . . The egg soup was boiling hot," the other commented.

Not a word about the burying of the young child-bride. It was as though the two of them had returned from a New Year's celebration, feeling nothing but satisfaction and happiness. I asked Second Uncle You how the child-bride had died and what had happened at the burial.

"What's the idea of asking me that? The death of a human being isn't as noteworthy as that of a chicken . . . just stick your legs out straight and that's the end of that. . . ."

"Second Uncle You, when are you going to die?"

"Your Second Uncle isn't going to die . . . now you take a rich man who lives in comfort all his life; the longer he hopes to live, the younger he is when he dies. Not even burning incense in the temple or going into the mountains to worship the Buddha will change the outcome. But then take someone like me who's been poor all my life; I get stronger with each passing year. I'm just like a rock that never dies! Like the old saying goes: 'The rich get but three measures of life, the poor hang on forever.' Second Uncle You is one of those poor ones, and King Yama won't even stoop to look at the likes of me."

That evening the Hu family invited the two of them, Second Uncle You and the old cook, over again to drink some more wine. This was their way of paying them back for all their help.

X

Not long after the Hu family's child-bride died, the wife of the elder grandson ran away with another man.

Later on the grandmother passed away.

As for the wives of the two sons of the family, one of them lost her sight in one eye because of the affair with the child-bride; she had cried every day over the fact that all of the family's wealth — more than fifty thousand coppers — had been squandered on behalf of the child-bride.

The other wife had suffered untold shame over the fact that her son's wife had run away with someone, and she spent every waking minute of every day sitting beside the stove smoking a pipe, never combing her hair or washing her face. If someone walked by when her spirits were high, she would ask them: "Is everyone in your family well?" But when her spirits were low she would spit in the person's face.

She had become half mad.

From then on few people ever thought about the Hu family.

XI

Behind our house there was a Dragon King Temple, to the east of which there was a big bridge we called Great Eastern Bridge. The ghosts of wronged people congregated below this bridge, and during inclement weather people crossing over it could hear the weeping sounds of those ghosts.

People were saying that the ghost of the child-bride had also come to this spot below Great Eastern Bridge. They said that she had been transformed into a big white rabbit who came to that place under the bridge once every few days to weep.

Someone might ask her why she was weeping.

She would say she wanted to go home.

If the person responded by saying, "I'll take you home tomorrow, . . ." then the white rabbit would wipe her eyes with her big floppy ears and disappear. But if no one paid any attention to her, she would continue to weep until the crowing of chickens ushered in the new day.

6

Second Uncle You

I

Second Uncle You had a very unusual temperament. If we had something to eat but wouldn't give him any, he would curse us. But if we took some to him, he would say: "I don't eat this stuff, you eat it yourself."

If we bought some things like peanuts or frozen pears and didn't want to give him any, we had to hide them from him, for if he so much as spotted them, he invariably began cursing: "God damn it, you little bastards . . . queer jack rabbits. There's plenty for dogs and cats, or for cockroaches, or even rats, but there's god-damn little for people . . . queer jack rabbits, queer jack rabbits . . ."

But if we took some to him, then he would say: "I don't eat this stuff, you eat it yourself."

II

Second Uncle You's temperament was strange indeed — he loved to talk to sparrows while they were flying in the sky and he also loved to have chats with the big yellow dog. But somehow he ran out of things to say when he was with people. Or if he did have something to say, it was of such a strange nature that it left the person scratching his head in bewilderment.

On summer evenings after dinner, when we all sat in the courtyard to cool off, we talked and talked about everything under the sun, and our spirited discussions were accompanied by the buzzing of mosquitoes and the croaking of distant frogs. Second Uncle You alone sat there without saying a word, flyswatter in hand, which he flicked from side to side. If someone asked him whether the flyswatter was made of horse's mane or horse's tail, he would answer: "Like they say: 'Everybody has his own thing, and even the ugly ne'er-do-well Wu Dalang had his pet duck.' Horse's mane is costly stuff, something reserved for people who wear silks and satins, with bracelets on their wrists and rings on their fingers. Each person is matched with his own kind of stuff to play with. We poor rootless souls must not become the butts of others' laughter by forgetting our place."

There is a fable concerning the evening star: When the Kitchen God ascended to the Western Heaven on his young donkey he carried a lantern in his hand, but because the donkey traveled so fast, in a careless moment the lantern got stuck in the sky, where it hangs today. I often asked Granddad how the lantern had gotten up in the sky and why it stayed hanging up there without ever dropping to Earth. I could see that he had no answer, but he knew that I wouldn't be satisfied without some kind of answer. And so he told me that there was a lantern pole in the sky, a very, very tall one, on which the evening star was perched. It was, however, invisible to the human eye.

"That's not true," I would say, "I don't believe you." Or I would say: "There's no lantern pole. If there was, why can't people see it?"

"There's a long thread up in the sky, and the evening star hangs from that," Granddad would answer.

"I don't believe you. There's no thread in the sky, or else I could see it."

"How could you, since it's so fine? There isn't a person

alive who can see it."

"If no one can see it, then how do you know it's there?" The others would all laugh, commenting on how clever I was.

Eventually my questions would back Granddad into a corner until there was nothing else he could say. I could see that his wild fabrications were a result of my persistent questions, and I knew that he really didn't have an answer. Still, the wilder his answers became, the more persistently I kept up the questioning. By the time I was finished I had even shot holes in the theory regarding the relationship between the Kitchen God's lantern and the evening star, following which I asked Granddad just what exactly the evening star was.

The others could see that I had reached the end of the line as far as Granddad was concerned, so someone recommended that I direct my questions to Second Uncle You.

I ran over to where he was sitting, but before I had even opened my mouth, and had barely brushed against his flyswatter, he gave me a scare by shaking the flyswatter and grumbling: "Come on kid, move back a little."

Forced to heed his command, I moved back a bit, then asked him: "Second Uncle You, just exactly what is that evening star up in the sky?"

He didn't answer me right away, as though he were mulling over my question; finally he said: "The poor concern themselves not with heavenly phenomena . . . dogs chase mice, cats watch the house . . . mind your own business!"

Thinking that he had misunderstood my question, I asked him again: "Is the evening star really the Kitchen God's lantern?"

"Even though your Second Uncle has a pair of eyes, he's never seen a single thing in his whole life. And even though your Second Uncle has a pair of ears, he hasn't heard a single thing in his whole life. Your Second Uncle is deaf and blind. You want to know why I say that? Take, for example, bright, shiny tile-roofed houses: I've seen them before, but what good has it done me? They belong to other people, so I might as well never have seen them at all. The same is true for hearing things; what difference does it make if you hear something that has nothing to do with you? Everything in your Second Uncle's life has had nothing to do with him... stars, the moon, winds, and rain, those are all Heaven's affairs that your Second Uncle knows nothing about . . . "

Second Uncle You was really strange. If his foot bumped into a brick while he was walking, stubbing his toe painfully, he would very carefully bend over and pick the brick up, then minutely examine it to make sure it was neither too small nor too big, but just right. Then, after examining the brick, he would begin talking to it: "You there, little one, I guess you don't have eyes either. You're just like me, blind as a bat. Otherwise, why would you move over and bump into my foot? Since you've got the nerve to bump people, why not aim at the high and mighty, those with boots or shoes on their feet? Why waste your time bumping into the likes of me? You're not going to get a thing out of bumping into me . . . like a chunk of stinking mud trying to roll itself into a stone, only to find itself stinking worse every minute."

His discourse with the brick finished, he would toss it away with a flick of his wrist, giving it one final admonition as he did so: "Next time find yourself someone who's wearing shoes and socks to bump into." The brick would fall crashing to the ground just as he finished what he was saying, but since he hadn't thrown it very far at all, it would wind up in just about the same place he had found it.

If Second Uncle You was walking in the courtyard and some droppings from a sparrow or swallow that was flying overhead landed on him, he would stop in his tracks and simply stand there. Then he would raise his head and begin cursing at the sparrow, which by then had already flown past. The gist of his comments would have to do with how the sparrow shouldn't have sent its droppings down on him, but should have aimed instead at someone wearing silks and satins. His comments would be punctuated by references to the sparrow's stupidity, blindness, and the like. But the sparrow, after having quickly let fly its missile, would have disappeared without a trace, so that Second Uncle You would be left with only the clear blue sky overhead as a target for his curses.

III

When Second Uncle You spoke he pronounced "this" as "dis."

"That man is good."

"Dis man is no good."

"Dis man has the heart of a wolf and the lungs of a wild dog."

"Dis thing's worse than nothing at all."

"What kind of year is dis, with house sparrows sending their droppings down on my head?"

IV

Besides this,
Second Uncle You didn't eat mutton.

V

Granddad said that Second Uncle You had come to our home thirty years before, when he was just past the age of thirty. Second Uncle You was now over sixty.

As a child he had been given the pet name Youzi, which

meant Little You. Now, at the age of over sixty, he was still called by his pet name. Granddad would say to him, "Youzi, do this," or "Youzi, do that."

We called him Second Uncle You.

The old cook called him Second Master You.

When he visited the house or land tenants he was called Second Landlord You.

When he went to the distillery on Avenue North he was called Second Proprietor You.

He was also called Second Proprietor You when he went to the oil store to fetch some cooking oil.

He was likewise called Second Proprietor You by the people at the butcher shop when he went to buy meat.

Whenever he heard people refer to him as Second Proprietor You his face beamed with a smile. His face also beamed when he was called Second Master You, Landlord You, or Second Uncle You. But he hated it like poison when someone called him by his pet name. Some of the neighborhood brats, for example, would throw rocks at him from behind, or spray him with handfuls of dirt, loudly calling him names like: "Little Second You" or "Big Oaf You" or "Little Runt You."

In situations like this Second Uncle You would never miss the opportunity to strike out at the kids. If he had his flyswatter in his hand he would use it to aim a swipe at them, and if he had his pipe in his hand he would hit them with the bowl of his pipe. For this made him as mad as a wet hen, and his eyes would be red with rage.

But as soon as those rascally kids saw him coming at them, his fists swinging, they would quickly call out: "Second Master You, Second Landlord You, Second Proprietor You, Second Uncle You!" They would clasp their hands in front of their chests and bow low to him. When Second Uncle You saw this new state of affairs his face would quickly break into a broad grin; he would stop swinging and resume the walk that had been interrupted.

But before he had taken more than a few steps, the kids behind him would start in again with their shouts of:

"Second Master You, the big queer."

"Second Uncle You plays with his own oar."

"Second Landlord You, out catching bastard turtles."

He would keep walking straight ahead, while the kids he had left in the distance behind him would continue with their taunts, raising clouds of dirt in the air as they shouted, and as the dust swirled in the wind, the whole chaotic scene would take on the appearance of a whirlwind.

Although no one could say whether or not Second Uncle You heard all of this, the kids behind him believed that he had. But Second Uncle You would walk on somewhat majestically, step after undaunted step, without once turning his head back.

"Second Master You," the old cook would call out. He preceded every sentence he spoke about or to him with "Second Master You."

"Second Master You's flyswatter . . ."

"Second Master You's pipebowl . . ."

"Second Master You's tobacco pouch . . ."

"Second Master You's tobacco pouch belt . . ."

"Second Master You, dinner's ready . . ."

"Second Master You, it's raining . . ."

"Second Master You, quickly look over there; the dogs are fighting in the courtyard . . ."

"Second Master You, the cat's climbed up onto the wall . . ."

"Second Master You, your flyswatter's shedding hairs."

"Second Master You, there's some house-sparrow droppings on the crown of your hat."

The old cook always called him "Second Master You." That is, except when the two of them were having an argument; then the old cook would say: "As I see it, if you took away the 'Second Master' from your name, all you'd have left is the 'You' *zi* [word]."

When he heard the words "You" and "*zi*" together it sounded to him just like his pet name, Youzi. With that, curses would begin to fly back and forth between them, as each tried to outdo the other. Their voices would grow louder and louder, and sometimes they would even come to blows.

But before long the two of them would be all buddy-buddy again, and once more we would hear: "Second Master You this," and "Second Master You that."

Whenever the old cook was in high spirits he would say: "Second Master You, as I see it, if you took the word 'You' away from your name, then you'd be left with 'Second Master,' wouldn't you?" Second Uncle You's face would be beaming with a smile.

He never got angry when Granddad called him "Youzi"; instead he would say: "When you speak to an emperor you refer to yourself as a slave. There's always a high and a low: a prime minister may be high, but he must prostrate himself before the emperor. Though superior to the multitudes, he is yet inferior to one man."

Second Uncle You was a very courageous man — he feared nothing. Once I asked him whether or not he was afraid of wolves.

"What's there to fear from a wolf? When I was young I took pigs out to pasture on a mountain where wolves were living.

I asked him if he had the nerve to walk down dark roads.

"What's there to fear from walking down a dark road? 'If one has done nothing shameful one has naught to fear from ghosts at the door.'"

I asked him if he had the nerve to walk across the Great Eastern Bridge alone late at night.

"Why wouldn't I? The only things your Second Uncle dares not do are shameful things. He has the nerve to do anything else."

Second Uncle You often talked about how courageous he had been when people were fleeing from the *maozi*, or "Hairy Ones" (during the Russo-Japanese War). The whole city's populace had fled, including our entire family. The "Hairy ones" astride their horses galloped back and forth through the streets, brandishing broadswords in their hands. Countless numbers of people were slaughtered by them during those days, as they pounded on every closed door they saw, then broke them down and butchered every person they caught. "When the 'Hairy Ones' were galloping back and forth," Second Uncle You said, "their horses' hooves made a great racket on the streets. I was cooking some noodles when they came pounding at my door and yelling, 'Is there anyone inside?' At times like that someone had to open the door in a hurry, otherwise the 'Hairy Ones' would break the door down with their swords and burst in. Things would look bad then, for there was sure to be some bloodshed . . ."

"Second Uncle You, you must have been afraid!" I said.

"I had just boiled some water and was putting the noodles in. The 'Hairy Ones' were outside pounding on the door, and your Second Uncle was inside eating noodles."

But I persisted: "You were afraid, weren't you?"

"Afraid of what?"

"If the 'Hairy Ones' had come inside, wouldn't they have killed you with their broadswords?"

"So what if they had? After all, it's only a life!"

But every time he and Granddad were talking of the past, he sang a different tune: "People are flesh and blood: They're all raised by their fathers and mothers! We've all got the same five organs and six bowels. Afraid? Who wouldn't be afraid? I was so scared I shook in my boots — I saw those broadswords with my own eyes. One slash with one of those swords and there goes another life!"

So I asked him: "But didn't you say before that you weren't afraid?"

At times like that he cursed me: "You heartless brat, just get away from me! Not afraid? . . . you show me a person who's not afraid . . ."

I don't know why, but he grew timid whenever he and Granddad discussed the subject of fleeing from the "Hairy Ones." The more he talked about them, the more frightened he became, on occasion even breaking into tears. He ranted on about the glint of the broadswords and how the "Hairy Ones" had ridden by on their horses in a frenzy of killing.

VI

Second Uncle You's bedding was a real jumble: if you opened up his comforter, cotton wadding oozed out of the corners; if you spread open his mat, shreds of felting skittered to and fro, making it look like a living map with all the provinces moving on their own. His pillow was filled with buckwheat husks, and every time he tried to fluff it up, a stream of husks poured from its corners or from rends in the middle.

Second Uncle You doted over this bedding of his, and when he had nothing else to do he picked up needle and thread to mend it . . . sewing his pillow, sewing his shredded felt mat, sewing his comforter. I never knew how his things could be so fragile, but every second or third day he had to get out his needle and thread and put them to work.

Second Uncle You's hands were so coarse and thick that he had to use a gigantic needle; he said he couldn't hold on to a small one. His needle was so large that when it lay in the sunlight it looked more like one of the silver pins women use in their hair. It was sheer delight to watch him trying to thread this needle of his. He would raise the needle and thread high above him, then close one eye and stare intently with the other, like he was taking aim. He would look as though he had spotted something up in the sky that he wanted to grab quickly but was afraid he might miss and knock away; wanting to study the situation carefully, he was also afraid that it would be gone if he waited too long. All this anxiety would make his hands tremble, and that was quite a spectacle.

When Second Uncle You woke up in the morning he always rolled up his bedding, then tied it up with a piece of cord, giving the impression each day that he was about to set off on some sort of journey.

Second Uncle You didn't sleep in any one prescribed place. One day he might stay in the bean-noodle mill with its creaky beams and posts, the next day he might sleep at the foot of the herder-boy's *kang* in the home of the family of hog raisers, while the night after that he might just sleep on a *kang* with Harelip Feng in the millshed behind our house. In short, he slept wherever there happened to be room for him. He carried his own bedding roll on his back, and whenever the old cook saw him carrying it like that, he shouted out loudly: "Second Master You is off to the market again."

Second Uncle You would answer him from a distance: "Since I'm off to the market, Old Wang, is there something I can get for you while I'm there?" Then he would continue on to wherever he was going — he would take up temporary lodging at whichever of the tenant's homes was convenient.

VII

Second Uncle You's straw hat had only a crown with no brim. Since his face was swarthy black and the crown of his head snowy white, there was a clear dividing line between black and white, which occurred exactly at the point where the straw hat fit down neatly over his head. Whenever he took off his hat the top half of his head was white, the bottom half black. Just like a melon in our rear garden — the side that faced the sun was green, the shaded side white. But the moment he put on his straw hat none of this was apparent any longer. He put the hat on his head very carefully, fitting it down so that it just reached the line dividing black from white. Neither above nor below, it rested precisely on that dividing line. Every once in a while he would put it on slightly higher than normal, but only very seldom, and not so that other people would notice. It just looked to them that there was a narrow white border at the juncture where hat and head met — just a single white line.

VIII

Second Uncle You wore a gown that came down only to his knees. It was neither a full-length gown nor a short jacket; rather it reached just to his knees. The gown, made of marine-blue cotton cloth, had a squared-off, high-pointed collar, broad flowing sleeves, and a row of brass-tipped hempen buttons. It was an old thing dating from the Qing dynasty that had been stored at the bottom of Granddad's chest. After Grandmother died, it gradually wound up draped over Second Uncle You's frame. And so when Second Uncle You was out taking a walk it was hard to tell just what period he belonged to.

The old cook often said: "Second Master You, with those broad flowing sleeves of yours, in the eyes of a Buddhist monk you, too, are a Buddhist monk, and in the eyes of a Taoist priest you, too, are a Taoist priest."

Second Uncle You liked to wear his pantlegs rolled up, so when farmers saw him they thought that he, too, might be a farmer, one just returning from planting rice.

IX

As for Second Uncle You's shoes, if one of the soles wasn't flapping, then a heel had dropped off. He glued the soles and nailed the heels on with his own hands, but he apparently neither nailed nor glued them very well, for within a few days the soles would invariably loosen and the heels fall off again.

When he walked it was either with a shuffle or with a flapping sound. If the soles had loosened, the shoes had the appearance of gaping mouths, his toes looking like tongues that moved back and forth inside those gaping mouths at each step; if the heels of his shoes had fallen off, then the heels of his feet made slapping sounds against the bottoms of the shoes as he walked.

Second Uncle You's feet never really left the ground when he walked, and Mother often said that they were weighted down with half-ton sluice gates. The old cook said that Second Uncle You's feet were locked in horse fetters.

But Second Uncle You himself said: "Your Second Uncle has foot-tie bands on his feet."

Foot-tie bands are ropes that are fastened around the feet of a dying man. That's what Second Uncle You used to say about himself.

X

Even though Second Uncle You dressed like a cross between a monkey trainer and a beggar, when he walked he did so with solemn, quietly dignified airs; he had great strength in his heels, which smacked loudly against the ground, and he walked with extremely slow steps, just like a great general. Whenever he walked into Granddad's room, the works inside the black clock that stood on the lute-shaped table often jingled and whirred a time or two, then grew silent. This happened because Second Uncle You's footsteps were much too heavy, just like big rocks crashing to the ground, causing everything that rested on the floor to bounce up and down.

XI

By chance I discovered Second Uncle You stealing things.

In the late autumn, when the big elm tree had shed its leaves, the rear garden grew dreary, and there was nothing for me to do there. The mugwort in the front courtyard had withered and lay flat on the ground. A layer of frost covered all the plants and stalks in the vegetable garden behind the house, and only a few sparse leaves remained on the big elm tree, though the autumn winds continued to cause its limbs to sway. The sky was ashen and covered with shapeless clouds, making it look like a water basin in which an ink-mixing stone had been washed; there was a mottled mixture of dark and light hues. Some of these clouds carried rainfall in them, others carried fine snowflakes. During weather like this, since I couldn't play outdoors, I went up into the attic above the backroom where old objects were stored.

One day, after climbing up by means of standing on a trunk, my hand bumped into a glass jar that was packed full of dried black dates. But when I tried to climb back down holding onto the jar, I found I couldn't, for there stood Second Uncle You, opening up the very trunk I had used to climb up into the attic. He was opening it not with a key, but with a piece of wire.

I watched him trying to open it for a long time; he was using his teeth to twist the thing in his hand — he would cock his head and gnaw loudly on it. Then after biting it he would twist it in his hands, then try it again on the lock of the trunk. He obviously was unaware that I was up in the rafters watching him, and when he finally succeeded in opening the trunk he took off his brimless straw hat and tucked the thing he had been chewing on for such a long time into the crown. Then he rummaged through the trunk several times; in it were some red chair cushions, a blue embroidered apron made of coarse cotton, some women's embroidered shoes, as well as a tangled wad of multi-colored silk threads. At the bottom of the trunk lay a dark-yellow brass wine decanter. He took out the embroidered shoes and tangled silk with his thick-veined hands and laid them to one side. Then he picked up the brass wine decanter from the pile of things. He placed the red armchair cushions on the floor and tied his belt around them, after which he placed the brass wine decanter on the lid of the trunk, which he then locked.

It seemed to me that he was going to take these things away with him, but for reasons known to him alone he walked out of the room without doing so. As soon as I saw him leave I jumped down onto the trunk and lowered myself down. But the moment my feet touched the floor, Second Uncle You reentered the room, scaring the daylights out of me. I was frightened because I was in the act of stealing some dried black dates, and if Mother had found out about it she would have given me a spanking for sure. Usually when I stole something it was merely things like eggs and steamed buns, which I took outside and shared with some of the neighbor kids. Whenever Second Uncle You saw me he was sure to tell my mother, and she was just as sure to spank me.

He first picked up the chair cushions lying beside the door, then came over to fetch the brass wine decanter from the lid of the trunk. Just as he had opened up his gown and tucked the brass wine decanter underneath it up against his belly, he looked up and saw someone standing in the corner of the room — *me*.

He had a brass wine decanter under his gown tucked up

against his belly, I was holding a jar of dried black dates pressed up against mine. He was stealing, so was I, and both of us were frightened.

The moment he laid eyes on me, large beads of sweat appeared on his forehead. "You won't tell?" he asked.

"Tell what . . .?"

"Be a good kid and don't tell . . .," he said as he patted the top of my head.

"Then will you let me take this jar out with me?"

"Go ahead and take it," he said. He didn't try to stop me.

When I saw he wasn't going to stand in my way I stopped by the basket alongside the door, picked up four or five big steamed buns, and darted off.

Second Uncle You also stole some rice from our grain storage shed. He filled a large sack, hoisted it up onto his back, then took it over to the grain shop on the eastern side of the bridge, where he sold it.

Second Uncle You stole all sorts of things: a tin cookpot, old brass coins, pipebowls . . . . As a rule, whenever something was missing from the house, he was accused of stealing it. Some of the things had actually been stolen by the old cook, but he passed the blame on to Second Uncle You. Some of them I had stolen to take out and play with, and Second Uncle You was blamed for them, too. Then there were things like the blade of the scythe, which hadn't been stolen at all, but was simply misplaced; yet when the time came to use it and it couldn't be found, Second Uncle You was accused of stealing it.

When Second Uncle You took me to the park he refused to buy me anything to eat. There was every imaginable thing for sale at the park: fried cakes, fragrant stuffed flatcakes, gelatined bean curd, and other delicacies, but he wouldn't buy a single one of them for me. If I merely stood for a moment near one of the stalls where those treats were sold, he would say to me: "Hurry up, let's keep on walking." A walk in the park with him was like an overland hike — he wouldn't let me pause even for a second.

There were all sorts of shows in the park: things like magic performances, a blind man and a dancing bear, and the loud gongs and drums produced a festive atmosphere. But he wouldn't let me watch any of it. If I stopped for a moment in front of a circus performance, he'd say: "Hurry up, let's keep on walking." I don't know why, but he was always chasing me on ahead.

As we walked up to a stall with a white awning where ices were sold, I noticed two big, yellow Buddha-fingers fruit in a glass jar; since I had never seen anything like them before, I asked Second Uncle You what they were.

All he said was: "Hurry up, let's keep on walking." It was as though someone might come up and start beating me if I looked at them even a moment longer.

Then we drew up alongside the circus grounds, where shouting and singing produced a great commotion. I was determined to go inside and take a look, but Second Uncle You was just as determined not to let me:

"There's nothing worth seeing in there."

Then he said:

"Your Second Uncle doesn't watch 'dis' kind of thing."

Then he said:

"It's time to go home and eat."

Then he said:

"If you keep it up, I'm going to hit you."

Finally he said to me:

"Your Second Uncle would like to watch it, too — who wouldn't like to watch something entertaining? But your Second Uncle doesn't have any money, and they won't let us go in if we don't have the money to buy a ticket."

There in the park, right where we stood, I grabbed hold of his pocket and checked to see what was in it. All I came up with was a few coppers, not enough to buy a ticket; again he said: "Your Second Uncle doesn't have any money."

Growing impatient, I asked him: "Couldn't you steal a little?"

Second Uncle You's face paled when he heard this, but in a flash the color came rushing back. With his face now all flushed, a forced smile on his tiny eyes, and his lips trembling, it seemed to me that he was on the verge of uttering a stream of his customary comments. But he didn't.

"Let's go home." After giving it some thought, that's all he said to me.

Once I even saw Second Uncle You steal a bathtub.

The courtyard at my house was generally quiet the day long; Granddad was usually asleep, Father was away from home, and Mother kept herself so busy with household duties that she didn't see much of what was going on outside. This was especially true during the summertime at midday, when everyone was napping, including the old cook. Even the big yellow dog would find himself a shady spot and go to sleep. As a result, both the front courtyard and the rear garden were deathly still, without a trace of people or sounds. It was on just such a day that someone walked out from the rear garden carrying a big bathtub on his shoulders.

The bathtub was made of galvanized iron that shone brightly under the sun's rays; it was longer than a person and made clanging noises as the man walked. It was scary to look at, as it reminded me of the fabled great white snake. The bathtub was so huge that, with it over his head, Second Uncle You almost completely disappeared from sight, and only the bathtub itself was visible. It was almost as though the bathtub were moving along under its own power. But more careful examination revealed that it was riding atop Second Uncle You's head. He walked along as though he had no eyes in his head, wobbling first to the left then to the right, leaning to one side then the other. Fearing that he would bump into me, I flattened myself up against the wall. The big bathtub was so deep that it covered Second Uncle You from the top of his head all the way down to his waist, which meant that he couldn't see the road ahead and had to feel with his hand as he walked along.

The scene that followed Second Uncle You's theft of the bathtub was a repetition of the one when he had stolen the brass wine decanter. As soon as the old cook discovered the theft, he derided him daily, directing every kind of taunt he knew at Second Uncle You.

Previously, when he had stolen the brass wine decanter, every time he picked up a wine decanter to have a drink, the old cook would ask him: "Second Master You, does it taste better to drink out of brass wine decanters or out of pewter ones?"

"They're all the same to me," Second Uncle You would say. "Either way it's still wine you're drinking."

The old cook would respond by saying: "I don't agree with you. I still think brass ones are probably better . . ."

"What's so special about a brass one?"

"I guess you're right, Second Master You. We don't have any use for a brass wine decanter, and we couldn't even get anything for ours if we tried to sell it."

By this time everyone else in the room would begin to chuckle, but Second Uncle You still didn't know what was going on.

The old cook would then ask him: "How much can you get for a brass wine decanter?"

"Don't know," Second Uncle You would answer. "I've never sold one."

After this the cook would begin guessing — five hundred coppers? Seven hundred? To which Second Uncle You would respond: "What makes you think you'd get that much? You can't even sell a great big brass wine decanter for more than three hundred!" At this, everyone would double up with laughter.

The old cook stopped bringing up the subject of the brass wine decanter following the theft of the bathtub; instead he began asking Second Uncle You about his bathing habits. He would ask him how many baths he took a year or how many baths he had taken in his lifetime. He even asked him whether people took baths in the nether world after they died.

"There's no difference between the nether world and this world," Second Uncle You answered him. "A poor man in this world becomes a poor ghost after he dies. King Yama of the underworld has no sympathy for a poor ghost, who's lucky if he isn't sent down to the lowest hell. There's no talk of a bath — he's afraid you'll muddy the water!"

Then the old cook said: "Second Master You, according to you, there's no need for a poor man to ever take a bath!"

Second Uncle You seemed to be getting the drift of the conversation, so he said: "I've never been to the nether world, so I wouldn't know."

"You wouldn't know?"

"I wouldn't know."

"I think you know very well, and you're going against your own conscience by lying," the old cook said.

At this point a fight broke out between them. Second Uncle You forced the old cook to tell him when he had gone against his conscience: "I've never in my life gone against my conscience. I've walked the proper road, done the things I was supposed to do, never straying from the straight and narrow."

"Straight and narrow? . . . That I'd like to see . . ."

"What is it you'd like to see?"

"If I told you, you'd die of shame!"

"Die! I'm not going to die. Don't treat me like that because I'm poor. Even the poor have a desire to live."

"Yes, I suspect you aren't going to die."

"That's right, I'm not!"

"Not going to, or won't? As I see it, you're one of those old fogeys who won't die."

Sometimes their arguments would last as long as a couple of days, and invariably it was Second Uncle You who got the worst of them, for the old cook would call him an "heirless old man." Whenever Second Uncle You heard these three words they hit him harder than any other, even including comments like "going to meet Yama." He would begin to weep and mumble: "That's exactly the way it is; after I'm dead there won't be a single person to take care of my grave. I've lived a whole life for nothing, and when I leave this world it'll be as though I hadn't even been here . . . no family, no profession . . . when I'm dead there won't even be anyone to mourn me."

At this point peace would reign once more between the two of them, and they would again pass their time peacefully as before, laughing and joking with each other.

XII

Later on we added three siderooms to the east of our five-room main house. As soon as these new rooms were completed, Second Uncle You moved back into our house.

Our house was very quiet, especially at night, when the chickens and ducks had all gone to roost, and the pigeons on the roof and the sparrows in the eaves had all returned to their nests to sleep. At such times I often heard the sounds of weeping coming from the siderooms.

Once Father beat up Second Uncle You; Father was just over thirty years old, while Second Uncle You was nearly sixty. As Second Uncle You got to his feet, Father knocked him back down. He got up again, and once more was knocked to the ground. Finally he could no longer get to his feet, so he just lay there in the courtyard with blood oozing out of his nose, or perhaps his mouth. The people in the courtyard who were watching the excitement stood off at some distance, and even the big yellow dog was frightened away, as were the chickens. As for the old cook, he continued gathering firewood and fetching water, pretending that he hadn't seen what was happening.

Second Uncle You lay there in the middle of the courtyard, alone and neglected. His brimless straw hat had been knocked off his head, so everyone could see that the top half of his head was white, the bottom half very dark, and the line that separated the black and white halves ran right across his forehead, just like the sunny and shady halves of a melon. He just lay there like that for a long time, until a pair of ducks waddled over to peck at the blood that had splattered onto the ground alongside him. One of the two ducks had a multi-colored neck, the top of the other's head was green.

It was on this very night that Second Uncle You tried to hang himself. At first he cursed, then he cried, and finally he stopped both his cursing and his crying. A short while later the old cook began to shout as though he had discovered some kind of weird apparition: "Second Master You's hanged himself! He's hanged himself!"

Granddad put on his clothes and took me with him, but by the time we had arrived at the sideroom we discovered that Second Uncle You wasn't there. The old cook called for us to come outside; when we got there we noticed a rope hanging from one of the beams of the southernmost room. It was a dark night, so we couldn't see a thing until the old cook held up a lantern and showed it to us. The rope hung limply from a crossbeam that was affixed to the beam of the southernmost room.

Where was Second Uncle You? Looking around with the aid of the lantern, we spotted him sitting quietly at the base of the wall. He was neither crying nor cursing. When I held the lantern up to his face to take a closer look I saw that he was glaring at me with eyes red from crying.

Not long afterwards Second Uncle You "jumped down the well." The news came to us from the water bearer who lived in the same compound, when he came banging on our windows and pounding at our door. We dashed over to the well to see for ourselves, but Second Uncle You was not inside it; rather, he was sitting calmly off to the side of the well on a pile of firewood that was some fifty steps distant. He was just calmly sitting on the pile of firewood. With the aid of a lantern, we could see that he was sitting there having a leisurely smoke on his pipe.

The old cook, the water bearer, and even the bean-flour sifter from the noodle mill had shown up — the incident had disturbed a good many of the neighbors. At first he didn't move, but when he saw that just about everyone had arrived he broke out running toward the well. But he was caught and stopped by several of those present. They couldn't have just stood by and watched him jump down the well, could they?

When he made his attempt at jumping down the well he took his pipe and his tobacco pouch along with him. Then when he was urged by everyone to go on home, he pointed to a small candle atop the pile of firewood and said: "Bring that candle along for me."

Later on, Second Uncle You's "jumping down the well" and "hanging" became laughing matters, and the kids in the street sang a little ditty about the incidents: "Second Master You faced the well, but came to no harm; his 'hanging' was all a false alarm."

The old cook said he was clinging to life out of a fear of dying, and others said he would live forever. From then on, whenever Second Uncle You "jumped down the well" or "hanged himself" no one went out to look.

And Second Uncle You still lived on.

XIII

The courtyard at my house was a dreary one. In the winter it was covered with a white blanket of snow, and in the summer it was overrun by mugwort that whistled in the wind and gave off mist when it rained. When there was neither wind nor rain we passed our days quietly behind a closed gate.

Dogs have their kennels, chickens their roosts, and birds their nests; everything belongs somewhere. Only Second Uncle You, among all the rest, never enjoyed a good night's sleep. There in that sideroom of his he talked to himself at all hours of the night.

"Accuse me of being afraid of death, will they! Well, if they think I'm so full of hot air, let a couple of them come over here, and I'll find out if they've ever been around death! Those shiny broadswords the Russian 'Hairy Ones' carried... they killed and butchered at will. As for all those fearless ones who disdained death, the instant they heard that the Russian 'Hairy Ones' were coming, they abandoned everything they owned and fled for their lives. If it hadn't been for this 'coward,' who took good care of their belongings for them, when they returned home after fleeing from the 'Hairy Ones' there wouldn't have been even a pair of pants left for them to wear. Now here they are today, with food to eat and clothes to keep themselves warm, though any thoughts of the outstanding debts they owe for their present situation have scattered to the farthest reaches of the universe. Their consciences are stuck between their ribs, those blackhearted wretches with their faces of steel . . .

" . . . So they say I'm afraid of death . . . well, I'm not bragging when I say I've seen wars and weapons, thunderstorms and killer winds. Like those Russian 'Hairy Ones' with their broadswords, slaughtering everyone they saw. But I wasn't afraid, and anyone who says I was . . . what are the times comin' to?"

A steady stream of Second Uncle You's monologue poured from the eastern siderooms: There was the time when the river overflowed its banks, and though others didn't have the nerve to cross it, Second Uncle You *said* he did. Then there was the time of the great fire, when everyone else fled, but Second Uncle You bravely stayed behind to snatch up several things. Then there was the time when he was a child out on the mountain gathering firewood and he met up with a wolf, a truly vicious beast; we heard him say: "The hearts of wolves and the lungs of wild dogs . . . the people 'dis' year all have the hearts of wolves and the lungs of wild dogs. They eat good food and drink good wine, and anyone who tries to be a good man in times like 'dis' is a bastard and a queer jack rabbit . . ."

"Queer jack rabbit, queer jack rabbit . . ." Sometimes on nights when Second Uncle You could not sleep, he would walk into the courtyard and begin to talk to himself in mid-sentence with "queer jack rabbit this," and "queer jack rabbit that." Chickens, duck, cats, dogs: all were asleep in the middle of the night; all, that is, except Second Uncle You.

Since the window in Granddad's room was covered by a curtain that blocked out the moon and stars, for all I knew, the evening star might have fallen from the sky, or the three stars might be lying on their sides. All I could see was the silvery curtain through which the light from the stars and moon shone.

I woke up to hear Second Uncle You talking to himself: "Queer jack rabbit this, queer jack rabbit that," and I wanted to run over and pull back the window curtain to look at him out in the courtyard. But Granddad wouldn't let me get up: "Now you go back to sleep, and we'll get up very, very early tomorrow morning and bake some corn for breakfast." He used this comforting method to keep me from getting up.

After falling back to sleep I dreamt I could hear sounds of a dogfight coming from the southern bank of the Hulan

River, or from some distant spot beyond the town of Hulan River. Then I dreamt about a great white rabbit whose ears were every bit as big as those of the little donkey in the mill. Having heard Second Uncle You's talk about a "queer jack rabbit," I dreamt of a great white rabbit; having heard the sound of the wooden clappers from the mill, I dreamt of the little donkey that lived there. And so my dreams were of a great white rabbit with ears as big as those of the little donkey in the mill.

I gave the great white rabbit a big hug, liking it more with every passing second; then I laughed out loud and woke myself up. When I woke up, Second Uncle You was still sitting in the courtyard talking to himself: "Queer jack rabbit this" and "Queer jack rabbit that." The wooden clappers in the mill behind our house were still being struck loudly.

I asked Granddad if the great white rabbit in my dream was the "queer jack rabbit" Second Uncle You was always talking about. "Hurry up and go back to sleep," he said. "The middle of the night is no time to be talking." When he finished he chuckled, then repeated himself: "Hurry up and go back to sleep. The middle of the night is no time to be talking."

But Granddad and I didn't go right back to sleep. We listened to the far-off sounds of the dogfight as they slowly drew nearer, and to some of the neighborhood dogs that had started barking. A few carts and horses were beginning to pass along the road beyond the outer wall, signalling the fast approaching dawn. But Second Uncle You was still out there cursing those "queer jack rabbits" of his, and the miller was still striking his wooden clappers in the mill out back.

XIV

As soon as I got up the following morning I ran over to ask Second Uncle You if the "queer jack rabbit" he was always talking about was my great white rabbit.

This really made him angry: "There's not a decent one in your whole family — you're just a bunch of rats! From top to bottom, all of your consciences are stuck in your ribs. The adults are a bunch of adult rats, and the kids are all baby rats . . ."

I had no idea what he meant. I listened for a while, but couldn't comprehend what he was talking about.

Harelip Feng

I

Harelip Feng lived in the mill. He struck his wooden clappers deep into the night, night after night. It was a little better during the winter, but on summer nights he struck it with great frequency.

The window of the mill faced out onto the rear garden of our house. Pumpkins, gourds, cucumbers, and other such creepers were planted at the base of the wall that ran all around our rear garden, and the pumpkin plants spread to the top of the wall, where their flowers bloomed. Some had even passed over the top of the wall out onto the street, where they showed off their bright orange blossoms.

The kitchen window was covered by that tenacious climber, the cucumber, whose tendrils were as slender as fine silver threads. A single cucumber plant put forth countless numbers of these tendrils, which caught your eye as they shone in the sunlight, their tips so clean they seemed like threads that had been formed out of beeswax. But the points were coiled back around, as though to show that while they were bold enough to climb great trees, wild vegetation, walls, and window sills, still they harbored some hidden reservations. The moment the sun came out, these tendrils, which had grown cold at night, suddenly took on a new warmth, pushing forward with increased speed — you could almost see them growing before your eyes, pushing ever forward.

The cucumber plant at the base of the mill window reached the window sill in a day, by the second day it had climbed over the frame, and by the third the window frame was covered with its flowers. Within a few days, before you even realized it, the cucumber stems had climbed above the window of the mill and had reached the roof. After that it was as though all the cucumber plants were signalling to each other as they gathered in great numbers to completely block out the window of the mill.

From then on the sunlight was kept from the man who worked the mill, as there was but one window, and now it was barricaded so that neither wind nor rain could penetrate it. With the inside of the mill thus completely darkened, there now existed two separate worlds — one inside the garden and one beyond — and Harelip Feng belonged to the world beyond. But looking from the outside, that window was a wonderful sight, adorned with all those flowers and cucumbers — it was virtually covered with cucumbers.

There was also a pumpkin plant that had climbed past the window to the roof of the mill and had formed a large pumpkin above the eaves. It almost seemed as though it had grown independently of the plant, looking rather like one that someone had placed on the tiles to soak up the sun. It was a lovely scene.

On summer days as I played in the rear garden, Harelip Feng would call out to me for some cucumbers. I would pick some and hand them in to him through the window, which was thickly overgrown with the vines. He would force apart the leaves that covered the window, then reach his hand out through the small opening he had made and take the cucumbers from me.

Sometimes he would stop striking his wooden clappers and ask me how big the cucumbers had grown, or whether the tomatoes were red yet. Separated from the rear garden by only a window, it was as though he were holed up a great distance away.

When Granddad was in the garden, the two of them would have a chat. He said that the little donkey that turned the mill was limping from a lame leg. Granddad advised him to send for a veteranarian, and Harelip Feng replied that he had, but with no results. When Granddad asked what medication had been given to the donkey, Harelip Feng said it was a mash of cucumber seeds and sorghum vinegar. Harelip Feng was behind the window, Granddad was outside; Granddad couldn't see Harelip Feng, Harelip Feng couldn't see Granddad.

Sometimes Granddad would walk away and return home, leaving me to play alone as I sat at the base of the mill wall; I could hear Harelip Feng say things like: "Haven't you been out to see the farms this year, old master?"

Sometimes when I heard him say such things I would keep silent to see what would come next. Once in a while I would be so amused by this that I couldn't keep from jumping to my feet and rapping on his window, laughing so hard that I would knock off many of the cucumbers that grew there. Then I would race home to tell Granddad what had happened. Just like me, he would laugh until tears came to his eyes. But he always admonished me not to laugh so loud that I'd be heard. On occasion he would quickly close the back door before he started laughing, as he was afraid that Harelip Feng would be embarrassed if he heard us.

But this wasn't how the old cook handled it. Sometimes he would be passing the time of day with Harelip Feng, then intentionally slip away right in the middle of their conversation. Now since Harelip Feng couldn't see out the cucumber-vine-covered window and was unaware that the other fellow had left, he continued the conversation by himself, but with no response.

Once when the old cook went out into the rear garden with a basket to gather some eggplants he chatted with

Harelip Feng as he picked them. Then without a word he slipped away back to the house, basket in hand, to begin preparing the meal. Harelip Feng continued talking in a loud voice from inside the mill: "The circus has come to West Park, but I haven't found the time to go see it. How 'bout you, Old Wang, have you seen it yet?"

But by that time there was no one in the rear garden; dragonflies and butterflies were darting back and forth, and the sounds of Harelip Feng's voice fell on the empty garden, where they were lost. They died away without a trace. When he discovered that Old Wang had long since left the garden he began striking his wooden clappers again and watched the donkey turn the mill.

Second Uncle You on the other hand, never once slipped away during one of his conversations with Harelip Feng. He would ask him things like how badly the roof leaked when it rained, or if there were many rats in the mill. For his part, Harelip Feng would ask whether or not a lot of rain had fallen in the rear garden that year, and whether or not the eggplants and beans were just about ripe. Then after the two of them had finished what they had to say, Second Uncle You would invite Harelip Feng to take a stroll in the rear garden, or Harelip Feng would invite Second Uncle You into the mill to sit for a while.

"When you've got the time come out to the garden and take a stroll."

"When you've got the time come in to the mill and sit for a while."

Then Second Uncle You would take his leave and walk out of the garden, and Harelip Feng would recommence striking his wooden clappers.

In the autumn the garden would look drearier with each passing day, as the leaves of the elm tree yellowed and the foxtails atop the wall were all dried up. It was at this time that Harelip Feng's window re-emerged, for the tangled cucumber vines that had blocked it withered and fell to the ground. By then I could stand in the rear garden and see Harelip Feng, and by pulling myself up to the window I could see the donkey turning the mill, its ears straight up, blinders covering its eyes. With every third or fourth step a snort of air emerged from the donkey's nostrils as it walked lamely along; when it stopped to rest, it stood on only three legs. Harelip Feng told me that the donkey had a lame leg.

Once the cucumber vines had withered and fallen away, I could see Harelip Feng every day: Harelip Feng drinking wine, or sleeping, or striking his wooden clappers, or playing the two-stringed *huqin,* or singing opera arias, or turning the windmill — all I had to do to see these things was pull myself up to the window ledge.

Once the glutinous rice was harvested in the autumn, for every three days Harelip Feng spent working the mill he spent two making rice cakes, which he covered with a layer of beans. They were composed of one layer of yellow and one layer of red — the yellow a golden yellow, the red a fiery red. He sold the cakes for three coppers a full piece, or two coppers for a piece sliced off with his knife, and he would sprinkle on some brown sugar if you wanted, or some white sugar, at no extra cost.

When Harelip Feng pushed his wheelbarrow along the street, he would be followed by a pack of children, some with money to spend, others just looking on.

Granddad was particularly fond of these cakes, and so was Mother, but I think I liked them the best of anyone. Sometimes Mother would send the old cook to buy some, sometime she would send me.

But there was a limit to how much we were permitted to eat. We were only allowed a piece as big as the palm of our hand, so we wouldn't upset our stomachs. As Granddad ate his he would say, "That's enough, that's enough," for fear I would eat too much; and when Mother had finished hers she too would say, "That's enough," for fear I would want to buy some more. But in all honesty, I really didn't feel that I'd had enough, and I could easily have eaten two more pieces. But once they had said this, there was nothing I could do; I would have felt embarrassed to keep clamoring for more, even though the truth of the matter is I hadn't had enough.

When I was playing outside the main gate and Harelip Feng came by with his wheelbarrow, he always cut a slice off of the big piece of rice cake and gave it to me, and I always accepted it. If I was playing inside the compound and heard him passing by the other side of the wall yelling, "Rice cake, rice cake," I would clamber up onto the earthen wall at the place in the southwest corner where part of it had crumbled away over the years, and look around to see Harelip Feng coming up the street, pushing his wheelbarrow with the rice cake ahead of him. When he came up alongside me he would ask: "Would you like a slice?"

I would neither give him an answer nor jump down from the wall, but would just stay there as if nothing had happened. He would then set down his wheelbarrow, cut off a slice of the cake and hand it to me.

When winter came, Harelip Feng spent nearly every day out selling his rice cake. He needed a great huge pot for making the cake. First he would boil water under a bamboo steamer, then spread a layer of the freshly ground rice over the steamer, followed by a layer of beans. Since he did all of this inside the mill, the place was filled with hot steam. If I went inside the mill to buy some rice cake, I could hear the crackling sounds of burning firewood, but I couldn't see a soul there.

Whenever I bought some I went over early, then waited until it was just out of the pan, all piping hot. There would be a great pall of steam inside the room, making it impossible to see anyone, so as I opened the door I always called out: "Hey, here I am!"

When he heard the sound of my voice Harelip Feng would say: "This way, I'm over here."

II

Once when Mother sent me to buy some rice cake, it was later than usual and the cake was already out of the pan. So I hastily bought it and ran home, but as soon as I arrived I discovered that I had mistakenly gotten some with brown sugar rather than white sugar, as Mother had wanted. I hadn't noticed it at the time, only discovering my mistake when I got it home. I ran back right away to exchange it, and Harelip Feng cut me some more slices, on top of which he sprinkled white sugar.

Then after I had taken the rice cake from him and was about to leave, I happened to turn and notice a curtain hanging in front of his small *kang,* I couldn't imagine what that was there for, so I ran over to take a look. I reached out, pulled the curtain back, and looked inside. Wow! There was a baby in there! I turned on my heel and ran home, where I gave Granddad the news that there was a strange woman sleeping on Harelip Feng's *kang,* and that there was a baby lying alongside her under the quilt. Only the baby's head was sticking out — it was bright red.

Granddad seemed perplexed as I gave him the news, but then he told me to hurry up and eat the rice cake before it turned cold and lost its flavor. But how could I eat it then? I was much too excited about this turn of events — not only was there a little donkey in the mill, now there was a baby there, too.

Because of all the excitement that morning I didn't eat any rice cake, and finally I put on my fur-lined cap and ran over to take another look. Harelip Feng was out when I went over the second time, though I didn't know where he had gone: he apparently wasn't out selling his rice cake, for his wheelbarrow was lying up against the millstone. As I opened the door and went in, a puff of wind parted the white bed-curtain. The woman was still lying there motionless, her baby lying beside her without making a sound. I looked all around the room: nothing had changed, except for the addition of a brass basin in which some old rags were soaking in water that had already frozen over. There were no other changes.

The little donkey that lived inside the mill during the winter was standing there placidly, its eyes covered with blinders, just as it was every day. Everything else in the mill — the windmill itself, the bolting frame, the millstone — all were right there where they should have been. Even the rats at the base of the wall were scurrying back and forth wildly and squeaking as loudly as ever.

I looked around for a while until I lost interest, then just as I was about to head back home I spotted an earthenware jar on the edge of the *kang* that was so frozen it looked like a little iceberg. This reminded me just how cold the room was, and I began to shiver uncontrollably. Then I noticed a gaping hole in the window that gave out onto the rear garden, and I could see sky showing through several holes in the tiled roof. I opened the door and ran all the way home, where the heat from the brightly burning stove hit me full in the face as I stepped through the door. Just as I was about to ask Granddad whose baby that was in the mill, Harelip Feng came walking up to the house.

You could tell it was him at a glance, wearing his four-flapped hat and the sheepish grin that always appeared before he said anything. He came into the room and sat in the armchair with the thick red cushion next to Granddad. He sat there looking like he was unable to say what was on his mind, all the while restlessly rubbing the red seat cushion with his right hand and pulling at his left ear with the other.

Several times he grinned as though he were about to speak, but each time he stopped short of saying anything. The heat from our stove was so strong it turned his face crimson.

"Old Master, I've got a problem . . .," he said at last.

Granddad asked him what his problem was.

Fidgeting on his chair, Harelip Feng took off his dogskin cap and started fumbling with it. Then after grinning sheepishly for a long while, which indicated he was about to say something, he finally managed to utter. "I've got a family now." Tears came to Harelip Feng's eyes as he spoke. "Won't you please help me, Old Master?" he continued. "I've got them in the mill for the time being, since there's no place else for them to stay."

As soon as he finished, I quickly looked over at Granddad and said: "Grandpa, it's freezing cold in the mill. An earthenware basin on the edge of the *kang* was cracked from the freezing cold."

Granddad nudged me away with the airs of someone engrossed in his thoughts.

"There's a baby sleeping on the *kang*!" I added.

Granddad gave his permission for them to set up temporary lodgings in a shed to the south of the mill where we stored hay.

Harelip Feng stood up at once: "Thank you!" he exclaimed, "Thank you!" Tears welled up in his eyes again as he was expressing his thanks, then he put on his dogskin cap and walked out, tears streaming down his cheeks.

The moment Harelip Feng was out of the room, Granddad turned to me and said: "Children should keep quiet when grownups are talking."

Since I was only six or seven at the time, I didn't understand what he meant. "Why should I be quiet?" I asked. "Why can't I talk?"

"Didn't you see the tears in Harelip Feng's eyes? He was feeling very embarrassed."

What was there to be embarrassed about? I really didn't understand it at all.

III

Toward noon we heard a commotion in the mill.

Harelip Feng was standing silently alongside the millstone facing his boss, the proprietor, who stood there, pipe in hand, cursing him. The proprietor's wife was abusing him in a loud voice and pounding on the windmill: "Are you trying to bring a curse on us, letting that dirty bitch of yours live here in our mill? I suppose you think it's all right for that woman of yours to anger the spirits! Harelip Feng, if we don't make any money after this I'm going to hold you accountable. Who the hell do you think you are! Do you call yourself a human being? You've got no pride left. If you had, you wouldn't have brought this dirty bitch over for everyone to see. . . . You just get the hell out of here . . . !"

"I was just getting ready to move them . . . they're going to move . . . ."

"*They're* going to move!" the proprietor's wife shouted. "I'm not talking about trash like them — I'm telling *you* to get the hell out. Thanks to you, we're ruined . . . !"

In the midst of this tirade, something on the *kang* caught her eye.

"What's this! You're using *our* grain sacks to cover that dirty bitch? Take them off this minute! I'm telling you, Harelip Feng, you've ruined us. You've absolutely ruined us!"

He had covered his newborn child with four or five grain sacks while it slept, its face nearly buried under the pile.

The proprietor's wife stood off to the side and railed: "Take them off, take them off this minute!"

So Harelip Feng walked over and removed the grain sacks, exposing the crimson hands of his child, which clenched and unclenched several times until the baby started to cry. Its breath rose white as snow in the air as it cried.

The proprietor's wife took the grain sacks from him, saying: "I'm freezing to death! You hurry up and move; I don't have the time to stay here and fight with you. . . ." So saying, she opened the door, hunched her shoulders, and ran home.

The proprietor, whose name was Wang Si, and who was also Harelip Feng's landlord, invited Granddad over to his house for some tea. We all sat on the *kang* in his place warming ourselves by a charcoal brazier and listening to the baby's cries from the mill. Granddad asked me if my hands were warm enough yet. I told him no.

"When they're warm we'll go back home," he said.

As we emerged from Wang Si's house I told Granddad I wanted to go back to the mill and have another look. He said there wasn't anything to see there, but if I felt like it, he'd let me go back after I first warmed up at home.

There was a thermometer at home, but none in the mill, so I asked Granddad: "What do you think the temperature is in the mill, Grandpa?"

He said it was below zero.

"How much below?" I asked.

"How can I tell without a thermometer?"

"How much below zero is it?" I persisted.

Granddad looked up at the sky and said: "Seven or eight degrees, I expect."

"Wow, that's cold!" I said with rising spirits. "That's the same as it is outside, isn't it?"

I began racing home: past the well, past the watering trough beside it, and past the discarded millstone; beneath the big glass window of our tenant, past Old Zhou's house, then past the big chimney at our place. They all flew past me, fading into the distance as I raced by. I was running so fast it seemed to me that the houses and the chimney were the ones moving, not me. I felt like I was traveling as fast as the wind.

If the temperature inside the mill was below zero, I thought, then it was the same as being out of doors. That really amused me — the temperature inside a house being the same as outside. The more I thought about it, the funnier it seemed, and the higher my spirits rose. Shouting with glee as I ran, I finally reached home.

IV

That afternoon Harelip Feng moved his baby into the shed to the south of the mill. The baby's cries were so loud they sounded more like those of a grown child than a newborn baby. With all the noise coming from their shed, I decided to go and take a peek.

This time the woman was sitting up, the quilt wrapped around her shoulders, her long braid hanging down her back. She was sitting atop a pile of hay facing the inside of the room, occupied with some task or other. She turned around as she heard the door creak, and when she did I recognized her as the daughter of the Wang family who lived in our compound, the one we called Big Sister Wang. This was strange — how could it have been her? I was really shocked when she turned to face me. I felt like turning around and running right home to tell Granddad the news and find out what this was all about. She smiled when she saw me. She had a large face and a pointed nose, which sort of crinkled whenever she smiled. As she smiled at me now her nose was covered with wrinkles, just like always.

Normally, when we had an excess of vegetables in our rear garden, she would come over with a basket and pick some of the eggplants and cucumbers to take home. She was a friendly, cheerful girl, and very straightforward; she always greeted anyone she met with: "Have you already eaten?" Her voice was as crisp and loud as that of a magpie perched on a roof.

Her father was a carter, and when she took the horse up to the well to drink she drew the water faster than her father could — two or three turns of the handle and the bucket was full. People commented when they saw her: "Someday that girl is going to put her family on its feet."

Often, after she had finished picking vegetables in our rear garden and was about to leave, she would pluck a purslane flower and stick it in her hair. Her glossy braid was bound with a red ribbon at the base and a green one at the tip, all neat and clean and topped with a purslane flower above her ear, which made her look very fetching. As she walked on, basket in hand, the people behind all voiced favorable comments.

To the old cook her beauty was in her large head and big eyes.

Second Uncle You said there was something auspicious in her broad shoulders and rounded waist.

As for Mother, she commented: "I don't have a son old enough, but if I did I'd choose her for his wife — such a bright young girl."

Third Granny Zhou from our compound said: "Gracious, this girl is as tall and large as a big sunflower. How old are you this year, girl?"

Everytime she saw Big Sister Wang, Third Granny Zhou asked her how old she was. I don't know how many times she asked, but it almost became a ritual each time she saw her; it was as though if she didn't ask, she would have nothing to say.

"Twenty," Big Sister Wang would reply every time.

"Twenty! Then it's time to find you a husband." Or she'd say: "Let's see who the lucky family will be. We'll just have to wait and see."

Whenever old Mrs. Yang from the next compound climbed up the wall to look at her she said: "That girl's cheeks are as red as fire!"

But now, although her nose crinkled as she smiled, her face was a bit gaunt and her complexion much paler than before. She was holding her baby in her arms. As I stood there looking at her, she grew embarrassed, and so did I. My feelings of embarrassment stemmed from my not having seen her for so long, and I guess the same must have been true for her. I wanted to leave, but would have felt awkward doing so right away; yet, if I stayed I didn't know what to say. So I just stood there quietly for a while watching her put her baby down on the *kang* and cover him with some hay. Actually there wasn't any *kang* to be seen, just piles of hay all over the room, on the floor and on the *kang* stacked in bales nearly to the rafters. The *kang* wasn't a very big one to begin with, and now it was completly covered with bales of hay. She had made a little nest for her baby, where he slept on a bed of hay and was covered by a blanket of hay.

The longer I looked, the more amused I was by the sight of this baby sleeping in what looked like a magpie's nest. Come evening I gave Granddad a complete account of all I had seen. He didn't say a word, but I could see from his face that he knew a lot more about what was going on than I did.

"She covers her baby with hay!"

"Uh-huh."

"She's Big Sister Wang, isn't she?"

"Uh-huh."

Granddad was evidently in no mood to ask questions or listen to me. But that night, as the whole family gathered round the kerosene lamp, the conversation turned lively. How the tongues wagged! Big Sister Wang such-and-such, one would say; Big Sister Wang thus-and-so, someone else would add. Back and forth it went, getting more vicious by the minute. After all her faults had been pointed out, the general concensus was that she was a bad lot. Everyone was of the opinion that her voice was too loud, proof positive that she was no good. No respectable girl would talk so loud.

"What's 'dis' world coming to," Second Uncle You commented, "when a nice girl like that falls for a man who works a mill?"

"A man's supposed to be rough and tough, but a woman's supposed to be dainty," said the old cook. "Who ever heard of a young woman who looks like a coolie laborer?"

To which Second Uncle You added: "You're right there! The Patriarch looks like a Patriarch, and the Immortal Matron looks like an Immortal Matron. Haven't you been on temple strolls on the eighteenth day of the fourth month? You know how awesome and stern the Patriarch in the Temple of the Patriarch is and how gentle and refined the Matron in the Temple of the Immortal Matron is."

The old cook continued: "Who ever heard of such a thing, a girl who can draw water better than an able-bodied man? I've never seen a girl as strong as that one."

"She's done for now," Second Uncle You lamented. "She was born to poverty, right down to her bones. Instead of falling for someone wearing silks or satins, she had to get hooked up with a grimy miller. Well, to each his own."

By the following day everyone in the neighborhood knew that Big Sister Wang had had a baby. When Third Granny Zhou ran over to our house to get all the news, Mother told her she could go take a look for herself in the shed. But she replied: "Gracious, I don't have the time to spend on seamy affairs like that."

Old Mrs. Yang from the west compound also came over when the news reached her ears. She was wearing a starched and shiny blue gown, a silver pin in her hair, and a white copper ring on her finger. The moment she stepped into the room, Mother told her that Harelip Feng had a son, but old

Mrs. Yang quickly protested: "I certainly didn't come over to ask about things like that. I only want to find out what the interest rate at the Guanghe Bank is these days. You see, my second son wrote home from Xihuang yesterday that his father-in-law wants to deposit a large sum of money for a relative." And with that she seated herself with great dignity.

Since our house was much too hot, old Mrs. Yang's face flushed a bright crimson almost as soon as she walked in, so Mother hurriedly opened the ventilation window on the north side. The moment it was opened the sounds of the baby's cries carried into the room from the shed — loud, harsh cries.

"Just listen," Mother said. "That's Harelip Feng's son."

"Well, well. I could have told you that Big Sister Wang was no good. And you mark my word, she'll never come to any good, either. Some time ago, when she upped and disappeared, I asked her mother: 'Where's your daughter gone to?' She told me that she had gone to visit her grandmother, but I was a little suspicious, since she'd been gone so long."

"Big Sister Wang cried so much during the summer that her eyes were constantly red," Mother said. "Her mother told me that she was a strong-willed girl whose constant arguing drove her to distraction."

Folding her arms, old Mrs. Yang exclaimed: "Strong-willed! She's got quite a temper. But now she's disgraced herself, and I'm surprised her temper hasn't killed her. That girl is just no good. Just look at those eyes, how big they are! I said long ago that she'd never come to any good." Then she whispered something in Mother's ear and walked off laughing and talking. Apparently she had forgotten her original purpose in coming over, which had been to inquire about interest rates, because she walked out the door without ever again mentioning the Guanghe Bank.

Old Mrs. Yang, Third Granny Zhou, even the people in the

bean mill — everyone was saying Big Sister Wang was no good. Some said there was something wrong with her eyes, others said she was too strong, and still others said her braid was too thick.

V

Once this affair became known, the entire compound was obsessed with Big Sister Wang: people discussed her, gossiped about her, and even recorded her daily activities.

According to one story, she had been raised from her youth by her maternal grandmother, spending nearly the whole of every day with boys, until she herself became a tomboy. Once she had even injured one of her cousins by hitting him with a pair of tongs. Another time during a windstorm she had stolen more than twenty of her grandmother's duck eggs and eaten every last one of them. Then on another occasion she had gone down to the stream to gather water chestnuts, but most of the ones she had brought back in her basket were other people's, which she had claimed as her own. She was said to be arrogant as could be, and no one dared try reasoning with her, for when they did she would curse and hit them.

The woman who spread these tales told them as though she had witnessed everything with her own eyes. She said that on the twenty-third day of the twelfth month, during the pre-New Year's festivities, the girl had even hit her own grandmother because she had been given one piece of meat less than she had expected; then she had run home.

"You see what a greedy little thing she is!" Everyone who was listening to her laughed at this. This self-appointed biographer of Big Sister Wang had collected a wealth of material for her stories.

Ever since the death of the child-bride, the whole compound had suffered a long spell of boredom, and now, although the atmosphere couldn't be called lively, there was at least full participation in the goings-on. Even though there was no sorceress-dancing or drum-beating, everyone felt that it was a good opportunity to have a little fun. So all the gossips and busybodies donned their fur-lined caps and felt boots and stood outside Harelip Feng's window on snowy evenings, waiting to pick up some juicy tidbit. Even if the news they gleaned was so small it would fit in the eye of a needle, as far as they were concerned, the wait in the freezing weather had been worth it, for that was the only way there would be news items for the next day.

And so for the next few days there was always a group of news-gatherers standing outside Harelip Feng's window. These news-gatherers, none of whom were trained or educated, were natural gossips and busybodies. Our old cook, for example, went over to gather some information, then came back and reported: "It's mighty cold in that shed! The wind howls right through it. The baby isn't making a sound, and I'll bet it's dead from the cold. Go on over and see for yourselves!"

Beside himself with glee, the old cook was waving his arms and jumping around. Before long he put on his dogskin cap again and went out to gather some more tidbits, but this time when he came back he reported: "Damn it to hell, the little brat isn't dead after all! It's at its mother's breast."

All of this news was being made a mere fifty steps from our house, but the news-gatherers twisted it all out of proportion and made a big sensation out of it.

Someone spotted a coil of rope on Harelip Feng's *kang* and quickly spread the rumor that he was planning to hang himself.

Talk of a "hanging" was a powerful stimulant. Women fastened on their scarves and men put on their felt boots; it's hard to tell just how many there were who came to watch the fun or who were making plans to come. There were more than thirty people, not counting the children, in old Yang's family from the west compound, and with the children there were more than forty. If just the thirty adults had come over to watch Harelip Feng hang himself, they would have crushed our little shed to pieces! Figuring that among them there were some who were too old or too sick to come, let's say that only ten of them turned out. That would make ten from old Yang's family in the west compound, and three from old Zhou's family in our compound — Third Granny, Fourth Daughter-in-Law, and Eldest Daughter-in-Law, plus the child Fourth Daughter-in-Law carried with her and the child Eldest Daughter-in-Law dragged along with her, as they customarily did — which means that there were five people altogether representing three generations of the Zhou family.

Then there were quite a few of the men — how many exactly is not known — who made bean noodles, stoked the furnace, or ran errands for the mill. At any rate, not less than twenty or thirty from our compound went to watch the fun. They were joined by countless others from the neighborhood who came as soon as the word reached them.

"A hanging!" Why should a good man choose not to live but prefer to hang himself? Hurry up and see! Besides, what harm is there in looking? After all, it isn't like a circus, where you have to pay admission.

That's why crowds always gather when a woman in the town of Hulan River jumps down a well or into the river, or when a man hangs himself. I don't know if this is true all over China, but at least it's true where I come from.

A woman who throws herself into the river is not buried immediately upon recovery of her body. Rather, her corpse is left on the bank for a couple of days for everyone to see. A woman who jumps down a well is not buried when her body is pulled out, either, but is displayed to the curious eyes of eager spectators just like an exhibition of native products.

And yet these are not pleasant things to see. If Harelip
Feng had hanged himself, it would have been a gruesome
sight. Timid women cannot sleep for several nights after
seeing the corpse of a suicide. But the next time some unfortunate person takes his own life, they flock around just the
same. The fearful and vivid impression they take home
causes them to once again lose sleep and appetite, but, as if
under some strange compulsion, they go a third time, even
though it frightens them nearly out of their wits. They buy
yellow paper money and a bundle of incense sticks to burn
at the crossroads, then kowtow three times each toward the
north, south, east, and west, imploring the evil spirits: "Don't
take possession of me! I've sent you off properly with
incense and paper money!"

One girl died of fright after seeing a hanged corpse, and I
heard of another who died of fright after seeing a body
brought up from a well. She fell ill from the shock and no
doctors were able to save her.

Yet people choose to look, and men, perhaps because they
are bolder, are not afraid. Most women are more timid, but
they screw up their courage and go. Some women even take
their children along to look. Long before they've even grown
up they're taken along, perhaps to accustom them to this
exciting world of ours; that way they won't be totally inexperienced in the area of suicides.

One of the news-gatherers saw Harelip Feng buy a meat
cleaver and quickly spread the word that he was going to
cut his throat.

VI

But Harelip Feng neither hanged himself nor cut his
throat; he got along just fine. In a year's time his child had
grown big.

Over the New Year's holiday we killed a pig, and Harelip Feng came over to help us remove the bristles. He stayed over for dinner and some wine, and as he was about to leave, Granddad told him to take a handful of the large steamed buns with him. He tucked them into his waistband and left. People were always poking fun at him by saying: "Harelip Feng now has an heir."

Usually when Harelip Feng did some work for us, whether it was grinding half a peck of beans to make bean curd or polishing a couple of pecks of the best red beans to make cakes, Granddad would have him come over to the house for a meal. Once, while we were eating, the old cook said in front of everyone: "Harelip Feng, you'd better eat a couple less buns so you'll have more to take home to your heir . . ."

But Harelip Feng wasn't the least bit annoyed by all this, not really feeling that he was being mocked: "He's got plenty to eat at home," he said very solemnly. "He's got food at home."

When the meal was finished Granddad said: "Why don't you take some home anyway?"

He picked up a few, but didn't know where to put them, since they were too hot to tuck up under his waistband, and they might drop out if he put them up his sleeve.

"Carry them in your cap," the old cook volunteered.

So Harelip Feng went home carrying them in his cap.

If someone in the neighborhood was having a funeral or a wedding, and Harelip Feng was one of the banquet guests, as the meatballs were served, someone would say: "Harelip Feng, you'd better not eat these. Don't forget, you have an heir at home." Then someone would pick up Harelip Feng's two meatballs with his chopsticks and place them on a small plate beside him. The same thing happened when the barbecued pork was served and when the dried fruit was put on the table.

But Harelip Feng was never embarrassed by all of this, and

when the banquet was over he would wrap the things up in his handkerchief and take them home for his son.

VII

Harelip Feng's son was like everyone else's, cutting teeth at seven months, crawling at eight, walking at a year, and running at two. In the summer the boy went naked except for a stomacher around his middle, as he tried to catch little frogs in the ditch in front of his house. His mother sat by the door embroidering another stomacher for him, while his father was in the mill striking his wooden clappers and watching over the little donkey as it turned the mill.

VIII

Two or three years later, when Harelip Feng's second child was on the way, he was in such high spirits that a grin was constantly on his face. When he was outside, people would ask: "Is it going to be another boy, Harelip Feng?" He would just laugh, trying hard to conceal his elation.

When he saw his wife carrying a big basin in the house he would say to her: "Just what do you think you're doing? Can't you let me handle that for you?"

He also stopped her if she was carrying a bundle of firewood: "Can't you let me handle that for you?"

And yet Big Sister Wang daily grew thinner and more gaunt. Her eyes seemed bigger, her nose more pointed. Harelip Feng said that she would be all right if she'd only eat a few more eggs during her lying-in period and get her strength back.

Harelip Feng's home was a happy one then; in front of the window he even hung a white curtain that he had bought in

town. There hadn't been a curtain at Harelip Feng's window
for at least three or four years — this was the first time. He
bought two catties of new cotton filling, several feet of
printed cloth, and twenty or thirty of the best eggs. He
worked the mill as always, while Big Sister Wang cut and
sewed some baby clothes out of the printed cloth. The
twenty or thirty eggs he had bought hung from a rafter in a
basket that swayed in the breeze every time the door or
window was opened. Whenever an egg seller passed by their
door, Harelip Feng would say to his wife: "You're not well;
I think you ought to eat a few more eggs."

But though he always wanted to buy a few more eggs, his
wife would never let him.

"You never got your strength back after the first baby was
born, so what's the harm in eating a couple more eggs this
time? I can go out and sell a few extra catties of rice cake
to make up for it."

When Granddad went over to his place to pass the time of
day, Harelip Feng would talk about his wife: "She's so
thrifty," he would say, "she won't burn a single straw more
than is needed during the day. She won't even eat an extra
egg, even though she's about to have a baby. You wait and
see, she's going to put our family on its feet." A look of
contentment was on his face as he finished.

IX

As August turned into September the crows came. Actually
there were already some crows in the sky in August, but not
nearly as many as there were in September.

The clouds in the sky at sunset in August were as red as
fire, forming unusual shapes: tigers, great lions, the heads
of horses, packs of dogs. But by September these clouds
appeared no more. We were no longer treated to the sight of

skies filled with bright red, golden yellow, purple, or cinnabar-hued clouds. None of them appeared in the sky again, either at dawn or at dusk — they were all gone. The September skies were quiet and empty; the black clouds of July and the red clouds of August were gone when September arrived — even the rains and winds ceased. During the day there was only the bright yellow sun, at night only the snow-white moon.

As the weather turned cold the people began putting on their lined jackets, and since no one went out to cool himself off after dinner, a cold and lonely appearance came to the compound. The chickens and ducks went to roost, pigs bedded down in their pens, the dogs curled up in their dens; in the absence of any wind, the mugwort in the courtyard stood motionless; in the absence of any clouds, the evening star shone as brightly as a little lamp.

On one such night Harelip Feng's wife died. The following morning, as flocks of crows flew overhead, they buried her.

The crows flew over only at dusk and at dawn. Where did they come from? Where were they flying to? They came flying from some distant place, darkening the sky like a huge black cloud and shattering the stillness with their loud cawing; then, passing quickly overhead, they were gone as quickly as they had come. Perhaps the grownups knew where they flew to, but none of the children knew, including me.

I had heard that the crows flew to the willow grove on the southern bank of the Hulan River, but I doubted this because there didn't seem to be anything they could do over there. The willow grove was a dark and gloomy place. I had no idea just what was in there, nor did I know what there was beyond the willow grove. Standing on the bank of the Hulan and looking over at that dark and gloomy grove of willow trees, which stretched for a number of *li,* I could see several large white birds circling overhead. Besides those birds I hadn't a clue as to what else might be there. I had heard that

that's where all the crows went, but what they did and where they flew to from there no one could say.

Harelip Feng's wife had died in childbirth, and legend has it that women who die that way can be accepted neither in large temples nor small ones, thus being doomed to become homeless spirits.

I wanted to go to the shed and take a look, but Granddad wouldn't allow it, so I waited at the gate. I saw Harelip Feng's son walking in front of his mother's coffin carrying a funeral banner. The banner went ahead, the coffin followed, and the whole procession was led by Harelip Feng as it headed toward Great Eastern Bridge.

The funeral banner, cut out of white paper, was shaped like a web and was honeycombed with holes, a number of streamers trailing from it. It was held aloft on a pole resting on the boy's shoulder. He neither cried nor showed any emotion, although the weight of the banner seemed to be too much for him.

Heading east, they walked farther and farther as I watched them from the gate, until they crossed Great Eastern Bridge; I remained standing there looking into the distance even after I could no longer see them.

Caw-caw. Crows were flying overhead. One flight passed over, then another. The crows were still flying by and screeching as we walked back into the house.

X

Now that Harelip Feng's wife was dead, no one gave him any chance of making it. He had been left with two small children, a four- or five-year-old and a newborn baby. Now let's see how he's going to manage this! "Now we'll see some fun," the old cook said. "Harelip Feng will start hitting the bottle soon, and he'll sit on the millstone and wail."

Everyone else in the neighborhood agreed that this time he was done for. All those people eager for some entertainment began preparing themselves for the excitement Harelip Feng's predicament would create.

But Harelip Feng, rather than completely losing heart as everyone around him anticipated, lived not as one in the throes of despair, but as a man with a firm grip on himself. The sight of his two children had a steadying effect on him, for he knew that he had to plant his feet solidly and make something of his life. It didn't matter to him whether he had the ability or not; he just saw what others did and knew that he would have to do the same. And so he lived on as usual, assuming whatever responsibilities fell to him.

He began feeding his newborn baby, starting unsuccessfully with chopsticks, then switching to a spoon. He fed the baby and minded the older boy. When it was time to fetch water, he did so; when it was time to work the mill, he did so. When he got up in the morning and opened his door, if he saw one of his neighbors fetching water from the well he would invariably say: "Out getting water, are you?" If he met a bean-curd peddler he would say: "Out selling your bean curd pretty early, aren't you?" He was blissfully unaware that in the eyes of others he was considered a hopeless case; he didn't know just how difficult they considered his position to be. He didn't realize that he was done for. It simply never crossed his mind.

Admittedly, he felt his share of grief, and tears sometimes welled up in his eyes, but the sight of his older boy leading the little donkey to water immediately brought a smile to his tear-filled eyes. "He'll soon be a real help to me," he would say.

Day after day he fed his younger son, but the boy's eyes kept growing larger and larger, his arms and legs thinner and thinner. In the opinion of others, this baby had no chance of surviving, but to everyone's amazement he held on tenaciously. Eventually the people grew bewildered by this young son of Harelip Feng's who just would not die — they were appalled: How could such a thing happen on the face of the earth?

Whenever Harelip Feng finished his work he held this child of his, and when the weather was too cold he lit a fire to warm him. The child's smile was a fearful sight, with something of laughter in it, something of crying. In fact it looked like neither, but rather, a mixture of the two. But it pleased Harelip Feng no end, and he would say: "The little rascal's playing with me," or "The little rascal really knows what's going on."

The child didn't know how to clap his hands until he was seven or eight months old, an age when other children were already crawling and sitting and on the verge of learning to talk. But Harelip Feng's child could do none of these things — he could only clap his hands.

Yet Harelip Feng's face beamed when he saw his son clapping his hands. "The child's growing faster every day," he would say.

In the eyes of others, not only was the child not getting any bigger, he actually seemed to be getting smaller, for the thinner he grew, the larger his eyes appeared. Seeing his eyes get larger, and nothing else, it seemed to observers that he really wasn't growing at all. The child looked more like a clay doll than a living person; there was no apparent difference in him even after the passage of two months. No one who saw the child for the first time in a couple of months would be amazed by a sense of how quickly time was passing, for although adults don't appear any older in that period of time, a child was supposed to have changed a great deal.

No one would be conscious of the passage of time by looking at Harelip Feng's child. Adults like to measure time by their children, but they could get no such satisfaction from looking at Harelip Feng's child, for there was no observable growth even after the passage of a couple of months. Far better to go out and look at the cucumbers in the rear garden: planted in April, they threw out tendrils by May, grew flowers in June, and by the end of June there were cucumbers ready to be eaten.

But Harelip Feng didn't see things this way; in his eyes, the child grew bigger every day. The older boy could lead the little donkey out to the well to drink, while the younger one knew how to laugh, how to clap his hands, and how to shake his head. He would reach his hand out to take food, and was already cutting a tooth. When he opened his mouth to laugh, that little baby tooth of his gleamed white.

Epilogue

The little town of Hulan River, in earlier days it was where my Granddad lived, and now it is where he is buried. When I was born Granddad was already in his sixties, and by the time I was four or five he was nearly seventy. As I approached the age of twenty Granddad was almost eighty; soon after he reached the age of eighty Granddad was dead.

The former masters of that rear garden are now gone. The old master is dead; the younger one has fled.

The butterflies, grasshoppers, and dragonflies that were in the garden may still return year after year; or perhaps the place is now deserted.

Cucumbers and pumpkins may still be planted there every year; or perhaps there are no more at all.

Do drops of morning dew still gather on the flower-vase stands? Does the noonday sun still send its rays down on the large sunflowers? Do the red clouds at sunset still form into the shape of a horse, only to shift a moment later into the shape of a dog?

These are things that I cannot know.

I heard that Second Uncle You died.

If the old cook is still alive, he will be getting on in years.

I don't know what has become of any of our neighbors.

As for the man who worked the mill, I haven't the slightest idea how things have gone with him.

The tales I have written here are not beautiful ones, but

since my childhood memories are filled with them, I cannot forget them — they remain with me — and so I have recorded them here.

December 20, 1940
Hong Kong

APPENDIX

How to Pronounce the Chinese Phonetic Alphabet

Following is the Chinese phonetic alphabet showing the pronunciation with approximate English equivalent. Spelling in the Wade system is in parentheses for reference.

a	(a)	Vowel as in *far*
b	(p)	Consonant as in *be*
c	(ts)	Consonant as in *its*
ch	(ch)	Consonant as in *church*, strongly aspirated
d	(t)	Consonant as in *do*
e	(e)	Vowel as in *her*
f	(f)	Consonant as in *foot*
g	(k)	Consonant as in *go*
h	(h)	Consonant as in *her*, strongly aspirated
i	(i)	Vowel as in *eat* or as in *sir* (when in syllables beginning with c, ch, r, s, sh, z and zh)
j	(ch)	Consonant as in *jeep*
k	(k)	Consonant as in *kind,* srtongly aspirated
l	(l)	Consonant as in *land*
m	(m)	Consonant as in *me*
n	(n)	Consonant as in *no*
o	(o)	Vowel as in *law*
p	(p)	Consonant as in *par*, strongly aspirated
q	(ch)	Consonant as in *cheek*
r	(j)	Consonant as in *right* (not rolled) or pronounced as z in *azure*
s	(s, ss, sz)	Consonant as in *sister*
sh	(sh)	Consonant as in *shore* strongly aspirated
t	(t)	Consonant as in *top*, strongly aspirated
u	(u)	Vowel as in *too,* also as in the French *tu* or the German *Munchen*

v	(v)	Consonant used only to produce foreign words, national minority words and local dialects
w	(w)	Semi-vowel in syllables beginning with u when not preceded by consonants, as in *want*
x	(hs)	Consonant as in *she*
y		Semi-vowel in syllable beginning with i or u when not preceded by consonants, as in *yet*
z	(ts, tz)	Consonant as in *zero*
zh	(ch)	Consonant as in *jump*

《呼蘭河傳》

蕭　紅著

葛浩文譯

三聯書店（香港）有限公司出版

香港域多利皇后街九號